THE MILLSTONE PROPHECY

JACK HARNEY

Second Edition

Coming soon to Kindle and CreateSpace:

Six: A Dax McGowan Mystery

Please visit: www.jackharneyauthor.com

Cover Design and Art by Victoria Landis

Copyright © 2011 Jack Harney

All rights reserved.

ISBN: 0-6154-9262-2
ISBN-13: 978-0615492629

DEDICATION

Barbara Blaine, founder and President of SNAP, Survivor's Network for those Abused by Priests. Her energy to seek solace and justice on behalf of victims of sexual abuse by religious clergy knows no bounds.

Visit to learn and take opportunities to support SNAP

at www.snapnetwork.org

(All the author's earnings are contributed to SNAP)

PROLOGUE

Nightmares are usually of the unexpected kind . . . but not for her. There was now a daily and hourly countdown as the time approached to face her horror. It was that day once again, as her limp arm was pulled into that room . . . that smelly, torrid room of sweat and violence.

She stood by the bed with her eyes turned up and away, her mind seeking a place to be other than where she stood. She managed to block her senses as furtive hands removed her clothes, but now the physical pain would always begin even before each attack . . . its anticipation too strong to repress.

Little girl's nightmares should be of a chase in a haunted house, or a fly over by the Wicked Witch of the West . . . never this.

CHAPTER ONE

Dax believed he loved his daughter, Grace, beyond what any parent felt for their child. His parents, Vinnie and Mary McGowan, were caring enough, but the bar they owned just across the border into Yonkers from the Bronx seemed to eat up all their waking hours. As a boy, he was told he was loved, and it seemed he received plenty of hugs, but those embraces were often followed with a brogue tinged, "Watch your sister, Eileen now, won't ya? We gotta meet the beer drivers early today to stock up for the weekend." He had concluded there was love enough in his childhood home, but he was sure his parents never felt for him or his sister the way he felt about his precious Grace.

His wife, Darlene, came from a similar background from the standpoint they both had hard working parents as role models . . . his, the nearly never at home bar owners, and hers, two attorneys in private practice together who often argued vehemently over personal issues behind closed doors while waiting clients in the lobby pretended not to hear.

Dax and Darlene immediately clicked when they first met at City College, as they were both intent on working tirelessly to reach their personal goals, he to become the best police detective in New York City, and she to get the needed advanced degrees to return and teach English Literature at City College. It was an instant partnership of two highly focused people, and the sex was as intense as their desire to succeed. Planning both a graduation and a wedding at the same time seemed the only right thing to do.

As Darlene later finished up her Master's Degree and earned an internship at City College, Dax was settling into his first assignment at the Bronx's Forty-First Precinct after graduating "Top of His Class" at the Police Academy. While they still felt a strong affection for one another, and both were on their most desired professional tracks, they struggled with the sense that their marriage was not all it might be. This was not something two driven, success is the only option people want to admit to anyone, especially themselves. Like many married couples who have unspoken fears about the longevity of their relationship, they began to talk about having a child. While this often-unwitting strategy to fill the void in a marriage is rarely the best of choices, it worked for the McGowans. Not quite as they expected, but it worked.

Grace's birth was met with great fanfare by the entire family. Darlene's mother, Marsha Olsen was ecstatic. "The perfect couple now had the perfect child," she could be heard to say for months afterward. Her husband, John, would scold her to stop repeating that. "It sounds too snobby!" That would set them off on one of their legendary arguments that caused Dax's mother, Mary, to openly cringe upon witnessing them. She, and her now deceased husband Vinnie, often wondered if Darlene had picked up that negative trait and caused their son any trouble. It was impossible, of course, for Darlene, as an only child, to be unaffected by such adverse modeling by both parents. Darlene's temper, mostly absent during their courtship, had become a full bloomed marriage affliction, but now hoped naively to be quelled by the arrival of a baby.

Grace truly was a beautiful child, and only became more so as she grew. Her mother and father were considered pretty and handsome in their respective rights, but Grace was judged by most to be well beyond that. Her immaculately smooth and fair skin was surrounded by flowing, almost white-blond hair, inherited traits from Darlene's Scandinavian background, and in stark contrast to Dax's dark Irish heritage which produced his jet black hair and deep brown eyes. Grace's star-flickering blue eyes, with exceptionally long dark lashes, drew stares from friends and strangers alike. Her father's high cheekbones, her mother's perfect nose, and lips too full for a child her age, all lent to adjectives about her future ranging from "royal beauty" to "man killer," dependent on the good or bad taste in the word choices of the admirer. One special thing Dax and Darlene did share was their acknowledgement of how beautiful Grace was. At times, they would catch each other peering at her in the same moment, and then smile in a knowing fashion.

Other than this one understanding, predictably, like everything else in their marriage, Grace became a separate, unshared emotional tie for each of them. It was as if they had unknowingly acceded to a successful joint custody arrangement of her while living in the same household. However, this unusual arrangement seemed to work well enough for the McGowans under normal circumstances.

The abnormal circumstances began when Grace was eleven.

CHAPTER TWO

"Have you noticed Grace acting oddly withdrawn lately?" Darlene asked.

It was Saturday morning and everyone was home on the same day for a change. Without answering, Dax slid from the kitchen where they were sharing breakfast making duties, to the living room where Grace was watching TV. As the couch was on the opposite wall from where he stood, he could readily see her staring obliviously at the screen. It was totally unlike her, as she loved her weekend morning cartoons.

"What's the matter baby? What's on your mind?"

"Oh nothing, Daddy," she said. "I'm just not feeling like myself today."

Grace often spoke in the manner of the precocious child she was, adding a degree of credibility to everything she said. However, Dax knew he should not let that evasive response go unpursued.

"Honey, Daddy can tell something is really bothering you. Please tell me what it is?"

Grace's face changed to her more smiling self. "No need to worry, Daddy, I'll be just fine." Then, only almost happily, "Are we still going to the zoo with Grandma tomorrow?"

"Yes honey, your Grandma is all excited about that. We're picking her up at noon after she gets home from mass."

Dax was unsure Grace's change of face and subject were genuine. He backed up all the way to the kitchen so he could continue to watch her. She gave him a weakened smile as she passed completely out of his view. He wondered how this sudden shift in Grace's demeanor had escaped his attention. *Of course!* He and Darlene had both been extremely busy in the past week. A guilt pang hit him as he remembered that virtually every evening of late involved a kiss on Grace's head well after she was asleep, the consequence of a drug related murder investigation that was keeping him out late doing surveillance. Darlene's week had not been much better, up every night grading long-winded essays of first-term freshmen who had yet to learn the skill of brevity in their writing.

He was sure Grace was fine the week before, his eidetic memory recalling each one of his limited encounters with her. He saw no signs of distress as far as he could tell. *What do you mean as far as you can tell? You're supposed to know what everyone is thinking, Sherlock.* Dax had long accepted that his exceptional memory and deductive talents somehow did not apply to Grace in terms of reading her cues and thoughts as clearly as he could read others. He had come to know his strong emotional attachment to her somehow muted those skills. Normally a sense of joy to him, he was now troubled by the barrier.

"Something is definitely up with Grace, Darlene. Do you have any idea what that might be?"

"Oh, I don't know. She's at that age where I hear little bits of things from other parents about boys she and her girlfriends are interested in. There's one kid I give a ride home after their CCD classes on Tuesdays and Thursdays, a Tommy O'Reilly, that I've heard may be an ongoing crush. He's in her sixth grade class at Lighthouse as well."

Dax was reminded that this had been the third week for Grace attending the Tuesday and Thursday Catholic Confraternity of Christian Doctrine classes at St. Mark's Church. She attended the K-8 program at the Bronx Lighthouse Charter School that he and Darlene had chosen because of its excellent Art Program, of high interest to Grace. It was located just a few blocks north of the Four-One where Dax was stationed, and was an easy two-block walk after school to St. Marks on Intervale Ave. for her and her Catholic friends. He only agreed to enroll Grace in the program at the constant insistence of his mother.

"You know Dax, just because you decided to give up your religion, you shouldn't deny your daughter the chance to learn about being a good Catholic. It's the religion of your family going back many Irish generations, don't you know?" was her constant admonishment.

Despite Dax's intense pride of his Irish ancestry, all religious beliefs and the deities offered by them held no logic for his Holmesian view of the world. His standard response to whether he believed in God was, "There may be a God, but I doubt it to be any of the ones picked so far." In the end, he agreed to allow Grace's attendance in these classes, partly because it made sense to him that if Grace were to make an educated decision for herself about religion she should at least, as he did, have had some exposure to it. Besides, his mother was at the stage of ranting on the subject.

Responding to Darlene's "crush" comment, "Well, let's keep an eye on her. I didn't like what I saw in her eyes, and if this kid is giving her any kind of trouble, I might have to interdict and straighten things out."

"Wow, listen to you . . . interdict! Aren't we getting all police state-like about some pre-teen young man you haven't ever met?" Darlene began to raise her voice in a manner Dax knew was but one step away from trouble.

"Okay, okay, I realized how that sounded as I was saying it. People do say that when daughters start getting interested in boys their fathers get a little crazy. I'm on a learning curve on this one."

He knew that as mature as that sounded, he was also sure he would never let anyone hurt his little girl. He would always protect her from any threats to her happiness.

Several weeks went by. Both he and Darlene had virtually no reprieve in their schedules. Grace seemed to have her good and bad days. She once walked in on her parents talking about her moods and caught their concern about this boy that might be the cause. After that, when she was asked about her troubles, she would say something like, "I just don't understand boys, they're such a pain" or "Don't worry, Daddy. I'm going to give up on boys for now."

Dax never quite bought that. However, she sounded sincere, and it was Grace, Grace who never told even the smallest of white lies. He simply had no other point of reference to judge beyond what he heard her say, and Darlene made it abundantly clear he was not to embarrass Grace by addressing the issue at school or her wrath would be the result. He finally resigned himself that the situation was simply a matter of patience as these childhood romances eventually faded away.

CHAPTER THREE

Father Peter Wendich was delighted that it was again a Tuesday . . . his day to teach CCD classes. It was always disappointing for him to wait from Thursday to Tuesday over the long weekend. He was especially looking forward to seeing his two favorite pupils, Grace McGowan and Tommy O'Reilly. He was impressed with their intelligence, and such beautiful children, he thought. *"God had blessed them mightily."* He would do his best to help them become the natural leaders in God's church he deemed them destined to be.

He was pleased that he had finally made it to the United States the previous spring after many different assignments in Europe over the last twenty-six years. He felt this time he would be able to finally blend in better with less stress, as the hustle and bustle of New York City lent itself to more anonymity. *"I am not a man who seeks recognition, just a simple life of love and serving God."*

Father Wendich was a short, rather portly man in his late fifties. Being old country, he was rarely seen in public without wearing his black cassock with its more primitive large black cloth buttons, that on him seemed to want to burst free of his protruding stomach. His rather large head sat stiffly on his cassock's collar, his neck jowls almost hiding its white insert. With his somewhat bulging eyes, a flattened face and pointed nose, he was a near dead ringer for the old movie actor, Peter Lorre, of *Casablanca* fame. Even his labored speech pattern of forcing air out to form his words was eerily similar to Lorre's. Were it not for a very warm, if not practiced smile, a soft German accent, and self-deprecating manner, he could be seen as a bit scary to young children. However, he was always very good at gaining their trust. Children felt safe and loved by him. *"My greatest asset,"* he thought. Yes, he was sure he had finally found a home for his talents and skills in God's work.

CHAPTER FOUR

Friday: December 11th

It was yet another early call into the precinct, this time resulting from an overnight murder of a gang banger the entire detective staff knew well. To Dax, it was one more time he was not home greeting his darling Grace with a good morning hug. The precinct wall clock told him that she and Darlene were likely just waking up. An hour earlier at 5:30, he had once again executed his well-rehearsed tiptoe routine to get out the door without disturbing them.

The Four-One Precinct building on Longwood Ave. in the Bronx, like many station houses that grew up as the city expanded over the last century, had its aging issues, but was an efficient physical plant for the capture and processing of criminals. The street level was home base for all the precinct's uniformed officers, and the main hub for citizens to enter and lodge their complaints. The second floor was the home of the homicide detective squad. With the exception of two interrogation rooms and two side-by-side private offices, one for the precinct's Captain, and the other for the second highest ranked officer, Lieutenant Dax McGowan, most of the floor consisted of an open bullpen of desks for detectives of varying grades. Often an arena of frenzied activity, it was not unusual for its inhabitants to grab calls at anyone else's temporarily unoccupied desk, as they were all so often "on the fly."

"Dax! It's line three for you."

Dax looked up to see the face of his good friend, Sergeant Dick

Daley, go gray, as his words trailed off with sheer horror in them. The entire squad stood still sensing something very wrong. He intuitively did not ask about the nature of the call as Daley's eyes were saying he would not want to answer that question. He looked with dread at the line blinking in front of him. His mind raced to reason what could have caused Daley's reaction, but no matter, all his instincts told him the call was from home.

Out of habit, "This is McGowan."

"Dax?!" It was Darlene. "It's Grace . . . you must come home. Please come home right now . . . please Dax?" The phone went dead. He flew to the door, no overcoat, no gloves. He fled the room impervious to his colleagues now swarming around Daley to learn what was going on.

Daley could only report to them Darlene's words. "My daughter is gone; my sweet Grace is dead." He had recognized her voice and could offer no reply, only to alert Dax. He sank down at the desk where he took the call as if he had been wounded by a deadly weapon, and hanging his head trying to imagine the immense pain his good friend would soon be facing. The whole floor was now at a full stop with ringing phones going unanswered. Street hardened men and women were distraught with grief for their precinct's star, Dax McGowan.

Dax hit the bottom of the stairs and raced to the Desk Sergeant, yelling on the way he wanted a squad car and driver to take him home immediately, full sirens and lights. No mistaking something of the gravest nature, the Sergeant simply replied, "Yes sir, Lieutenant."

The shortened emergency ride home still seemed to never end. Part of his thinking was in chaos that anything had happened to Grace, the other wanting desperately to call Darlene to tell him nothing was seriously wrong. More than once, he looked at his phone and decided not to call, knowing from the sheer despair he had heard in her voice she wouldn't be able to speak again until he got there.

As the squad car turned the corner onto Lafayette Ave., he saw an EMS bus. Its sight gave him a ray of hope that maybe Grace was in danger and they were inside saving her. Everyone, including neighbors, police, and medical staff quickly stepped aside as he navigated the crowd and jumped the steps to their red brick walk up. He was desperate to find Darlene. He needed to know what was wrong, to prepare before seeing Grace. She bolted around at the back of the house in the kitchen when she heard him call her name, and flew to meet him halfway down their home's central hallway as he rushed toward her.

"Darlene! Grace? What's wrong with her?"

He could see the blood go out of her face, and felt her knees buckle as she tried to speak. "She's gone Dax. Our amazing and beautiful Grace is gone."

He felt as if his heart exploded as he and Darlene slipped slowly while in each other's arms to the floor in a dirge of emotion neither could fathom. They sobbed openly for a time as medical staff and fellow officers watched in paralyzed silence. Then in a sudden call of clarity and anger, he cried out, "How, how did this happen?! Where is she?!" He was unintelligibly shaking a non-responsive Darlene, expecting her to direct him to Grace, his only thought now was to see and hold his daughter. But his wife's eyes were blank, lost in shock. He looked around for anyone who might answer his questions. He saw the young male officer who had brought him home gesture to a female EMT that she should go over to him. Reluctantly, in what seemed like slow motion, she broached the several steps toward him.

Her voice quivering, "Sir, it appears, sir . . . that your daughter may have committed suicide." Her eyes were now expressing a full out flight response, but she managed to stand her ground long enough to continue. "I'm so sorry for your lo . . . Sir, I don't know what to say, Lieutenant, really sir I . . ." Her voice trailing off, she turned slowly and walked away.

NO! NO! His mind was screaming, then "NO!" Unbridled remorse overcame him. "Beautiful little girls don't commit suicide unless their parents weren't doing their job of protecting her. Little sweethearts don't hurt themselves when they are loved. Only the children of rotten bastard parents do that. How did I not protect my little baby?"

The haunting words shook everyone in earshot, but he was oblivious to their reactions. His only thought was to discover how he had failed his little girl so he could kill himself for that unforgivable sin. Then it occurred to him that Darlene may have somehow allowed this to happen. Even so, he thought, it didn't matter. It was on him to be sure his baby was safe at all costs, even from her. *"Nothing else makes a difference . . . NOTHING! It's my fault . . . only mine."*

Before he could take his despair any deeper, he was being lifted by the same officer who brought him home, and another officer was helping lift Darlene. A couple of EMTs moved in to assist taking them upstairs to their bedroom at the direction of a tall, dark haired woman, who Dax would discover was a doctor immediately dispatched by his Captain after Dick Daley's report to him of Grace's death. He was in no shape to disagree and moved willingly. As they topped the stairs, he looked to his left down the hallway and saw the open doors to Grace's bedroom and bathroom, realizing she was in one of those rooms.

He stiffened, "I want to see her," and began to lean in that direction.

The doctor pushed back against the officer nearly carrying him, "Lieutenant McGowan, you don't want to see her now. I'll make sure you and Mrs. McGowan see her when the time is right. Please sir, just come with us so we can get you a bit settled."

"How did she die?" the cop in him coming out.

"She cut her wrists, sir, sometime in the middle of the night. She's in the bathroom." was her honest response.

He began to picture the countless bodies he had seen in a tub of bloody water. Try as he might, he could not place Grace there; his mind would not let him. Shock was now engulfing him. He barely felt the needle pierce his arm as he and Darlene were laid across their bed, thrust into an abyss of sleep, deep enough, even Dax's normally vivid, dream induced recollections could not penetrate.

CHAPTER FIVE

Sliding off the bed as he drifted into consciousness, Dax was at first unaware of where he was. He had never before slept like that, without dreaming. Then, as the realities of why he had just awakened began to overtake him, he shook his head in an attempt to become more lucid. Still wobbly, he struggled to get up off his hands and knees. Darlene was still unconscious on the bed.

"How long have I been out?" he queried to anyone who might hear him.

"About three hours, Lieutenant." He turned to see the doctor coming into the room peering at him with concern. "You need to sit down and get a bit more oriented. Let's talk . . . let me help you."

He obeyed the request, sitting back on the bed next to Darlene. "I want to know everything that's happened! But first, where's Grace . . . . I have to see my Grace." He accessed his memory of when he left that morning and mentally looked down the hallway to Grace's room and her bathroom. Both doors had been closed. He thought, she could have still been alive as he crept toward the stairway. "*Was there any clue I missed that should have made me check on her? There had to have been . . . there must have been.*"

"Lieutenant McGowan, my name is Dr. Eleanor Kirkwood. Let me tell you everything I know. But first, I'm sure you're thinking this is somehow your fault. However, let me say, these things are most often beyond the control of good parents like you and Mrs. McGowan."

That was his confirmation she was a shrink. "Listen, I don't need you telling me anything about what goes on in this house when you have no goddam idea." He then recalled, when as the investigating officer, he had called professionals in to handle distressed family members after a death, causing his next words to soften some. "Please, I just want answers . . . all the answers."

"Okay, Lieutenant. Your daughter has been taken to the mor . . . , taken from here and forensics has left as well. It appears she got up somewhere around three in the morning. Her wounds were pretty deep and she . . . it appears she used a very old straight razor, one that might fall into some kind of antique category."

Dax remembered the collector's item which was passed down to him from his father. It had belonged to his grandfather and male relatives well before that in Ireland. He had stored it downstairs in a drawer in the dining room's buffet table. *"Why did I ever save that old piece of worthless junk?"* He thought, grabbing his thick black hair with both hands.

"And sir, the M.E. reported," she swallowed hard to prepare, "there appears to be signs of vaginal and anal tearing from repeated rape, sir; SVU has already been and gone." She closed her eyes and lowered her head in empathy, knowing the powerful impact of what she said.

"What?! What do you mean rape?!" he said standing instantly. His words were on fire. He was now entering a realm of mental and physical responses that he had never known. The blood in his heart was pounding its way into his head. He could feel every muscle in his body tighten into some form of attack mode. His hands felt like weapons with untold power to tear and destroy. His head turned violently in every direction with a look of total madness in his eyes. With no thought and no effort, he reached for a heavy leather bedside chair, lifted it and smashed it through the bedroom wall into the hallway, destroying drywall into powder with 2 x 4s breaking like toothpicks. He turned with blood red eyes toward the doctor causing her face to go pale in fear.

"Dax? Dax, are you there? Where's Grace, Dax?" The loud crash had awakened Darlene still suffering from disorientation.

Her soft words, gently speaking Grace's name, were like tiny cloth snaps, one by one, quietly releasing his rage. He turned to Darlene and began to breathe huge full gulps of air. He had lost himself for those few seconds, not aware of what he had done, except for the evidence of destruction before him. He allowed himself to collapse down to the bed next to his wife, knowing it was now on him to help her navigate the information he had just been given. For the next moments, he simply waited as the fog of the drugs wore off, and the reality of what had happened began to seep back into her consciousness.

CHAPTER SIX

Tuesday: December 15th

Dax was sitting at his forty-year-old hand-me-down desk in his precinct office. Only now, it felt like he had never occupied it before. It had been four days since Grace's death and the day after her funeral.

On the way in, his walk through the open squad room was met by a piercing silence as his fellow detectives and staff could not find an appropriate word to offer. It was no different for them at the funeral, as they all remarked at never seeing anyone so distraught and unapproachable with grief. They each made sure they were visibly engaged in work that required their line of sight to be away from his to caringly allow him the privacy his demeanor demanded.

His desk was covered with hundreds of cards, flowers, and all forms of condolences from people everywhere in the city and beyond. The faded gray tile floor was half covered, as the desk could not hold such an outpouring of responses. Everything in view seemed foreign to him. Walls consumed with citations, educational achievements, and pictures with city luminaries appeared to be a history of someone else's life. *"So many smiles on those faces,* he thought, *"smiles that could never have predicted this horror."*

When he sat there last, he was a good cop who lived a good life. He and his wife both held dear a daughter they loved beyond description. Today, his life was broken like a tree trunk bent in half after being struck by lightning. While he and Darlene had drifted even further apart each of the last few days, the gap between them now seemed impossible to traverse.

With Grace's passing, he could not give it a name, that part of him that was torn away forever, that part that defined a major purpose for his existence as a man and as a father, but it was gone. The tears rolled slowly down across his fists pushed up against his face as he struggled to gain a direction for his emotions.

Yesterday, after the funeral was the first day Dax began to realize that blaming himself for Grace's death was getting in the way of finding the *fucking bastard who caused it.* It was getting clearer he had been wasting too much time castigating himself for missing the signs of her troubles rather than tracking down her murderer . . . *yes, the murderer who really killed Grace.* He never pictured himself ever taking advice from Catholic clergy, but Father Wendich, her CCD instructor, led him to realize the futility of where his mind was in self-pity. As he stood at the cemetery, the last person still standing over her lowered casket, the priest approached him.

"Herr McGowan," he began with a forced breath, "Grace was such a beautiful child. Oh my, the essence of purity, sir. Only the best of fathers could have produced such a child. I hope you are not feeling in any way to blame. Der is evil in the world, as you well know being a policeman, and this evil reached out and caused her death . . . not you. It will be up to God to judge this transgressor, and the Devil will no doubt exact his punishment. Let God take his vengeance, but you sir need to press on and keep being the good and honorable man that you are."

Dax was ruminating on those words once more. *"Yes, there is evil in the world, and it did reach out and destroy my Grace. But it won't be at the hands of any God or Devil that this evil will suffer."*

He sat there wondering how such a rotund and seemingly lone figure of a man could have such insight into the heart of his Grace and the special little girl she was, or that he knew just the right words he most needed to hear at that moment. They were helping him change direction. *"The priest was right."* He knew he was not directly responsible for Grace's death and may never fully sort that out, but there was one thing he could do, and that was to destroy the man who was. Surely, he thought, the priest did not intend to encourage his revenge, but his words nevertheless were releasing him from enough of the blame he was experiencing that was getting in its way.

As he fingered away his tears, sitting there amongst all the goodwill of others, he peered around his office reminding himself it was a place that strove to exact justice, and that was precisely what he would do. He knew, that as a man of the law and seeking personal revenge were at odds, but refused to dispel any of his anger. He needed it to move ahead to break out of any disabling grief that was keeping from avenging Grace's death.

He leapt from his chair with a new resolve wiping away the last vestige of any wallowing in sadness. There was a noticeable return of a missing mental sharpness. Clarity and purpose were creating a sensation he could feel all the way down the back of his legs. He headed to his Captain's office to discuss a plan he was forming in his head, though only those parts he could wisely divulge.

CHAPTER SEVEN

Captain John Pressioso was the kind of leader who would never ask anyone to do something he had not already experienced during his own career before being declared "Head of the House" at the Forty-First Precinct. When it came to hunting down killers, he had taken bullets more than once while leading charges against them. He was also one of the many unsung heroes still carrying a latent cough after harrowing rescues at the Towers on 9-11. Though a good number of years had passed since those days of heroics, and a full crop of white hair now topped his craggy and stress lined sixty-three year-old face, there was no dilution in the respect and admiration of the men and women serving under him.

The Captain had immediately recognized Dax's exceptional skills upon his arrival at the Four-One, and sponsored his unheard of rise from being a uniformed cop to a Detective Lieutenant in record time. It was inevitable that Dax would eventually be recommended for his own Captaincy, which Pressioso could only endorse, except that Dax wanted nothing to do with management responsibilities that would take him off the streets solving crimes. Even the approval for his last elevation to Lieutenant, with no administrative assignments attached, went all the way to the top brass at the "Big House" at One Police Plaza in Manhattan. One of the major factors in supporting that compromise was that One P.P. had borrowed the Four-One's best detective on several occasions. Those were times when the crime of murder had paid a visit on the lives of its wealthy, well-connected constituents, and the pressure to close a tough case had reached an increased level of political necessity. What eminently established Dax's superior skills in both the eyes of the Department and the public, was an uncanny sorting of disparate facts that he managed to piece together to uncover a terrorist plot to kill the President upon a visit planned to Ground Zero. All the wire services later carried the Pulitzer nominated photo of the President surveying the construction progress there, with a huge grin, and his arm around the shoulders of his hero, Lieutenant Dax McGowan.

Dax and his Captain had a unique working relationship, each appreciating the other's standout commitment and reputation. The Captain never resented the amount of publicity his charge attracted, and Dax felt no hesitancy in answering to or being under the tutelage of a superior officer with Pressioso's impeccable skills and character.

While never previously expressed, the divorced and childless Captain had come to consider Dax as his surrogate son. In the days after Grace's death, he was seen sitting alone in his office fighting back tears, leaving his staff on edge, wanting him not to feel they were catching him crying. Dax's return found him no less emotional.

"Welcome, son." Both he and Dax caught the unexpected ascription. Toughening his posture a bit, "And how's it going on your first day back? Don't you think this is too soon? You need a good deal more time than you're giving yourself, my boy."

"So I'm told, Captain. I suppose you've seen all the stuff in my office. I'm not complaining of course."

"There are a lot of people who care about you, Dax. You know that. Not everyone gets invited to Sternberg's office or gets a call from the President when they lose their . . . you know, when they have a family loss like this," he said wheezing, trying not to cough.

"I know sir, but I'm sure you understand that I just can't go through all those memories right now. I'm just trying get my head back on straight, and I need to deal with what's ahead of me. In fact, I'm planning on taking some time off as you suggest. I have a good deal of unused vacation time to fall back on."

"How's your wife holding up? She seemed in pretty rough shape at the funeral. I suppose you need this time to be with her, and take care of yourself."

"That's it Captain, sorting out to do." Dax responded knowing that was not his agenda. What was going to become of his relationship with Darlene was hardly now in question and secondary to the mission in front of him. "Captain, I know I can't be directly involved in my daughter's case, but I would appreciate it if I could be kept up to speed and get to review the file when I want to. I may be able to catch something, maybe any little thing that could help. I promise I'll stay out of the way and let Daley do his work." He knew that was a lie.

"Of course you know, Dax, we're lucky to be involved at all since it's a Special Victims case assigned to the Four-Five. We're supposed to be on a strictly need to know basis. It was only that Daley pleaded with the lead detective over there, his old partner, Janet Meehan, that she agreed to keep us more closely informed."

Dax was pleased that Daley was assigned to follow up on his precinct's end. Daley was one of the best, and told everyone how committed he was to seeing this perp go down, especially after taking the call from Darlene, an experience he still claimed having nightmares over. More importantly, Daley's ex-partner relationship with the lead detective at SVU, Janet Meehan, "a ball busting, take no prisoners, damn good cop," as Daley described her, would mean less filtered and more solid information. "She hated perv perps," Daley had once said, and enjoyed it when they would try to run so she could tackle them and drive their faces into the pavement.

Dax liked this recipe of people. "I know Captain. I just want to help if I can."

"Listen young man, I know you well, and your sounding all cooperative to other people's methods isn't your style, and I'm sure that will be even more so the case where Grace is concerned," he said wincing, wishing he had not used her name so directly. "For the moment, I'll take what you're saying on face value." A deep cough exploded a wide spray onto his desk.

"I get it, Captain. I don't want to cause any problems" he tried to say convincingly.

Unconvinced and fearing for his protégé's professional future, Pressioso jumped in more harshly. "Just don't fuck this up. I'll look sideways knowing you'll be getting your hands into it, but I don't want to see my best detective disciplined, or worse, if you overstep where you don't belong. You hear me Dax?"

"Yes sir."

Pressioso, still fearful of Dax's intentions, then chose a different tack in the conversation. "You know, you've had a great history at the Four-One. You need to remind yourself about the reputation you've built here, and you know how hard I've worked to get you whatever you needed."

"Yes, sir. I've appreciated everything you've done for me . . . very much."

"Well, you've earned it! Do you remember when you first made detective and I hooked you up with those two different guys who I thought might teach you something?" Pressioso said grinning broadly.

"Yes, sir." Despite his dour mood, Dax grinned back, falling victim to the Captain's infectious smile, and recalling the comedy of those experiences.

"I still crack up when I think about those times, young man. You of course know the first guy quit after two cases because he felt you were embarrassing him in front of everybody else, but did I ever tell you what the second guy, Sergeant Tortelli, said to me before he transferred out?"

"No, sir."

The Captain leaned as far forward as he could over his desk without standing. "He says to me, "Captain, I really like McGowan, and I think he's the best detective I've ever seen. But, I have to be more involved than just getting this guy his coffee while he out thinks me on every case." Pressioso burst into a coughing laugh that was impossible for Dax to avoid joining in on. Tears rolled down the outer edges of the Captain's eyes matched by one from Dax. Both men appreciated they were sharing together their first experience of any joy in the last five days.

Dax was savoring his mentor's attempt at helping him heal, but also observed his now trying to compose himself back into the comportment of being his boss.

"So. How long do you think you'll be out? Anticipating you would, I used a good part of yesterday to get most of your cases re-assigned. You will have to check in on those once and awhile too, I hope? Some of these folks don't quite get your notes, or how your mind works on those things."

"Hey Captain, they all have my cell number. I'll be available whenever anybody needs me. I'll work on some before I leave today. As to time off, I'm not sure, but I imagine three or four days might do it."

"Okay, I'll tell everyone to get off the eggshell dance and start calling you if need be. This is still the best goddamn precinct in New York and I plan on keeping it that way. I do understand how you must feel, and that you want to get your fists into the middle of it." Pressioso's eyes softened as he leaned forward again, "I really feel your loss, son. I really do." There was no mistaking the clear meaning and his open use of the word this time.

The Captain ended the conversation abruptly by turning his chair around as if he had something behind him that needed his attention. He hoped he had not exposed his personal feelings too much, and that Dax did not catch his last attempt at clearing his throat was anything more than that.

In most cases, three or four days were enough for Dax to narrow clues down and arrest a prime suspect. In this case, the result would be to wipe his existence off the face of the earth. As he would soon discover, three or four days would just be a warm up.

CHAPTER EIGHT

The upstairs bullpen of the Four-One was always relatively deserted during the early evening dinner hour. The day shift had gone home, calls were routed through the front desk downstairs, and the second shift was more of a skeleton crew before ramping up the numbers again around nine. Most civilians were home eating, and it was at least two to three hours before the "crazies" came out of their lairs to engage in their usual mischief. Dax and Dick Daley had retreated to the privacy of the only place on one-half of the entire floor with a light on, Interrogation Room One.

"Okay Dax, I know this is going to piss you off, but I'm going to say it anyway." Daley began. He remained standing to feel more in control of what might happen next. He was holding several files with the Special Victim's Unit's, "Precinct Forty-Five" stamped on the front and back.

"You know that ninety percent of the time the perp in these cases is a family member or a close friend. We've already talked to your wife. Your dad has passed on. Except for Grace's funeral, the Olsens, your in-laws, have been in Florida for a month. Your sister Eileen lives in L.A. and Darlene has no siblings. You and your wife lead a crazy busy life. All your friends are related to your work, and neither of you spend enough social time with any of them to give them the opportunity to do the long-term damage the M.E. says your daughter showed. Either you or your wife managed to get Grace wherever she had to go, and the seventy-eight year old lady next door to you, who occasionally filled in at times to watch her, is not in question. That leaves you."

Dax knew this was coming. He had prepared. "I totally get that Richard. What do you need from me?" Dax asked with a smirk.

"It's not what I need, but what Meehan and her partner at SVU need to cover their asses. They want to schedule a sit down, ask you all the right questions, record your answers, and move on after the real perp. The question is can you do that without grabbing any chairs and heaving them through walls or getting into it with those guys? I've seen your bedroom wall . . . or what's left of it."

"No problem, I've already practiced my answers while squeezing my balls to keep my mind from getting into a rage. So, what have you got so far to share with me my friend?" Dax asked within his attempt at levity to put his friend at ease.

Daley had not expected that. He was trying to remain serious, and not into laughter at the unexpected humor. A muted chuckle, tinged with a degree of relief made it through his lips instead.

"Okay," he went on, "as I said the usual suspects aren't there. The only place that makes any sense is at Grace's school. But Meehan has already checked out the staff there . . . no hidden sex offenders . . . no newly hired or old staff with any kind of related record that slipped under the school's radar. And shit Dax, she was in the sixth grade at a charter school with only eight grades, blocks and blocks from any high school. They're not ruling out any adult at that school just yet, but it looks like we might be narrowing it down to some over-sexed twelve or thirteen year old boys."

Dax pointed mildly at him as he responded. "I'd like Meehan to first check out a kid named Tommy O'Reilly. Darlene was hearing talk about a possible crush going on, or whatever they call it now, between him and my daughter."

"They still call it that, I think." Daley offered.

"Yes, well Grace would never verify that, only hinted at it." Dax felt his breathing heave as he realized it was the first time he had openly said her name that day. "Can you leave that file copy with me so I can check it out? I'll have them back to you by morning . . . promise," implying he did not see there was much else to cover for now. Daley took the hint and put a supporting hand on his friend's shoulder as he headed for the door. "Sure man, that works," he said. "Be sure and call Meehan right away, will ya? She wasn't too keen on calling you . . . and Dax please do that yet tonight to set it up? She really wants to get that interview behind her. I'll call her now too, and see how soon she can get the O'Reilly boy in for questioning."

Dax sat frustrated after Daley's exit. The information in the files in front of him revealed nothing. He needed to be there looking into the eyes of anyone who had been personally contacted, to catch them lying if they were, reading their reactions and their tics. Somehow, he had to figure out a way to be involved when Meehan interviewed the O'Reilly boy. Logic told him it wasn't likely an eleven year old was directly involved, but it was more than probable he had knowledge of who was.

There were other aspects of the whole affair that were troubling him now, making no sense. His mind began to take on a familiar thought process. It would always lead him to employ his most successful strategy when faced with a slowdown in solving any case. It was to consult his alter ego. He turned off the light in the interrogation room after also verifying no sound could be heard from it. It was a perfect setting for him to engage in open verbalization . . . *as Sherlock Holmes.* He felt he needed these times to "become" the fictional detective of Sir Arthur Conan Doyle's creation, having as a boy, committed to memory all his now famous works. In fact, it was Dax's boyhood game of copycatting Holmes that led him to discover the value of crossing over to a different persona. He used this same technique to solve the countless mystery stories he had read before the authors revealed the ending in their last chapters. His current day use of the strategy was a simple, consistent repeating of the process ever since his teenage years. It provided him more than the benefit of removing distracting, extraneous information from his thoughts in order to lay out an orderly pattern of facts from which he could draw helpful conclusions. It was also a required escape from his endemic high-strung emotions, which could often cause a loss of self-control and mute his deductive skills.

At age thirty-five, if he were willing to admit it, he actually considered himself the current century's version of the Baker Street phenom, and reveled in utilizing Holmes' distinctive style of pontification and English diction. This indulgence of accessing a better-controlled altered self would likely appear as a form of crazed puffery to his peers, so it required he do this only in private. He always engaged in this theatrical portrayal of Holmes while mimicking the voice of actor Basil Rathbone, his favorite icon for the sleuth. He would often begin by stating a few basic facts.

"What is it that we know so far Watson? Grace's life consisted of a simple schedule. This was no stranger who had briefly entered the domain of her life. On-going abuse required continuous encounters. Yet complete searches of her room, her belongings, and her clothes have produced no tangible clues. How could this scoundrel perpetuate such an unconscionable crime at so many intervals and not leave at least some shred of evidence on the victim's undergarments, other personal belongings, or physical signs on her body that any observant parent might readily discover?"

As Holmes often did after presenting a puzzling question to his protégé, Dr. Watson, or Inspector Lestrade of Scotland Yard, he might answer it before they could respond.

"I think it's quite clear. First, the clothes would have to be placed a good distance from the horrific acts to prevent any possible contamination. Then, this progenitor of evil would have to be sure the body was cleansed thoroughly to leave no incriminating residues. This would require a very controlled environment in which the rapist felt at ease and in total control. Moreover, he would have to be a master of manipulation in order to dominate his victim and prevent her from physically resisting, which might leave bruises that would reveal his acts, and potentially his identity. These undeniably necessary elements also make it clear that this perpetrator must be cunningly experienced at committing this crime. He is at the very least, a serial paedophile . . . a man of the most fiendish nature. We must now discover who this yet unknown person was in our poor Grace's life, and what venue he employed to commit these heinous acts."

At other times, this foray into fantasy included voicing Dr. Watson's words of reply filling the air in the tenor of actor Nigel Bruce, Rathbone's constant cohort.

Yes, he thought; he had honed in on a profile of who this perpetrator might be and the conditions necessary for him to commit his crimes. He was also sure, that while he needed this exercise, due to his lack of experience in child related sex abuse cases, the SVU people were no doubt ahead of him in this thinking. Staying ahead of them to reach this monster first and destroy him was his highest priority.

However, it also hit him hard. This was no ordinary victim from whom he could remain at least somewhat detached. It was his dearest Grace he was talking about now. He acknowledged the coupling of words like contamination and residues with the memory of his daughter as disturbingly out of place and sickening to his senses. A fury now wanted to replace those ill feelings as well as a disgust at having to include such vile terms in the process of remembering the loss of his lovely daughter.

He knew he had to quell his anger for now, saving it for the day he would face his prey. He would need a much more composed and diplomatic posture if he was to maintain the cooperation of all the other official players in this investigation, to use them as a conduit to accomplish his goal. He was hoping that would start with SVU Sergeant Meehan's acquiescing to allow him to sit in on tomorrow's interview with the O'Reilly boy.

CHAPTER NINE

Wednesday: December 16th

At 8:15, joined by Janet Meehan's partner, Ted Laney, inside the listening booth for an interrogation room at the Four-Five, Dax was observing her interview getting nowhere. It was clear to him that the O'Reilly boy was totally distraught and uninvolved criminally in his daughter's abuse. Yet her line of questioning continued to pursue that path.

Despite her several years on the force, Sergeant Meehan was a new introduction for Dax. He had little interaction with SVU over the years. Their involvement in sexually based homicide cases created a very clear line of jurisdiction. While in earlier years, he socialized with his fellow officers at various "police" bars, he dropped attending those activities before Meehan arrived on the scene. His growing notoriety not only required his attendance at other social gatherings, but his desire to fraternize with the temptations those hangouts often offered became less alluring after the birth of his daughter. He had heard the rumors about Meehan's drinking prowess and party stamina, but never had their paths crossed until this morning.

When they met earlier for his required suspect elimination interview, as requested by Daley the night before, he discovered her to be a very solid cop, though burdened with a common trait held by most females in the NYPD. She was cordial, but held up a guard against appearing emotional in any way to avoid discriminatory criticism from her male counterparts. She had short brown hair and brown eyes with brows that were left in their natural, un-plucked state, and no makeup. He would not describe her as pretty, but a person with a pleasant face. He also surmised her stocky build had more to do with gym time than food intake. Her clothing was sharp and stylish, though more unisex than female, a buttoned white cotton shirt with a dark blue amorphous tie adding to the look. He was sure of several things. She was street wise, intelligent, committed, and not a person you would want unhappy with you, all great traits for anyone tracking down sex offenders.

As understanding as Meehan seemed at first when he tried to convince her to let him sit in on the interview, she stood her ground against the idea. She was adamant about taking no chances that anything the boy revealed about his possible involvement could be tainted due to any pressure from the presence of the victim's father, cop, or no cop. He knew she was right and came to accept her offer to listen in from the booth, especially after she explained all the promises that were made to the boy's parents he would be treated gently.

"I don't think we're going to get much from this kid," Laney said shaking his head.

"No, because it's clear he's not criminally involved." Dax responded.

"Maybe we'll need a shrink to be really sure." Laney retorted, and Dax caught the regret come over his face at questioning the Lieutenant's reputed judgment on such things.

Dax tried giving him a half smile to put him at ease, but was getting more edgy by the minute. He was sure the boy could not take much more without completely breaking down. It was all Dax could do to keep from barging in.

He finally decided on a more direct approach to employ with the boy. With a short salute to Laney, he quietly slipped out a side door and worked his way downstairs and outside. He wanted to approach the boy's parents at just the right moment so they would not feel put upon. As they walked from the station door, he could see the O'Reilly's were visibly shaken and trying their best to console their whimpering son, both attempting to hug him, and losing no time getting to their car as fast as they could to remove him from the environment. He noted with a twinge of concern that their wear worn thin coats were inadequate for the day's frigid morning as they headed toward a car whose sight leveled doubts about its ability to even start. He waited until Mrs. O'Reilly had hugged him one more time and put Tommy in the back seat on the passenger side. Mr. O'Reilly was already in the driver's seat reaching back with a calming hand to his son. She looked up. "Oh my God, it's you Mr. McGowan," she said startled, immediately recognizing him from all the media coverage surrounding Grace's death.

"Hello Mrs. O'Reilly. That's one brave boy you have there."

"Well sir, Mr. McGowan that's very nice of you to say," her thick Irish brogue coming through and evidencing the family's likely immigration to the U.S. not long before their son's birth. "This whole thing has been quite the ordeal for our boy. Oh, I am so, so sorry, that's not to make any less of what you have suffered, sir. No, no, not at tall. My dear God, I can't even imagine what you and your poor missus must be goin' tru." Tess said trembling in her attempt to apologize for what she deemed a terrible error.

"Mrs. O'Reilly, we parents have it very tough indeed when we lose a child, but we forget sometimes the terrible loss that is felt by their friends, young things like your son, not able to cope with such tragedy." Dax's diction instinctively reverted to a well-remembered cadence of just off the boat relatives in his own family, but avoided the strong urge to add the accompanying brogue in full empathy with the distraught woman in front of him, not wanting her to feel condescended to in any way by such a slip.

"Oh, to be sure, Mr. McGowan, sir. No one realizes that fact to be so true. My Tommy and your daughter were such good friends. And we all much appreciated the rides home your good wife gave him from their religion classes every week. And please Mr. McGowan, we apologize most sincerely for not comin' to ya daughter's funeral. Poor Tommy . . . well, he just couldn't . . . he just couldn't handle it. Besides, he hasn't been hisself as it is these past many weeks."

Dax felt his eyes blink hard as he honed in on her words. "Has the lad been out of sorts of late, unable to focus at times? Poor Grace seemed to have that problem as well," he offered.

Mr. O'Reilly was standing outside the car now leaning with both elbows on the roof to join the conversation. Dax grabbed a glimpse of little Tommy laid out in the back seat with a blanket over him; his eyes closed attempting to sleep. "Sure it is, Mr. McGowan. I work a good many hours and have to rely on Tess here to watch over the boy. But she can't figure out what's botherin' him so, and we can't afford the kind of doctor he might need."

All manner of suppositions were going off in Dax's head. The possibilities of the boy's involvement had suddenly become wide open. He was fighting the notion of entering the car to question him. He knew better, and that giving him time to recuperate and get back to the comfort of safe and familiar surroundings was necessary if there was any chance of his opening up.

"Mr. and Mrs. O'Reilly, I think I can help. First, I want you to know I was aware that Tommy and Grace were friends. I think as Grace's father, I might be able to relieve some of the pressure on your boy if he and I could have a little talk."

Dax waited knowing the request could go either way. To his pleasure, a look of relief appeared on both their faces as Mrs. O'Reilly said sighing, "Oh, Mr. McGowan, that would be most appreciated. Are ya sure with all ya have to deal with, ya know . . ."

"Really, no problem. It's clear your Tommy is suffering and I very much want to do this. How about I contact you in the next hour or so and we plan for later this morning? I suggest we meet at your home so Tommy can feel more at ease."

"Oh, but of course, sir," she answered. "Whatever is convenient for you would be just fine."

After offering their phone number and address with smiles of anticipation, the O'Reillys sped off as if the sooner they might reach their home and take his call, the sooner their son might somehow be freed of his stresses.

CHAPTER TEN

Before he could schedule a meeting with the O'Reillys, Dax was to stop home at the insistence of his mother. During Grace's funeral, she had correctly diagnosed the growing chasm between him and Darlene. As he walked from the grave to his car that day, she put both her arms around one of his in that certain way a mother shows special concern and is about to offer some advice. In a disarming manner, she started, "Who was that priest you were talking to? I don't know him."

He's Grace's . . . was Grace's CCD teacher over at St. Marks, Father Wendich. He was trying to be supportive, a decent guy."

Having only asked the question as an ice breaker, she launched into her real concern. "Dax, how are things with you and Darlene? You sat next to her during the service, but it seemed you hardly touched her, or were looking out for her like, you know, the way a husband should. This is the time when a husband and wife need each other the most. My God Dax, you can't let this somehow come between you!"

He knew the futility of trying to explain the history of his relationship with Darlene, how any interdependence they shared was based solely on their love for Grace, to say nothing of Darlene's temper issues.

"This isn't the time right now, mom," was all he said knowing the inevitability of a future follow up conversation. The meeting today was the result. He decided not to wait to see how long it might last. *Too much at stake.* He was dropping his phone into his coat pocket as he entered his house, having set the time to meet the O'Reillys in less than an hour. He was not relishing listening to what was coming his way, especially with Darlene sitting there, though he noticed upon pulling up, her car was nowhere to be seen. No matter, he thought; he now had a deadline to leave regardless.

The meeting went as expected, except that Darlene had exited before his arrival telling his mother that she needed some down time away from everything, and was going to spend the next few days with a college friend in New Hampshire. This left his mother at a loss in her strategy to get them to communicate with each other.

Dax listened and nodded a lot simply repeating that whatever the future held it would be between Darlene and him. He knew she was not ready to be told that they had already spoken about splitting up as being the best thing, and had contacted an attorney to represent both of them in an amicable divorce. Through their pain, they were somehow able to admit to each other that beyond their shared love for Grace, their secondary attentions were directed toward their careers, and their previously active sex life had become a collateral damage victim of those priorities. Left unsaid, they both realized, that rather than a comfort, they had now only become a stark reminder to each other of their loss. Their last discussion, filled with tears, had ended without even the slightest semblance of an embrace.

Darlene's welcomed no-show for the meeting led to its shortened duration, leaving Mary McGowan in a state of disappointment. For Dax, it meant he would get to the O'Reillys all the sooner.

CHAPTER ELEVEN

"Ah, welcome Mr. McGowan, sir, or should I be sayin', Lieutenant?" Tess O'Reilly greeted at the door, her husband also walking up to shake his hand.

"Mr. and Mrs. O'Reilly, please . . . please call me, Dax."

"Dax it will be sir, if you'll be callin' me Tess, and you remember me husband Vincent?"

"Aye, that was my father's name" Dax replied, a bit of the brogue slipping out. He realized he was not likely to get them to drop the "sir" title and he was sure this Vincent was not a "Vinnie" like his old man. "Good to see you again, Vincent."

Once seated, Dax accepted an offer of coffee, and a small piece of layered jelly cake it appeared had just been purchased for his visit. As they exchanged pleasantries and the O'Reillys expressed good wishes to both he and his wife "during this terrible time," Dax took in his surroundings.

The O'Reillys lived in a small apartment on the second floor of a six story building on East 147th St. Well-known to Dax, this neighborhood had more than its share of crime. To make sure his car was left unmolested, while approaching the building, he held his coat open so the delinquents loitering about the front stoop could clearly see the gold shield attached to his belt. The strong odor of urine coming off the small black and white porcelain tiles in the cramped entranceway was not unexpected. From there, he walked a long narrow hallway to a back stairwell going up to their apartment, 2C.

Upon entering, Dax passed Tommy's tiny bedroom on the left

just inside the door. He was lying on his side on a bed against the far wall with his back to them. The kitchen was opposite Tommy's room on the immediate right. From it exuded the aroma of beef gravy and potatoes, staples of Irish cooking. Two steps down the hall further on the right past the kitchen was the only bathroom, and the parent's bedroom another two steps on the right from there. On the left, just down from Tommy's bedroom, was the small living room where they were now seated. He had been offered a worn, but clean, cloth covered chair in front of the only window in the room on the far wall facing its doorway. Tommy's parents sat against the wall to his right on a love seat that subbed for a couch, Tess sitting closest to him. A large blanket stretched over it entirely. However, the edges of large holes in the cushions beneath it were quite evident. The only artwork in the room consisted of a small picture of the Virgin Mary hung over an ancient looking television on the wall to his left, and a crucifix over the arched doorway to the room. The still damp, early 20th century birch wooden floor had been mopped clean only minutes before, but unable to hide decades of apartment dwellers wear.

As Tess was now going on apologizing for the condition of their home, Dax could discern Vincent's old country shame for not providing better for what he thought he should for his family. His weather worn face and hands were those of a man who worked the most menial kind of outdoor construction jobs, doing all that his likely limited education might offer. His clothes were clean, evidencing an unmistakable hand-washed look, with holes nearly worn through at the elbows and knees. Dax pictured maybe one other set, if that, in his bedroom drawer, with possibly an outdated suit hanging in the closet which he wore to church on Sunday. It probably still fit him well, Dax thought, only because the family could not afford to eat well enough to put on the extra weight most Americans complained about gaining. Tess's light blue jumper covering a plain black blouse was a match to one worn by the matriarch in Frank McCourt's book and movie, *Angela's Ashes*, the saga of a destitute Irish family burdened with the patriarch's poverty driven alcoholism.

It was clear to him the courage it took for this struggling family to invite someone they discerned to be from a much higher social station into their home, but for the sake of the child they loved so dearly. To control the lump gathering in the back of his throat, he took an extra sip of coffee before responding to Tess' apologies.

"Tess, please, most of us New York City Irish folks know all about tough times when we started out raising our families. Oh the stories I've heard . . . both happy and sad they are."

Dax knew this wasn't the slightest bit true of his background, but was the only thing he could think to say. The resulting grins on their faces and Vincent response of, "True it is, sir . . . true it is," seemed to break the ice on the issue for them.

"How's Tommy?" Dax asked.

"He's not doin' well." Tess said with a fear filled face. "That ip to the police station unnerved him it did. And Dax," his name coming out clumsily, "he's not so sure he should be havin' this talk with ya. We . . . me and Vincent, told him we thought it best he does, but he's frightened somethin' terrible. We don't know why, or what to do."

Her statement had Dax struggling with how to get the critical information he believed Tommy most likely possessed, and at the same time address the valid concerns of his parents.

"Tess . . . and Vincent, I've spoken with many, many people under the most trying of circumstances, and I can assure you, this conversation will be good for Tommy," he said, wanting desperately for that to be true. "Talking is what sets a child free from hurt and pain. Bottling it up only makes things worse." Dax suddenly found himself fighting to focus on Tommy, attempting to push from his mind how he knew he had failed to apply that same simple logic where Grace was concerned.

Tess turned to her husband, as if to get his approval, but got only a shrug, saying it was up to her. With but a moment's hesitation, "Well, we'll be doin' it then." Tess dropped her head for a long minute, then raised it slowly and looked directly into Dax's eyes, "Ya will be very careful now won't ya, Mr. McGowan? Me Tommy seems near the edge of a cliff."

No more informality. No more just Dax. Tess was openly demanding that the Lieutenant get through to her child and do no damage in the process.

"You have my word," was all Dax could say, determined to keep that promise.

CHAPTER TWELVE

Dax was thrust into an excruciating alliance with Vincent O'Reilly. They both sat speechless in hopes that Tess could talk Tommy into coming out and speak with, "Grace's lovin' father" as she was describing him. From the short distance to the boy's bedroom, they heard every word of her entreaties and every word of his sobbing refusals. Then, in a desperate attempt to have Tommy agree, his mother grabbed both his arms and insisted he look her squarely in the eye.

"Tommy, your father and me are thinkin' this may be the most important conversation you may ever have in your life. I know that Grace was your very good friend, and she's callin to ya right now . . . I can hear her callin' to ya to talk to her daddy. She has a message for ya Tommy, and only he can give it to ya. Do ya understand how important it is for that poor girl to rest in peace?" Her last words ended in a near shrill of emotion.

Dax had no place in his worldview for liaisons with the dead, but Tess's approach to Tommy was brilliant. Tommy's unselfish response of, "I'll do anything to help Grace," was also the key he knew he needed to get through to the boy. As Tess brought Tommy into the living room, her arm around him, her raised eyebrows and knowing look in his direction reminded Dax of how genius abounds, even in poverty.

After several more hugs and entreaties from Tess for Tommy to "tell Mr. McGowan everything," the O'Reillys exited to the kitchen and knowingly turned on a radio to provide sound cover for their conversation.

Tommy was sitting on the edge of the love seat now, turned toward Dax, but with his head lowered considerably. Dax wondered how anyone could have ever thought this distraught little freckled faced boy was ever a threat to his Grace.

"Tommy, its good being here with you. I know you and I have never met before today, but I already know that Grace loved you and cared about you very much."

"Did she say that?" he asked looking up hopefully.

"Well, when we would talk about this boy, 'Tommy,' that she knew at school, I could tell she cared about you very, very much." Dax attempted to stay as close to the truth as he could. "Now I get to finally meet that special boy."

Tommy half smiled before lowering his head again. Dax went on. "I'll bet you loved her and cared about her very much, and want to do everything you can to help her."

"Oh yes, Mr. McGowan, sir . . . anything, sir."

"Tommy, I think someone was hurting Grace, and that same person was hurting you, and you know what Grace wants Tommy? Grace wants her daddy, the policeman, to put that man in prison and stop him from hurting you anymore. Grace wants that very much, Tommy. She told me that," he said hoping the strain in his voice was not as evidenced as he felt it to be.

He waited, knowing this was the point when he would not say another thing no matter how long it took. Tommy had to absorb what he said, and decide for himself whether it was important enough to him that Grace get what she wanted, more than he was afraid to tell what he knew.

"But, Mr. McGowan . . . if . . . if I tell . . . I will lose my daddy, and Grace will lose you." Tears were streaming down his face, small sobs interrupting his words as the distraught boy was fighting off the need to weep openly.

Dax was searching to say the right thing now. He had to keep Tommy going in the right direction without making him aware of, or scaring him with the anger that was now rising up inside him. It was his deciphering the obvious method of the abuser's manipulation that was driving it. He recovered enough to go on. "Tommy, whoever said you would lose your daddy was lying."

"But God doesn't lie, does he sir?" Tommy asked puzzled.

Dax understood the boy was saying it more as a test, hoping he could explain to him how God doesn't lie, but that he also wouldn't lose his daddy. "Tommy, it's true that God doesn't lie, but it is true that people sometimes lie. Whoever told you you'd lose your daddy was lying." He waited again.

"But priests don't lie . . . right, Mr. McGowan?" Dax's mind immediately reverted to Holmes' train of thinking. Tommy's last question confirmed what was becoming clear. The bottom line was their abuser was the priest. He began to fix timelines and situations in his head. He thought through his previous logical discourse with "Watson" injecting the priest as the perpetrator and it all fit perfectly. Of course, the controlled environment for the crime had to be the church, or more likely the rectory. The nature of the manipulation was clear. To keep the children silent in exchange for his sexual perversions, he threatened the power of God to control the life and death of their fathers. And of course, he thought, it would be in the early morning on a Friday, after a Thursday and her second CCD class of the week that his sweet Grace would be in the greatest despair, having been raped twice in three days. He instantly pictured Wendich's face with the fiendish sneer of a master manipulator. The intense takeover of rage was back now, except this time he had a known target for it. Picturing his hands around Wendich's throat, strangling him with all his strength, and wanting to respond sanely to this tortured boy's question, were fighting over the control of his mind.

"Of course they lie!" he shouted.

Tommy jumped back raising his hands in fear and began crying loudly. His reaction immediately broke Dax free from his anger, the little boy's anguish too critical to ignore. Stirred by the outburst, the O'Reillys rushed into the room. Dax leaned over to Tommy and said in the calmest tone he could garner, "Tommy, your mother was right. This was a very important conversation, and you have helped me solve a major police case. You Tommy are a hero. You Tommy have helped Grace more than you could ever imagine. And you know what, Tommy, I can guarantee you that Father Wendich will never have any power to take your daddy away from you . . . ever!"

His words had the desired effect. Tommy sat expressionless for a moment. Then he dropped his head and in a faint voice, "And I can stop going in that room with him?"

"Oh yes . . . absolutely Tommy! You will never have to go anywhere near him again. Not only will your daddy be safe, but so will you. We're going to make sure you never get hurt again and we're going to fix anything that has been hurt. You're such a hero, Tommy my boy, such a hero!"

Tess and Vincent, now sitting on either side of their son, were both hugging him and each other as tightly as they could as Tommy was again in a state of complete breakdown, only now from the major relief he had just been gifted.

Dax went on to tell them everything their conversation had revealed. He could see their emotions visibly vacillating between intense anger and their own version of relief. He assured them that Tommy would need plenty of professional help, and he would personally arrange for him to get whatever was needed. While he was relating everything he could think of to put their minds at ease, knowing there would be a long road of recovery for their son, his cop's mind took over.

"Have you had any recent contact with the priest?"

"Sure we have," said Tess. "He called just as we came home from the police station. He was wonderin' why Tommy missed class yesterday, the fuckin' son ov-a-bitch. Can you imagine that? Your poor little girl only two days in the ground, and the bastard wants his perversions satisfied again already. I'll kill him . . . I will Lieutenant! Forget me soul's destination! I'll kill the bastard dead on sight!" Likely, a bit out of character for her use of such language, Dax thought, it was clear Tess was beyond livid. And, while Vincent had now begun to talk about murdering Wendich with his bare hands, Dax was sure he would never beat his wife to the deed.

"Did he say anything else?"

"No sir, but he seemed more than a wee bit nervous when I told him you'd be over to have a heart-to-heart with our Tommy. Sure, he'd be most nervous. He knew you'd get Tommy to expose him, the fuckin' bastard. "

Dax knew he had to move quickly now. He made quick mention of his need to capture Wendich as he jumped to his feet. It seemed only a few short steps to get to the kitchen to grab his overcoat off the back of a chair, when he felt a small but strong hand grab his arm. He looked down at a suddenly calmer, Tess O'Reilly, whose warm brown eyes were now filled with tears. "God love ya, Dax

McGowan. Fa sure, you saved our boy's life and maybe his soul at the same time. We can't never repay that. I can only pray for ya to have the best of rewards in heaven."

"Thank you, Tess. But, I'll have to get their first. Though I'm sure if anyone has sway with the man upstairs, it's you."

As he turned to leave, he reminded himself that he didn't believe in punishing Gods, but defiantly thought that if there was one, he would surely be in the deity's sights, as he was assuredly going to beat the O'Reillys to the demise of Father Peter Wendich.

CHAPTER THIRTEEN

Dax knew that Wendich, like most serial criminals, would have heightened instincts about his imminent capture, and Mrs. O'Reilly's revelation to him about his scheduled talk with Tommy was sure to send him packing. Being the first to discover his identity and availing himself of the opportunity to corner and kill him was decidedly diminished by the realization that he was likely already on the run. He would take his shot if he had it, but was already accepting he would need plenty of help to prevent Wendich from getting somewhere he would have trouble finding him. He had heard about priests disappearing in some of these sex abuse cases, squirreled away somewhere in the bowels of the church's worldwide bureaucracy and lost forever. Being Meehan's case, she would have to coordinate the BOLO, the Be On The Look Out, and other means to search for the perp.

"This is Lieutenant Dax McGowan. I want to talk to Sergeant Meehan right away."

"Yes sir, just a moment," was the dispatcher's response.

"Meehan here; what's up Lieutenant?"

"Meehan, it's the priest. It's the fucking priest who was abusing Grace and the O'Reilly boy. Listen, we've got to grab this guy before he leaves town. He's already spooked. And, we . . ."

"Whoa, whoa there Lieutenant. This isn't your case and nobody's going to be arrested until I say so." Meehan was coming off more than pissed at what she read as him trying to push her around.

Dax took a deep breath, backed off a bit, but remained direct.

"Listen, I just spoke with the O'Reilly boy. He told me that Wendich threatened both him and Grace, that if they didn't cede to his wishes for sex, and keep it a secret, he had the power to ask God to take the lives of their fathers from them."

"You mean the CCD teacher?" she broke in. "He was our next stop on this." she said a bit defensively. "Where are you now?"

"I'm headed over to the rectory at St. Marks. Listen, unwittingly Tess O'Reilly told him that I was going to have a sit down with their son, and she said he reacted agitated to that information. This guy is a pro. I suspect we're already too late."

"Alright, I'll grab my partner and meet you there. If you get there first, you just keep an eye out for him and wait for us. We don't want to fuck this up by screwing with procedure," she added while summoning her partner from across the room with a wave of her free hand. "I mean it McGowan, hands off till we get there."

"See you there," was his only response.

Dax had waited to call her until he was already pulling up the long drive off 163rd St. to St. Mark's rectory. It was going to take Meehan and her partner more than a few minutes to travel west from the Four-Five in Throgs Neck, giving him ample time to take out Wendich if the now slim possibility presented itself.

Dax had never been to St. Marks, but could easily recall how to get there and the location of the rectory in the back of the property from simply taking a mind's picture of it once as he drove by. There was only one car in the parking lot, an older, black Ford Taurus sedan with a clergy emblem in the back window. He pulled in next to it to check its interior. A large plastic bag of groceries on the front seat with a pharmacy package on top sporting a Medicare billing was an immediate indication it didn't belong to Wendich. Being a newly transplanted European would make him ineligible for the coverage. While there was a slim chance that Wendich might still be inside, Dax's instincts told him otherwise. He reached in his pocket for his phone.

CHAPTER FOURTEEN

"I'm driving this piece of shit as fast as I can." Laney finally said after a litany of requests from his partner to go faster.

"Listen Ted, everything tells me we've got to get there before he offs this bastard. We both saw the results of the tirade at his house. My old partner Daley warned me to watch out for this. He doesn't give a shit about the perp, just doesn't want his buddy getting trashed for doing it."

Laney's response was interrupted by the crackling sound of dispatch breaking in, "Sergeant Meehan, its Lieutenant McGowan being patched through to you."

She grabbed the mic, wondering if McGowan might be telling her about something he may have already done. Cautiously . . ."Meehan here."

"Hey Meehan, I'm certain he's not here," Dax said, creating some relief in the center of her chest. "We're going to need a warrant to search this place. Can you get that process in the works?"

Annoyed again at his controlling tone, she shot back, "Already done . . . on its way . . . made that call the instant we got in the car."

"You already got a judge to agree to sign a warrant based on my talk with the O'Reilly boy?" Dax said in a pleased disbelief.

"Hey McGowan," she started authoritatively, "remember that Monsignor MacEachin over at St. Michael's caught diddling those four altar boys? Well, one of those kids belonged to that hard ass judge, James Ripley. Ripley was always a stickler on warrants before that happened. Now he'd sign scribbling on a napkin delivered by his paperboy if I called and told him it was a warrant to search the premises of one of these sick fucks. When I tell a friend I have at the D.A.'s office that Ripley has already agreed to sign it if they process the paper, it's an instant go from there. One of our newbies is probably already at the judge's office as we speak. Hell, the warrant might beat us there," she said sarcastically, and with an air of being totally in charge.

"Well, that's impressive, Sergeant. See you in a few."

Unable to fight the temptation, Dax quickly loped up the steps of the cement stairway and brick front porch. He knocked hard on a thick wooden door framed with leaded glass sidelights. In answer to his third fist pounding, Dax heard "Coming, coming," from somewhere in the back of the residence.

A tall, very thin man pulled the door open and began with the expected, "Can I help you? Sorry, I was just putting some groceries in the fridge and still need to retrieve the rest from my car."

Dax was face to face with a man who looked as though life had been tough on him. He wore an open-at-the-top green and white striped flannel shirt with a frayed collar, revealing a torn white t-shirt underneath. Over that, his leather winter waistcoat looked like it had seen better days before it was run over by a truck, or so it seemed. Baggy khaki pants hung far enough over heavily scuffed brown loafers to touch the floor. No one was going to argue that this man had taken a vow of poverty if he'd ever claimed one, Dax thought. There was also no joy in his face. His wrinkles were stacked with wrinkles of their own, signs of an existence that tripped on most of life's hurdles instead of jumping over them. Dax guessed him at mid-sixties, though he looked a good deal older, a classic case of it's not the years, but the mileage.

Flipping out his gold shield, "I'm Lieutenant Dax McGovern, NYPD. Is Father Peter Wendich here?"

"I know who you are, Lieutenant," he said blandly. "No, Father Wendich is not here."

"Do you know where I can reach him? It's important." Dax struggled to keep his voice from quivering and exposing his tension about how much head start his prey had in escaping.

"No, I don't. He left some time ago, I suspect while I was out shopping. I have no idea where he is."

Dax was picking up that tone cops get from people who consider themselves too busy to be annoyed or have something to hide. He was betting the latter. "And who is it I'm addressing?" he asked.

"I'm Monsignor Murphy."

"Well, Monsignor, since you know who I am, then you're aware there is an investigation into my daughter's death, and since Father Wendich was a teacher of hers, I need to find him and ask him a few questions. Do you have any idea how I can reach him?"

"Since when, Lieutenant, do cops investigate the deaths of people in their own family?" the Monsignor's demeanor changing from annoyance to defiance.

"Since when did monsignors become so acquainted with police procedure?" It was clear the Monsignor was not going to be the least bit helpful, but he decided to give it one more shot. "When Father Wendich left, was he alone or did he leave with someone else?"

"I'm sure you'll have to ask him that when you see him as it's his business until then." was the acidic reply.

"Well Monsignor, the lead detective and her partner on this case will be here any minute." Dax turned his head only slightly, assuming the sound of a car speeding up the driveway was them. "A search warrant for the premises won't be far behind. I suggest you might think about being more cooperative than you're sounding right now. Obstruction of justice carries a nasty sentence, white collar or no white collar."

The Monsignor smiled haughtily, which Dax read as the cleric's belief that the white collar did in fact have its perks. He turned as Meehan and Laney walked up to the door. With no chance to wipe out Wendich for now, he stepped aside.

"I'm Sergeant Meehan with the Special Victims Unit and this is my partner Detective Laney," she began. "We're investigating the sexual abuse and death of Grace McGowan, and we want to meet with Father Peter Wendich, now!"

"I heard the girl committed suicide, Detective, and I was just telling her father here . . ."

Dax clenched his fists hard. *"This bastard is trying to portray Grace's death as something unrelated to the abuse?"*

Meehan jumped all over that. "Listen buddy. Little eleven-year-old girls don't commit suicide without reasons, and this little girl had plenty. Would you like to come down to the station and have a debate about that with all the staff at SVU . . . one at a time?"

Meehan was hot. She turned to Dax. "Is this here guy some kind of clergy, McGowan?" she said with as much disrespect as she could summon.

Dax was settling down. He was in sync with her tirade. "He's the Monsignor around here."

"Oh good . . . one of the higher-ups who has always been so helpful in these cases." The sarcasm was dripping from her mouth. "Listen, we believe the perp may not be here, but we need to search his room. Are you going to let us in, or do we go and have that debate at the station house I just suggested."

The issue was moot as a patrol car with siren blaring was turning up the driveway. Without turning to look, she shoved her face to within an inch of Murphy's. "The cop in that car back there will give you all the necessary paperwork. Now get out of my way." She pushed by the Monsignor with a not-so-minor shoulder jab to his and headed into the long hallway behind him.

Dax was right behind her and Laney. They passed a stairway just inside the door on the right that he surmised led to the living quarters upstairs. There was a large sitting room on the left and across from that on the right, before reaching the kitchen, an old den serving as an office.

"You know we have to check all these rooms out McGowan, including the storage building out back, just in case this dick is hiding somewhere. We'll go through the kitchen's back door," she said pointing to a rear exit off that room, "and be right back. I know you'd like to begin the sleuthing stuff there, Sherlock. You can start upstairs if you'd like. I'm counting on you to not touch anything, of course."

He nodded and mouthed a silent thank you as he mentally reminisced on Daley's previous comments about her "take no prisoners" approach. He suspected it was the effect of case after case of children's innocence being stolen and their trust destroyed, coupled with the constant stonewalling and protection of criminal priests by the hierarchy. Those conditions had created a monster . . . *a monster for the good guys,* he thought.

Heading back to the stairway by the front door, Dax caught the monsignor in the office on the phone speaking in hushed tones making a frantic call, likely, he surmised, to his superior, the Archbishop. He considered for the moment that his tracking down

50

one rogue priest who had killed his daughter was surely going to evolve into a wider range of players and bad guys. Any larger number of players was going to make it substantially more difficult to isolate Wendich and take him out. Focused on homicide his entire career, he admitted to himself that he was navigating unknown waters. He would have to sit down with Meehan and become better educated on what might lay ahead if Wendich was going to be aided by the entire Catholic institution in his escape.

As he began to turn away from watching the Monsignor's call, his eyes caught what seemed to be an anomaly in his totally disorganized office. Papers were strewn everywhere, some sitting on the floor yellowing with age. But, in the far left corner of the room was an almost shrine like display. It was populated by neatly arranged sets of newspaper clippings and copies of military school commendations hanging on the wall next to numerous pictures of a young man, obviously a student at the Naval Academy. In some of those pictures, the Monsignor appeared much better dressed and in high spirits, beaming large smiles. *"Even in the longest of unsuccessful lives there are moments of brightness."* He moved on after taking special note of what he had just seen.

As he passed the sitting room again, now on his right, he observed two severely worn, old Victorian style tufted couches facing each other on either side of a soot-covered fascia, centrally located, fireplace. A large mahogany coffee table placed directly in front of it and between the couches, felt right at home being well marred and covered with dust. Three soiled armchairs, strewn randomly about the room, sat on several grossly faded oriental rugs. The underlying dark wooden floor was in dire need of sanding and re-staining.

The room's perimeter walls were covered with a series of pictures of men wearing various forms of head coverings assigned to Monsignors, mostly reddish violet zucchettos and miters. Aside from being a place designated to congregate for social occasions, the room was also a monument to past supervisors of the very old St. Mark's parish . . . its longevity evidenced by one wall containing some 19th Century black and white photos of prelates. Unfortunately, the dimly lit room with its velvet drapes drawn, made the dust covered visages within their frames appear more like characters from a haunted house.

Dax wondered how far back it was that this room would have

been brightly lit and ornately decorated for the Christmas season, exhibiting freshly painted walls and smartly polished furniture. The oft-dusted photographs would have glistened from the flickering of firelight revealing the positive smiles of their inhabitants. The setting would have been unmistakable evidence of the fastidious care given it by a full time housekeeper who would have met them at the front door with a wide smile and an Irish brogue of joy at their arrival. It was a sad state, he thought. The Catholic Church had brought this precipitous fall from grace and dignity upon itself, a loss even he felt some empathy for. Though, his desire to inflict punishment on Grace's killer was no less diminished by these observations.

His much higher priority than insipid nostalgia was the desire to observe Wendich's quarters. The result of fast paced, energetic leaps, Dax found himself at the top of the stairs. He observed what was a dormitory of bedrooms. Three on the left and two larger ones on the right, as the stairway came up into the center of the hallway. A quick check of the open doorways revealed only one bedroom on each side was occupied. The larger of the two was the Monsignor's. A pair of small-waisted pants across the bed, and on the nightstand, a near empty prescription bottle containing the same anti-depressant he had observed in the Monsignor's car made for the easy determination. The smaller bedroom on the left had to be Wendich's.

Dax stood in the hall and drew a deep breath. He was about to enter the room where he suspected his sweet Grace had been violated. With all the crime scenes he had attended, witnessing the remains of gruesome murders with little reaction or afterthought, he was struggling now to enter this empty room. While Wendich had been careful with the children before releasing them from his evil hands, he would likely have let his guard down in this place, his lair. Dax was sure there would be some degree of incriminating evidence at hand. As he mustered the courage to proceed, he heard Meehan's voice barking orders as her feet hit the steps hard on her way up. He was glad for the company.

"And Laney" she was yelling, "post a guy down there. I don't want anyone but CSI coming near here. Some Twitter freak has probably already got the word out about our surrounding this place, and the press won't be far behind."

She walked over to Dax at the entrance to the bedroom, "You probably have the same problem in homicide, eh Lieutenant? No quiet time to process a scene anymore with cell phone cameras and Twitter heads out there."

Straight faced, he nodded, pointed and said, "This is Wendich's."

Meehan immediately blew by him into the center of the bedroom with her hands on her hips, craning her neck in every direction. "Pretty damn austere in here!"

She continued with one derogatory remark after another as she pointed out the lumpy unmade single bed on the right, a small beat up chest of drawers opposite it on the left and an old style sink on the far wall, commonly built into bedrooms when the rectory was originally constructed. It contained an aging chrome fixture with a badly rusted drain that stained all the porcelain around it.

"No mirror in here, Dax. I guess if you're a sick fuck like this guy is, you wouldn't want to look at yourself either."

It was clear, that for Dax's sake her remarks became ever more ruthless. Only affording himself a moment's enjoyment of them, he knew he had to but didn't want, to look at the bed and imagine what went on there. Meehan's constant, humorous banter was at least a bit distracting.

Thanks to her forethought, it was only another five minutes before two CSI reps with paraphernalia in hand showed up. Removing the latex gloves he had donned earlier as a habitual precaution, he once again ignored who was in charge. "Good timing you guys. Please, as fast as you can on this one. This perp has a head start on us, and anything you can find indicating where he might be we'd appreciate knowing it immediately." They nodded and moved into high gear.

Realizing what he had just done . . . again, he turned to Meehan expecting the worst, but she had something else on her mind.

"Hey Dax, I want to clear something up . . . why we weren't on to this guy sooner."

"Hey Janet, no need to explain anything to me. I'm just as guilty for not thinking of him before now. Isn't it always that a priest is the last person anyone would think of . . . and a church building as an ongoing place of crime?"

"Well, that was true once." Meehan began. "With me now, if there's a priest anywhere near a sex abuse case, I'm right on him. We just didn't know until we interviewed some of the other kids today that this CCD class even existed. I hope you're not feeling like we were too slow to focus on him."

Dax raised his hand and shook his head. "Not at all. Hey, and I know I was stepping over the line to directly question the O'Reilly boy. Sorry . . . couldn't help myself." He managed to sound sincere, despite his personal motives belying the apology.

"Yeah and I should be all over you for that, but I'm glad for what you did. The guy may be on the run, but he's no longer hurting the boy or anyone else . . . at least for now."

"Meehan, I'd like to know more about what you've been facing with the church hierarchy and what roadblocks you've run into catching these priests. As you know, it's easier when you're tracking someone with local ties and known associates that speed the process. Tracking a pedophile priest, who not that long ago emigrated from another country, and who's now in the wind has to present its own set of challenges. I'm sure you've run into this before and have ideas on what we should do next?"

Disregarding the "we" reference and smiling slyly, "You have no idea my friend. I have a significant confidential resource that no one else has access to but me. Let's go outside clear of anyone's hearing. By the way, Laney whispered in my ear bud that the Monsignor just lawyered up.

CHAPTER FIFTEEN

Dax was sitting in Janet Meehan's car listening to her pass instructions to the precinct dispatcher for the BOLO on Wendich. Standard checks for travel venues and passport usage out of the city were included. She also relayed a lengthy list of specific physical features for Wendich which Dax had recorded on his Blackberry and emailed to her precinct's sketch artist.

Waiting on her, he began "playing his tapes back" to recall his cemetery conversation with the priest. The exercise only served to remind him once again of how muted his powers of observation became when his emotions were in a state of flux. *"How did I not catch something in his manner or voice to alert me to his possible involvement? Hell, the bastard's plea to allow God to take his vengeance, and no one else, should have set something off in my head!"*

Seeing Meehan replace the mic, his thoughts turned to more immediate concerns. "Janet . . ." Dax's witness of her performance with the Monsignor was changing his perception of her, seeing her more as a partner rather than a competing detective of a separate division of jurisdiction, "we really have no idea where this guy is from originally. His fundamental language is German, but it's uniquely mitigated by having lived somewhere else before he came to the States. I'd say possibly England, but more likely Ireland."

"Whoa there Lieutenant, how can you possibly draw that conclusion?"

"Well, as you know, this city is populated by large numbers of people from all over the world that have varying homeland based dialects. Variations to those accents occur as individuals are exposed to other forms of speech. Their age at the time of the introduction to a new speech pattern, and how long they are exposed, determine the extent of their personal variation . . . elementary really." He instantly wished he hadn't added that last affectation, aware it could be taken negatively.

"Well la di da! And while I totally understand what you're saying, just how would you know the difference . . . Bronx boy?"

"Well," Dax offered in a tone of bring contrite, "it's one of those things I've given special attention to over the years."

She nodded an acceptance of his explanation, and based on what she had heard about him, "Okay professor, I'll buy that. And hey, that description you just recorded for us? I've never heard anything like it. Left leg a good inch shorter than the right, a malformed finger nail on the left pinky finger and fuck, the location and size of wrinkles on the bastard's face . . . in centimeters? Where do you get all that shit? I mean I'm not complaining. I wish we could get something even close to that from all our witnesses. This is that Sherlock Holmesy thing everyone talks about isn't it?"

While Dax's transference into that alter ego was his most closely held secret, he reveled in knowing that others described him in those terms. While Janet's question found him squelching a flattered grin, he responded in a less conceited manner. "Hey, it's what I love about being a detective. I'm like you; I love catching the bad guys, and I've worked hard on whatever I thought would help."

She smiled at him like an old friend as his words perfectly described her own commitment, and now thought it a good time to check something out.

"And every once and a while, you just want to take one of those bad guys and blow the motherfucker away . . . right?"

Dax remained stolid, but correctly read her face as having deduced his intentions for Grace's killer. Saved by the interruption, they both looked up to see the Monsignor being escorted to the car for further questioning by Detective Laney. Dax suggested he follow them in his car to the Four-Five so they could discuss that confidential resource she had referred to earlier. He exited her car attempting to compute a reasonable response to her last inquiry, which he knew would inevitably be repeated.

CHAPTER SIXTEEN

Dax was navigating the length of the Four-Five's bullpen toward Janet's office to a bevy of supporting words from his "comrades in arms." It was a litany of, "I feel your loss man," and "We're gonna get that bastard." He smiled and nodded to each contributor, appreciating the solidarity that all cops shared when any one of them had become a victim themselves.

He saw Ted Laney heading from his left to meet him at the end of the large room. "Hey Lieutenant." "Hey Laney," they exchanged.

"Before you get with Janet, she asked me to catch you up. We haven't heard anything from the people at the airport, or any other means of travel, and as far as finding any connections within the city, he's a ghost. Even the local grocers and other storeowners near the rectory don't know him. We're trying to track down a passport photo from Homeland Security because there were no pictures at the residence. But hey Lieutenant, I listened to that recording you sent our sketch artist. Hell, sir," he chortled, "I've got money that based on your description, her drawing will be a better likeness than his passport photo."

Dax laughed. "Thanks Laney. Anything from the Monsignor?"

"Nada! It's clear he knows things he's not telling us because he's just not answering any questions. Oh, and his attorney was already on site waiting for us when we arrived. He's an expensive suit, not one this guy could afford on his own. Between him and the attorney, I don't see us getting anywhere. We can hold him till tomorrow morning, but unless we can come up with some leverage, we'll have to spring him."

"I'll work on that leverage thing if you don't mind . . . you know, maybe come up with an idea of my own," Dax said, trying not to seem intrusive. "Maybe some overnight jail time might help loosen him up. But just in case, I'll work on something."

"Hey . . . anything that helps." Laney shot back as he headed to his desk. "It would be nice to finally get one of these guys to fess up instead of the same old, same old nothing on these clergy cases."

Dax could see Meehan through the glass walls and door to her office. She was spreading out files on a display table on the opposite side of the room from her desk. She spied his approach and waved him in.

"Hey Janet, Laney just caught me up on the search so far and the lack of headway with the Monsignor."

"Yeah, it's déjà vu all over again with these red hats. It royally pisses me off, that for every priest perp we bring in, there's a Monsignor, or other higher up immediately covering for him. Then, if we bring that higher up in for questioning, there's always an attorney ready and waiting before we even get back to the precinct. By the time we settle down to question the guy, we've had calls from upstairs telling us we shouldn't be so hard on these pricks, or we have to be extra careful not to ruffle any feathers. It's a bunch of bullshit. If this were Mafia underlings selling heroin and their bosses covering it up, the brass and the fucking politicians would be singing our praises and looking to get their pictures taken with the prosecutors who'd be trying their cases. But hell no. The Archbishop's office makes a call to a city council member and eventually one of the dominos falls on our head. And you'll never see any of these smart ass politicians looking to get any face time in the press on these cases as if they're behind us cops in solving these atrocities . . . don't want to piss off the Catholics hierarchy around here, right?" The sputum was now flying on the ending "t" letters in her words.

"We've heard a good deal about that over in homicide, but I have to admit, I didn't realize how bad it was until now being involved so personally." Dax said, slipping into one of the folding chairs at the display table.

He began to consider what effect his own case might have in the realm of what was ordinarily a lukewarm legal response to these crimes. Never wanting to appear to be throwing his weight around, he had succeeded in avoiding ever playing that card. But he was well aware that he could raise substantial hell on any issue with his contacts downtown and his pull with the press. However, another factor was hanging over his head. *"How are you going to make life easier for SVU by personally killing Wendich . . . eh McGowan?"* He quickly decided this sudden pang of conscience was simply a distraction from what he knew he must do and cleared his mind to better listen to Meehan.

Still highly irate, she continued. "It's terrible Dax. Do we have to get pictures in the newspapers of the anal tears on these kids in order to get everyone's attention? But hell no, that'll never happen. We wouldn't want to offend anybody's sensibilities, now would we? We can't be upsetting any politician's constituency, right?" After a short pause, "Sorry for the ranting man. I reach the limits of my patience on every one of these priest cases."

As a further avoidance of his moral conundrum and her reference to anal tears, Dax was now observing what a dichotomy Janet was. She had a mastery of the Queen's English when she wanted to. The "magna cum laude" on her Master's Degree from Michigan State posted on her wall said she had the intellectual prowess to hold her own with anyone. However, she could also run several sentences with the word fuck in them often enough to compete with any street criminal. He could easily see her landing in SVU and dealing with the frustrations of clerical abuse cases had a good deal to do with that.

As if having read his mind, she turned more serious. "Listen, you're a pretty perceptive guy; so I'm going to fill you in on some things. But please just keep this to yourself."

"Okay . . . sure," he readily responded.

"I grew up in the small town of Haslett, Michigan after being born an 'OOPS!' child of the Catholic rhythm method. I worked hard and got a scholarship to enter the Criminal Justice Program at Michigan State less than ten miles from where we lived. My dad was a State Trooper.

I had a much older sister, Karen, who I loved dearly. Shortly after I began my education at State, she moved here to New York to work as a paralegal for Legal Aid. In my junior year, Karen was murdered and raped post mortem just outside her apartment on 77th street off Central Park West. She shared the higher rent of that place with five other girls so they could afford to live in a safe neighborhood . . . a lot of good that did. They were never able to prosecute the guy they liked for it due to a lack of hard evidence. It was already in Cold Case by the time I got here. I pull it out every once and awhile, hoping I've learned something new about being a detective that I can apply to the old evidence. No luck so far."

She was standing, bent at the waist with her head hanging quite low. Dax was watching her come off less like a confident cop, and more like the "kid" he imagined she was when she first arrived on the job.

"Anyway Dax, I worked my ass off to make sure I ended up in SVU, determined to find my sister's killer and be in a place where I could make a difference in getting these sociopaths off the street. So, if I come off a little hot sometimes and sound a little rough around the edges, it's this job. I really don't care about much else. But, I have all I can handle with these clergy abuse cases . . . especially when I can't get the system off its ass and do what's right by these kids and their families. And I want to tell you, this thing is a whole bunch worse than people know."

Janet was beginning to regain herself, pacing now. "Look, I know procedure says I've got to keep you out of this thing, but I need the kind of help only a connected cop like you can give. You and I share much the same thing now. You know the real deal pain personally, and you're getting better educated about what's really going on with these cases. Any help and influence you can bring to bear on this . . . we need it. I also know you want to off this son of a bitch. I really don't care if you do. Just be sure you don't do anything that gets in the way of making sure we get all the clerical players in this case . . . do you hear me Dax . . . all the fucking perps. With your juice, maybe we can get the big guy this time . . . the Archbishop, if he's involved. You've got to be open to the fact that in many of these cases the higher ups are just as responsible for the priest's actions as they are, maybe more so because they were either in a position to prevent it, or moved these bastards around from parish to parish to protect them. And, if you kill this motherfucker just to satisfy yourself, you could blow any chance of us getting him to flip on the higher ups that were involved."

Dax hadn't anticipated this. Janet was laying out his inner dispute right in front of him. He knew she was totally credible in doing that given the circumstances of her sister's death. He was at a loss as to how to respond. His first instinct was to defend his position.

"Tell me Janet. You find the proof and identify of the man responsible for your sister's death, and you have the opportunity, does he live or die?"

"All I can tell you is that I've reached a point where I don't know the answer to that question anymore. And hey, that's coming from a place not long ago when I would have readily said, he's a dead man. But, I also don't want to spend the next fifty years in prison, and not just for my own benefit. I'd be sitting there all that time thinking about all the kids I could save by taking these sick fucks off the street, and I've gotten pretty damn good at it. So, at this point, I don't know is all I can give you. This just happened to you. I guess I already know the answer if I asked you the same question. All too raw for you right now."

He had no response to her perfect logic. But Grace wasn't like his sister Eileen, or just some other close family member. He only knew that no other person ever in his life was so precious to him, and for whom he was so totally responsible to protect than Grace.

Regaining his composure, he leaned back in his chair. "Look, you and I are definitely on the same page, and I'll admit to maybe being short-sighted in terms of limiting my anger to just this particular priest. However, I won't make any promises just yet if for no other reason than I just can't. Just know I support everything you're saying. Maybe you can teach me some things along the way I need to learn . . . we'll see. Let's just be sure we find this guy, and not let him disappear on us. You referred earlier to a resource you might have to help?"

Dax watched her stare at him knowing she was making judgments about what she thought he could be counted on going forward. Then, as if finally dispensing with that line of thinking, she pulled up the chair next to him. "Have you ever heard of an organization called CABS?"

CHAPTER SEVENTEEN

Nothing could seem more normal than the arrival of three black cassocked priests at a JFK terminal gate. In fact, there were certain times of the year when it appeared that the black togged travelers outnumbered the general population. It followed that the Vatican, as well as many other Catholic enclaves around the globe would dispatch large numbers of its clerical representatives to and from the city that is one of its largest financial supporters. Today was no different.

At this busy travel hub, spectators observe all manner of priestly fashion . . . from the old world cotton cassock, with its unmistakable broad white collar, to well-tailored suits with only a hint of a white insert . . . all accessorized by distinctively styled ebony shoes, only the educated fashion eye was able to determine the wearer's country of origin.

The faces sitting upon those collars ran the gamut. There were the youthful and optimistic smiles of the very rare, newly ordained, to the older more stoic prelates of higher station, dressed down to basic priestly garb, either for travel comfort or much desired anonymity. Whatever the style and whoever the wearer, black was the color du jour today at any number of JFK gates.

So maybe today, it didn't appear that unusual for three priests travelling together to be dressed exactly alike. However, it might be a bit uncommon that their heads were completely shaven, their attire lacked any white collar, and out of character for clergy so young, their faces exhibited such a menacing and chilled expression. But, in the major rush of the hectic Christmas season, such anomalies might easily go unnoticed in such a sea of black.

CHAPTER EIGHTEEN

"CABS?" No, I assume that's an acronym of some sort?" Dax answered.

"Correct." Janet said. "It stands for <u>C</u>lergy <u>Ab</u>use <u>S</u>urvivors. It's a non-profit support organization founded some twenty years ago by a woman named Rebecca Bain. She was an abuse victim herself. She's still the President and driving force of the group. They're based out of Chicago. Dax, these people are extremely well organized with thousands of members, a chapter in every state, and a good many throughout the world. Their main mission is to provide support, counseling and legal referrals to clergy abuse victims. This woman, Rebecca Bain, is no stereotypical do gooder trying to overcome her own abuse by helping others. She has advanced well past that, and I think could run any major corporation. On the road to her recovery after repeated sexual abuse through middle and high school by a priest, she got a Master's Degree in Social Work, a Masters of Divinity from a theological seminary and a Juris Doctorate from Harvard. I know for a fact that her name strikes fear in the hearts of the Catholic hierarchy."

Dax was nodding in appreciation. "She surely perfected all the necessary variant parts of her education to match her life's work. That's a rare accomplishment in itself. But how can her organization help us?"

Janet was now smiling like a cartoon cat that had just captured a bird in its jaws. "Dax, my man, they have a system where they track the comings and goings of priests . . . not just known pedophiles, but all priests."

"You mean they'd have information on Wendich's last assignment before New York?"

"It's probably our best shot at this point." She reached for the files on her table. "Look, as you know, Wendich shows up out of nowhere at St. Marks. The prick lives a low profile existence so no one in the neighborhood really knows anything about him. Laney, along with a large group of uniforms, checked with a good number of the parishioners and all they can tell us is that this guy says the six am mass during the week and hears some confessions. Except for a few remarks like, 'seems like a pretty good guy,' the church members don't know him any better than we do."

"And, as we said, the one logical place for him to escape to is where he came from," Dax added.

"Exactly. Your guess of England or Ireland is no doubt a good one. But even if you're right, the next question is, where in either of those places he might be?"

For Janet, a flow of adrenaline was clearly at work. "I have four case files here where we had similar situations. This one was right in my precinct; two were out of the Four-Three, and one I received from a good friend up in Albany who called me for help. In all these cases, being able to track down where these perps came from helped us eventually locate the bastards. And goddammit Dax, only one got prosecuted because the diocese in the other three bought off the victim's families, getting them to drop the charges. Even in the prosecuted case, in Albany, they only got the priest, not the Bishop who knew he was a pedophile and placed him in that parish anyway. But, we were at least able to track them down and we did it with CABS' help.

"Did any of these cases involve priests who came to these assignments from outside the country?"

"Yes actually, one had transferred here from South America. Hopefully they have something on this guy. If anyone can help us, it's these people."

Dax put his right hand up in a "let's stop for a minute" fashion.

"Janet, I know that a victim or witnesses getting bought off happens, and we see our share of that over in homicide. But explain to me how any parent of a sexually abused child would let the perp get away with it, especially since kids can give testimony in some form of isolation so they don't have to go through the stress of a full court room, or have to stare down the defendant who raped them."

"It's a whole bunch of things. First, there's the money . . . there's always the money. In most of the cases, these families are pretty poor, and have no idea how they're going to afford the years of intensive counseling their kid is going to need . . . and needs right away. They can't rely on taking the long-term chance on winning or losing a civil suit. If the parents even try to go the legal route, the diocese purposely stretches them out till they can't handle it anymore and have to settle."

"The O'Reilly's definitely fit that profile," Dax said. "And I promised them I'd see to it Tommy would get the help he needs. I have to get on that right away."

Janet went on. "Not only does the hierarchy and their attorneys sit with the parents dripping honey from their mouths about how wonderful they are for providing the needed psychological help, in the name of Jesus of course, but they prey on these people's loyalty to the Mother Church. They all but accuse them that their negative testimony could lead to . . . and get this . . . the destruction of the one true church on earth. How's that for a Class A guilt trip?" Janet followed her words with the universal forefinger pointing to gag the back of her throat. "Most of these kids and their families are loyal Catholics with little or no education, and they fall for that bullshit."

"Okay, that more than answers the question of why most of these cases don't go to trial," Dax started, "but what about the Bishops and Archbishops who move these pedophiles from place to place? I'm not sure I've heard of any of these prelates being charged or convicted of felony child endangerment, accessory after the fact, or any number of the other obvious charges. Under the right circumstances, those charges can be brought by the D.A.'s office whether the victims press a complaint or not. Please explain that to me?" he asked in a non-accusatory tone, wanting her to be sure he did not think that state of affairs was due to any incompetence on her part.

"That's what's so crazy," she responded. "The hierarchy first claims that it's their right to handle these things internally because the sinful acts of any priest fall under their domain. Like the legal system has no fucking jurisdiction over them. Or the Bishops/Archbishops, state they got these priests counseling and thought they were cured . .

. like that ever happens! Worse yet, they claim they had the promise of the priest to stay away from children and sin no more. The problem is that the brass and the D.A.'s office buy that shit. They just sit there like dumb fucks nodding their heads saying, 'Yes, your Excellency, or yes, your Eminence.' Jesus fucking Christ, Dax, that's like letting a Mafia captain off because he says he told one of his henchmen to stop killing and was sure he wouldn't do it anymore. You see how fucking insane this gets?!"

"Then you add into the recipe people who look at everything from a political standpoint all the way up to the D.A.'s office." Dax added. "While the Catholic Church is required legally not to use the bloody pulpit to influence elections, the politicians know they will whenever they want to anyway, and in a city like New York, with such a large Catholic population, they understand how that could swing results."

"But Dax . . . Dax, this is about sexually abusing and raping children! When does that ever get to matter more than all that other bullshit?" Janet was now collapsing into her chair with breathes of exasperation, her head dropping in despair. After a moment, she clenched her fists and began to raise her face, a distant icy stare coming over it. "One thing is for goddamn sure. None of this means that I will ever stop hunting these bastards . . . not ever."

Dax was sure her mind's eye was now filled with the image of her sister. Inching closer, "Okay, how do we get CABS to help us track down Wendich?"

After taking a second to compose herself, "Well, honestly, I think you're going to have to go to Chicago and talk directly to Rebecca Bain, right away . . . today or tomorrow. This worldwide tracking they do is highly confidential stuff. I've just told you about something I'd sworn to keep a secret. I only know about it because a victim's family member who is involved in the reporting network slipped it out during an investigation, and I drove him nuts till he told me the whole story. It took me weeks to track Rebecca Bain down before she'd even talk to me, and more time after that before she would trust me with any information on any of my cases. She's not going to be happy that I spilled this to you, and I think the only chance we have of recruiting her help is for you to appear in person, use that McGowan charm, and plead with her on this. I can't get away. You're on leave. But most of all, you're the victim's father. She'll see you as a victim who needs her help as well. It has to be you."

"Why should I spend the time travelling to Chicago to meet someone who is only a phone call away? That just kills more time leaving us that much farther behind in catching this guy," Dax replied.

"Listen, when I tell her I revealed their network secret to you, I'm expecting major blowback. She isn't going to give us anything unless she gets to drill you personally and assesses your credibility to even be involved. I know you're thinking I could act like it's just another case of mine, but she never tells me anything until she drags me through a third degree on it for every detail. What Rebecca is most worried about is her program getting hijacked by law enforcement to suit only their purposes. She's rightfully concerned that once the word gets out the program exists, all priests, especially the most dangerous ones, will get moved even more secretly than they are now. The whole system breaks down and the kids will suffer for it. And Dax, I can't play this anyway but with the truth. I won't lie to this fine lady. She's my friend. She counts on me, and I need to keep her confidence for help on future cases. Let's just hope when I contact her about you coming, that doesn't just blow up the whole relationship right there."

Dax was calculating all the variables in terms of Wendich's possible escape routes and the time-lines involved. He mentally re-visited the state of their information on him so far. He could see no other alternative. "Okay. You've made your case. I'll make the trip if I have to. I sure hope you can set it up quickly. At least there are always dozens of flights going to Chicago from here, and it can easily be a quick in and out day trip."

"Depending on traffic, driving to and from the other side of Jersey can sometimes take longer than that," Janet added for levity. "Listen, I never catch her the first time I call, but I'll get back to you as soon as I reach her. I'm going to tell her about your reputation here, and how your involvement could lead to prosecuting someone higher than a priest. That will have strong meaning for her. But hey, there's another reason that you've got to meet this woman. She's about your age, mid 30s, and she's hot."

Dax was taken aback. Not only was her sudden turn of subject so extreme, the thought of this trip involving a romantic element seemed absurd. He wondered if the near obvious chasm that now existed between him and his wife Darlene had begun to circulate in the department's rumor mill.

"Look, I have no interest in pursuing any kind of romantic interests; we have a murderer to catch. You've talked me into this trip, and that's fine. "But that's it."

"Hey, I'm just sayin'. She's beautiful and smart . . . your kind of smart actually."

Before he could respond to her knowing smile, she changed the subject. "One other thing before I forget. CABS has contacts with the very best of counselors for abused children, some pro bono for the poorest folks. Be sure and check with her. She can probably get you hooked up with just the right people for little Tommy here in New York."

"Oh, that's great. I won't forget to do that. Thanks."

This last suggestion helped him rationalize the trip to be more palatable. He stood, stretched, and turned to her with the face of a friend. "Listen Detective, I appreciate your letting me in on your personal family history. I also understand the limb you're going out on with your relationship to this Dr. Bain. When this is all over, I'm going to owe you big time. Really Janet, I'd be a lot crazier right now if it wasn't for your help."

"No problem, we're helping each other out . . . you don't owe me anything. Let's just catch this motherfucker and maybe, just maybe, we'll be able to nail a higher up for once. I'm tired of just taking pawns in this chess game. I'll call you as soon as I get through to her."

"Actually, I may drop back in later on my way home," he suggested. "I have to make a stop back at my precinct first."

Dax's discussion with Janet had created an unexpected challenge irresistible to his alter ego. Employing the assistance of his good friend and her old partner, Dick Daley, made the stop at his precinct a requirement.

CHAPTER NINETEEN

To become the very best detective he could be, Dax continuously improved his education and honed his skills of observation at every opportunity. Filtering variations in dialects to pinpoint a person's place of origin or their last place of residence was but one of many abilities he had all but mastered. Breaking down street smells and victim's body odors into their essential elements, identifying cars by their engine sounds or horn bleats, even divining psychological inferences from walking gaits and posture positions fell into his bevy of accreditations.

Regardless of whatever appeared to have his attention, he was also acutely aware of his surroundings. He was obsessed with absorbing and deciphering any knowledge available to him, and in his thinking, New York City was the Library of Congress of human traits and behavior.

A valuable byproduct of the relentless engagement of his five senses was the development of an extraordinary sixth. Patterns of city life were etched in his memory causing anything outside those patterns to catch his scrutiny. To Dax, well-known places had a certain identifiable rhythm, an almost musical syncopation to them. The street area around his Four-One Precinct was one of those places, and Dax knew its "chorus" very well.

At his planned stop there, the walk from his car caught a note in the music out of tune. He stopped at the building's entrance to turn and see if he could discover what he sensed was out of place. As he pivoted around, it seemed the flat note faded out. Returning to face the building to enter, the aberration was there again. One more swift turn back and it disappeared completely. *"The flat note is hiding!"*

A sixth sense has no vocabulary to translate specifics, only that it perceives something. Unlike other easily identifiable off-key notes, like a person who has suddenly fallen or another who has burst suddenly from a building, a flat note that chooses to hide evokes danger and calls for heightened vigilance.

CHAPTER TWENTY

As Dax ascended the stairs of the Four-One on his way to see Dick Daley, his Blackberry signaled an incoming text. "RB not available. Promises to get back asap. Call u as soon as I know. " jm

While quietly waving to his friend to join him, Dax managed to enter his office without gaining the attention of his Captain next door. He was not sure what he had heard about his unauthorized encounter with the intractable Monsignor Murphy, and wished to avoid any possible queries about it.

Daley entered talking. "Jesus Dax, every time I call Janet to get an update that I can pass on to you, I find out you're already up to snuff on everything. She's been honest with me that you're almost as close on this case as if it was yours and I know the way you operate. I expect you're running it. So, if you really don't need me to do this? I mean I'll do whatever you want, but it looks like --"

"Hey Richard, that's one of the reasons I stopped by. First thing though, Janet is everything you said she is. If we had ten of her in every SVU unit in the city, it would be all the pedophiles who were in danger, and all the kids would be safe. She's one of a kind, and thanks to her, I've already learned a good deal more about the whole clergy abuse issue. To answer your question, yes, she's given me free reign, which I would appreciate you keeping to yourself, but make no mistake, she's running the case. As far as keeping me informed, you're right. You can relax on that."

Daley looked sideways as if to be sure some unseen person wouldn't hear his next words. "Well old buddy, I'm going to have to at least pretend I'm keeping up because the Captain is extremely interested. I saw you kinda skirt in here without him seeing you. He's heard about your questioning that Monsignor and he's a bit uptight about it."

"Ouch. I'm going to have to stop in and explain that I was only there as an observer with Janet in charge, though I will have some difficulty glossing over the direct confrontation I had with the man. Listen, I'm heading out of town for a time and maybe that will put his mind at ease," Dax offered, hoping he could at least use this somewhat unwanted trip to Chicago to an advantage indicating he was less involved, though he disliked the thought of misleading his mentor.

"Since you've been working with Janet, I want to ask you. How is Ted Laney managing over there? I don't worry at all about her, though with Ted as a partner . . . well I was just wondering how they're making out together."

"Are you asking about the fact that they're both homosexuals?"

"Well . . . yeah. I felt really bad about leaving Janet at SVU when I did. But I just couldn't handle seeing all the physical abuse that was happening to all those women, the gay guys, and especially the little kids. It was keeping me awake at night thinking of my own children being in harm's way. Really, dead bodies over here at homicide are much easier on me.

"So, anyway, when I did transfer, Janet pushed hard to get Ted under her wing. I think she did it partly to protect him. You know how the pecking order is. Tough lesbians are sometimes more accepted than straight women, and gay guys are still last on the list. I just hope no one at the Four-Five is giving them any trouble."

"Not that I can tell, Richard. In fact, my guess is no one's aware of Ted's orientation. I know because . . . well I just know. It's too bad they can't both be more in the open about who they are. They're not only living proof it doesn't affect their police work, but that homosexuals and pedophiles are two completely different people despite what the right wing religious nuts have to say. Actually, I had something else I wanted to ask your help on."

"Sure . . . name it buddy."

"You were Janet's partner for a good while, so I'm sure you know the story about her sister Karen's murder."

"Yeah, I do. Janet doesn't let her soft side show very often, but whenever she'd been back to reviewing that file? Well, you could just tell."

"So, what do you say you and I see what we can do to work that case, Mr. Daley?"

"Hey, if I could do that for Janet . . . man she carried my ass over there for a long time. I owe her big."

"Great, but let's keep this to ourselves. I don't want to get her hopes up. This case is ice cold, and we can't be sure we'll solve it."

"What do you want me to do?"

Dax reached into his overcoat's inside pocket. He pulled out a set of notes and information from Karen Meehan's SVU file he had just retrieved from the Cold Case room in the basement at Janet's precinct. "Okay, here are a couple of things I think are worth checking out."

Before he could proceed, his phone rang. It was Janet. "Hey Dax, are you still planning to stop here on your way home? I've talked to Rebecca and you're set up to meet her tomorrow morning. You'll probably need to catch a plane tonight."

"Uh, yes I can still stop. That's good news, I suppose. Did you manage to make the arrangements without any trouble?"

"Yeah, well, I'll have to fill you in on that when you get here. Catch you later," was her goodbye, and she hung up.

For but a moment, Dax sat mulling over the confusion embedded in Janet's voice, and decided he would find out its meaning when he saw her later. He smiled, turned to Daley, and began the instructions he wished him to pursue on her sister, Karen's case.

CHAPTER TWENTY-ONE

Walking the length of the bullpen to her office, Dax was able to observe Janet in what seemed a lengthy pensive pose as she sat at her desk. "So how did it go?" he said as he entered.

Janet was clasping a mug of a mid-afternoon caffeine boost. "Well, I'm a little tossed up about that. I was about to tell her I had a big favor to ask, and hoped she wouldn't be angry about my revealing her tracking program to a third party I believed could help us, especially with maybe nailing someone in the hierarchy. She scared the shit out of me before I could finish my first sentence. She screeched into the phone, 'Who . . . who did you tell?!' All I could say was his name is Lieutenant Dax McGowan."

"Were you able to calm her down?"

"Actually, after giving her your name, she didn't say anything for what seemed like a year. Then she asks me, 'Does this concern the death of his daughter?' Shit Dax, I know CABS keeps track of thousands of abuse cases, but she was definitely up on yours. So, I said yes and started to apologize. But, get this. Her voice starts to crack as she asks me what she can do to help. I explained our plan was for you to come and visit her with all the details, but we needed help tracking down the priest who was responsible for your daughter's death, and suspect he may have escaped to Western Europe. I also threw in we thought with her help and your high profile we might just net a Monsignor or an Archbishop on this one."

"So, it sounds like I may not have to make that trip after all . . . she'll help us anyway?"

"That's what I thought at first too, but no. She asks if she can call me back after she makes another call. I say yes, and she gets back to me maybe fifteen minutes later. First, she explains it could take a good twenty-four to forty-eight hours to track down any information on Wendich in Europe. But, she would like to meet you at her office tomorrow at ten o'clock to discuss the process. She has also arranged for you to meet with a colleague of hers at two in the afternoon."

"Did she say who that other person was, and why it's so important for me to meet them both in person?"

"Hey man, she didn't offer and I didn't ask. I was so relieved she wasn't going to dump all over me, I didn't object to any conditions she wanted met."

Dax was now seated in one of the folding chairs at the display table across from her desk. He was attempting unsuccessfully to decipher the meaning behind these clandestine meetings. *"Even Holmes needs sufficient data to deduce answers."*

"Still no word on Wendich from any of the travel venues?" he asked reaching, knowing the answer in advance.

"No, nothing . . . and the bitch of a task of looking at all the security footage from the airports, hasn't produced a thing either."

"Even if he pops up there, and we can determine a flight's destination, as we said, we are going to need this Dr. Bain's help for something more specific. Though, I'm feeling as if I'm going there to feed some agenda I know nothing about . . . a quid pro quo to get what we want."

Janet shrugged; he gave a friendly salute; she saluted back, and he left.

By the time he had reached the stairway at the other end of the floor, he had memorized the remaining flights to Chicago for the rest of the day from both JFK and LaGuardia from his Blackberry. He was again realizing that tracking this priest was involving more and more players, invariably complicating his efforts to isolate Wendich. It also appeared that the most likely place he would be putting a gun to his head was going to be somewhere across the Atlantic. No matter, he thought. *"The where was of no concern, only the final result."*

But first, he had to make another dreaded stop at home to ready for this last minute trip and once again face its excruciating silence. With both the women who were part of his life now forever absent, he was not cherishing entering yet again, what he expected was an empty house.

CHAPTER TWENTY-TWO

Coming to a stop in front of his house, Dax reached over to the passenger seat to grab his briefcase. Pulling up on its leather straps, he slid out the driver's door, closed it and hit the remote to lock it. Then it hit him; something was not right. There was that scary flat note in the symphony again, only this time the danger was palpable. He sensed being watched, but chose not to peer around and give that away. He threw his arms up, and hit the side of his head as if in punishment for inadvertently leaving something in the car. Hit the remote, opened the door, and re-entered.

"Okay, if this was a sniper hit, I'd be dead by now. Therefore, whoever is in wait is expecting me to enter my front door. Surely an attack inside would reduce the potential for outdoor witnesses. But first, you have to figure out what caught your attention . . . what note was flat? It registered somewhere. Play your tape back and SEE it.

Dax realized he had sensed the danger immediately upon his exit from the car before he had a chance to even look up at his house. So it must have been something that registered before that. He decided to start his "tape" from when he first turned the corner onto his block.

He saw it now. Out of habit, when coming home late in the evening, he always glanced up at Grace's 2nd floor window to see if her bedroom light was still on. When it was, he was assured to get to tuck her in and kiss her goodnight. The replay of today's autonomic glance "saw" that her window was opened just a crack; he knew it had been both shut and locked after her death. Like focusing a

78

binocular lens, he strained harder on the image in his head, and made out a small black tube hanging over the windowsill aimed at the street. Someone was inside and with the aid of a lens at the end of that tube watched him pull up in his car.

There were now alternatives to consider. He could simply leave, but then run the risk of being set up again later in a place where he would have substantially less control. He decided his best strategy would be to turn the tables on his pursuer, literally having the "home court advantage."

He calmly re-exited his car, and walked around to the trunk and popping it open. This allowed him to appear in the normal activity of cleaning it out. The open lid effectively hid his removing his gun from its belt holster and covering it with loose paper and cellophane plastic he retrieved from the trunk. Instead of heading to the front door, he stepped down the four steps to the right of his front stoop to the location of his garbage cans. His peripheral vision picked up the tubular lens at the window turning to examine his activity. As he lifted a garbage can cover, he appeared to accidentally drop some paper over a rail onto three short stairs leading down to his basement door. A bulging bay window above hid that area from the view of the intruder's lens. He threw up his arms again in feigned disgust, and headed down to supposedly retrieve the refuse.

Several minutes passed. Suddenly, the whole house was filled with a screeching sound like the screams of a large bird in the throes of death after an attack by a predator. It lasted but ten seconds and then stopped. Several more minutes of total silence passed, then several more. Eventually, amidst the total silence in the house, two lowered voices were speaking at the top of the stairs at the bedroom level.

"He has to be inside," said one.

"But where? You think he knows we we're waiting for him?" said another.

"It's been fourteen minutes and twenty-seven seconds since we heard that god awful noise," said the first.

Steps could then be heard walking the length of the hallway from Grace's bedroom to join in the conversation. "He's not out front and his car is still there," added a third voice. Three pairs of feet then quietly descended the stairs to the main level. They split up in different directions. One went left toward the living room, the second right into a den with an adjoining bathroom, and the third proceeded the furthest down the hall to a large area housing both the dining room and kitchen.

Every few seconds, a muted "clear" could be heard as they checked out their assigned rooms. Finally, all three stood together at the very back of the house in the kitchen. They remained rigid at first, still unsure of the location of their target, and then relaxed only slightly as they began to debate his whereabouts.

Dax had an excellent view of them. He was sitting stone cold still, curled up inside a dumbwaiter located in the kitchen and was peering at his wannabe assassins through the peek-a-boo slits of its door covering. They looked like triplets in terms of height and weight and clothing. Only their fully shaved but different shaped heads told they were not. He guessed them to be in their twenties. Ninja black was the only color to describe their clothing which fit very tightly from the waist up over muscled shoulders and arms. However, there was no mistaking that they were wearing full-length black cassocks, priest garb, absent any white collars. What made their attire both hideously bizarre and threatening was that their faces were covered by ashen colored masks shaped in the face of a wolf. The forehead of those face coverings contained the deep furrows and curled eyebrows of a lupine engaged in intense anger, making their real eyes underneath appear in full attack mode. The nose and mouth were shorter than a normal wolf, but in no way diminished the danger exhibited by its snarling lips and exposed ivory white teeth, the two large upper canines curved and honed to a piercing point. *"The only thing missing on those faces is the dripping blood of their last victims."*

He recognized the gargoyle expressions, having seen a number of them on the rooftops of Catholic cathedrals in Europe built in the Dark Ages during the Spanish Inquisition. The masks fit very tightly on their faces so as not to hinder their vision, and the military issue Browning semi-automatic pistols with custom silencers, left no doubt in his mind. These were highly trained killers.

Their speech gave them away as mid-westerners. He surmised, that due to their young age and geographic upbringing, they were likely unfamiliar with dumbwaiters, which were more associated with times well past on southern plantations or in eastern seaboard homes and apartments. The previous owner of his house had covered its opening with fascia to match the other kitchen cabinets to visually hide its location for décor purposes. Dax correctly predicted the "nerve tingling screech" of the rusted metal pulleys on their rusted metal axis was not a sound most people would readily identify. As expected, his stoic patience and long silence afterward had left them all the more unnerved. However, he also realized he would not be surprising them, as he would have liked. He might get two of them with perfect shots to the head as they were clearly bullet proof vested, but he would be a goner before he could complete the kill of all three. No, while the element of surprise was in his favor, it was not sufficient to survive the encounter, not against these experts. *"Who are these guys?"*

He expected their next move would be to check the basement where he boarded the dumbwaiter. The apparent leader was already motioning them toward the inside basement door.

Scratches on the lock to the outside basement door told Dax these assassins had entered his house from there as he did. He was hoping, due to some fortuitously placed large plastic storage bags, they had not noticed the open dumbwaiter platform sitting on the floor or, its exposed pulley ropes as they entered. Once he climbed on the platform and pulled the ropes to raise himself, he had fished the ropes up inside with him. When the platform was locked in at the kitchen level, it sealed the shaft at the bottom. To the unknowing eye, it looked like any other wooden covering against a basement's ceiling, likely housing a plumbing or electrical utility.

He could hear them now inches below him checking for any sign of his presence. He was struggling to breathe very shallowly. He wondered if his heart pounding in his ears was audible to his attackers. He knew the slightest sound would mean shots fired into the bottom of the platform draining his body of all its blood onto the basement floor. He concentrated on not blinking, concerned that the one additional sound, though minute, might make the difference, and cause his discovery. He pictured the stoic and motionless stare of an extremely pensive Sherlock Holmes as his model of silence. It worked.

Then one of the intruders broke the stillness. "We clearly have no idea where he is," it spit out in frustration. "This guy is supposed to be pretty sharp. We're going to have to find another time and place and probably take him out in a smash and go, if we can get permission to do that. Arranging his death to look like suicide may not be possible for this one. Let's head out."

"So that was it." Dax was almost appreciating the strategy. Suicide might be an easy sell for everyone else to buy based on his current emotional state and the hole in his bedroom wall. *"But why are these men trying to kill me in the first place? What's their motive, and who put the hit out on me? There's a lot at stake when assassinating a New York City detective. No doubt, I'm onto something bigger than just one priest's pedophilia and that has somebody very spooked. I'll relish not only putting down this mad dog priest, but anyone else who thinks they can succeed in such a plot against me."* He readily accepted his own arrogance in those thoughts.

The outside basement door closed with a loud slam. He smiled. Several minutes passed as he continued to stay cold stone still. The door then opened for a few seconds and closed again, just barely making a sound. He smiled again. He checked his Blackberry for the time. He still had a plane to catch.

CHAPTER TWENTY-THREE

Dax liked Chicago. Much like New York it was a city built on the western shore of a large body of water. When you stood on its beaches, Lake Michigan's immense size made it look not much different than the Atlantic Ocean. He loved the city's energy and its Midwestern take on life. Its downtown was especially clean for a metropolis its size. The Chicago River that stretched through its center added a taste of Mother Nature much like Central Park did for New York. He remembered getting wasted with a few of his Irish college buddies on a trip there for a St. Patrick's Day weekend when the city dyes it green for the occasion. He had chosen a window seat on the left side of the plane to get a view from the night sky of the city, ablaze in the red, green and white lights of the Christmas season as it passed just north of downtown heading a short distance west to O'Hare Airport. *"My first Christmas without Grace."* He only just now considered what that might be like.

He had booked a stay at the Water Tower Hotel in the city's heart, only a three-block walk from there on East Chestnut St. to the CABS offices in the Spencer Building. His arrival at the hotel found him still considering whether he should inform Janet about his encounter with the gargoyles. If he was somehow later killed by them, it would be best to have someone have at least a faint idea who they might be looking for. These assassins were good enough, and so far outside the loop of possible suspects, Dax could easily see the file on his death sitting in the letter M section of Cold Cases not far from Karen Meehan's. However, this attempt on his life might also be seen as all the more reason he should be excluded from any involvement in his daughter's case. Janet herself might draw that conclusion, as it could put her career in grave jeopardy for allowing him as far into it as she had. No, he could not take that risk and reduce his opportunity in any way to discover Wendich's whereabouts and send him straight to hell. Not believing in hell, however, did not deter him from the enjoyment of picturing his prey suffering in such a place.

While his next thoughts steered clear of Janet for the moment, Dax knew he should contact her partner Ted regarding the lack of cooperation on the part of Monsignor Murphy. It was now time to set in motion a plan he had devised but five minutes after stepping into the rectory at St. Marks.

"Hey Laney, how goes it with the Monsignor?"

"Nowhere Lieutenant; he won't budge and his attorney's been practically living with him just outside his holding cell. As you know, we're going to have to let him go in the morning."

"I assume he'll be without his attorney tonight until what time tomorrow?"

"The attorney said he'd be here to pick him up at ten."

"That's good. I mentioned that I'd be working on something and have an idea in mind. It might involve you stepping over the line somewhat, but I'm relatively sure I can protect you from any trouble. Are you game?"

"Hey, I'm in Lieutenant."

"Good. Here's the strategy. I need you to purchase a prepaid, unregistered cell phone. Then I'd like you to somehow, unseen, slip the Monsignor a note with that phone at least an hour before 10:00 am. If our plan works and he cooperates, that should allow plenty of time for him to come clean with you and Janet before his attorney gets there. Please write down this name . . . Adam Murphy . . . got that?"

"Yup. It'll magically appear under the cover plate over whatever he gets served for breakfast. That usually arrives shortly after eight o'clock anyway."

"Okay, all the better. On the note, under that name, write down my cell phone number and a time. This is very important Ted. That time should be no more than a minute or two after he gets his food tray. I don't want him to even consider calling anyone else before he calls me. Are you with me so far?"

"Got it Lieutenant."

"Good. Then keep an eye on him. As soon as he finishes making the call, you need to come up with a defendable excuse like retrieving his food tray to roust him and recover both the note and the phone. That way, if this doesn't work and he cries foul, the only available proof that the call ever happened would be a record of my phone receiving it at that exact time. Then I'll be the only one who has to answer for it. If asked, you can play dumb and I'll back you? Does that work?"

"You bet." Then pausing, "Uh, Lieutenant, I can't keep this from Janet . . . you know what I mean?"

"Sure, of course. If this works, tell her that it was my doing. Tell her you don't know what I discussed with the Monsignor, which will be the truth, and that I will fill her in later. If this doesn't succeed, all the better she knows nothing about it. She'll have no culpability. Okay?"

"Sounds good to me," Ted said in a satisfied fashion.

"And Ted, when this guy requests to spill to you guys, like I expect he will, you'll need to give Janet that heads up just before you take him to an interrogation room. Besides the both of you having to act appropriately surprised, you also need to be prepared to hit him hard on the information. We want to know anything he knows that will lead us to Wendich. I have an important meeting after I take that call and I'll check back with you later to see how you made out. I know I can count on you Ted. Have a good night."

Dax heard Ted's return "Goodnight" fading off as he blinked his phone closed and put it on the hotel room nightstand. He caught the time at 9:13 and was ready to call it a day. Much had gone down since his early interview with Janet at 7:30. He was tired and thought a stiff Southern Comfort Manhattan at the bar downstairs might reduce the barrier between his often non-stop mind and a good night's sleep. Then he thought. *"It might take two."*

CHAPTER TWENTY-FOUR

Thursday: December 17th

Dax showered after a half hour of intense stationary bike work at the gym on the tenth floor, seven floors above him. He rationalized it might make up for some of the lack of his usual exercise regimen that had been absent for several days, though the second and third Manhattan the night before had made itself known during the entire workout.

The time being 6:50 am, and the one-hour time difference in New York, he expected the call from the Monsignor to come within the next fifteen minutes. He was buttoning the left cuff of his dress shirt when his cell phone rang.

He started with a simple "Hello," moderating his tone so that it might pass for any male voice the party on the other end might expect it to be.

"Adam?"

"No Monsignor, it's Dax McGowan, but I do want to talk you about Adam."

There was an expected silence as the Monsignor digested the information. Then, "What the hell are you doing talking to me? You have no right. My attorney will be here soon. This is totally out of bounds. I have no idea how I got this phone except that you somehow arranged it, and I'm going to end this conversation right now!"

Dax judged he would not do that based on his expected concern for his nephew. However, he took no chances by referencing him again.

"Your nephew might end up paying dearly for that decision, Monsignor."

"What the hell does any of this have to do with my Adam?!" he screamed back.

"I'll tell you. Right now, we have enough forensic evidence from Wendich's room to firmly establish that these crimes committed against my daughter and the O'Reilly boy took place there. While we have a missing priest, we also have a totally uncooperative Monsignor. We're now questioning whether that Monsignor was aware of these crimes being enacted right under his nose. Maybe a little digging might produce enough evidence that he was even complicit in the acts. Maybe we have two pedophile clergy on our hands. All we know is that you're stonewalling continues to keep you under suspicion."

"Yeah? So what? There won't be any proof I was involved because I wasn't."

"Well, as with any news story containing a lurid backdrop plastered all over the papers and television, suspicion and open ended conjecture develop a life of their own. Right now, we have the rectory cordoned off as a crime scene . . . no reporters in there yet. Once they get the okay as we're pulling out, they'll be viewing that shrine you have in your office of your nephew. After it hits the wire services, it won't be long before the Annapolis, Maryland press starts tracking him down wanting his opinion on whether these suspicions about you are true. They'll be driving the Naval Academy nuts trying to hound him for a statement. And Monsignor, how is he going to react when he's asked the inevitable question by some low life tabloid huckster if you ever touched him in any of the wrong places, and the press reports his answer as something like "no comment" which his military superiors are going to instruct him to say?"

"No, no, my God no, you can't let that happen!"

"I'll do whatever I can to prevent that Monsignor, but you have to cooperate with us if you want my help."

"What do you want?" he said still shaken, but sounding open to complying.

"Look, I don't think it's likely you're directly involved, but it's also apparent that you and the other hierarchy want only to protect your own asses, and as far as I'm concerned it makes you just as guilty. But, it's Wendich we want. We want to know where he immigrated from to New York, the circumstances that brought him here, and any knowledge you have as to his current whereabouts."

"Yes, but if I help you, what do I tell my attorney?"

"Realistically Monsignor, we both know he's not your attorney. His number one role is to protect the Archbishop and the diocese. Besides, unless it becomes necessary at some future date for you to testify, no one will ever know what you told us. When your attorney arrives, you just leave with him like nothing happened."

Dax knew he needed to get the Monsignor back on track about his concern for his nephew and off his own issues with the Archbishop. He was straining now to hold his train of thought and not allow his anger to interfere with getting what he needed from this man.

"Listen Murphy, you guys who live in secluded rectories, have no idea of the pain and suffering these kids have gone through, even enough to commit suicide. You also have no concept of the collateral damage done to the families from these horrific acts. But I'm telling you that unless you give us information that helps us track this son of a bitch down, you're going to find out first-hand from your nephew how these crimes can inflict irreparable damage. Are you getting what I'm telling you? Do you hear me you prick?!"

"Okay . . . okay." the Monsignor said soberly. "I really don't know that much. I was kept in the dark on a lot of things, but I'll tell you what I know. But, you have to promise me my nephew stays totally out of this."

Dax breathed hard to re-gain his composure. Very directly . . . matter of factly . . . with no intent to seem friendly, "I will do everything I possibly can to accomplish that. You have my word. You need to ask for detective Laney, the man who brought you in. Give him both the phone and the note you have, and inform him you want to talk to him and Sergeant Meehan right away. As soon as I get their full report, I'll take the necessary steps to protect your nephew as long as they've assured me you held nothing back."

With no goodbyes, Dax simply pressed his phone off. It did not escape him . . . the Monsignor's reference to being kept in the dark. He was implying someone higher up wasn't telling him all there was to know about Wendich. Following up on those details could be most interesting, not only in the pursuit of Wendich, but also to Janet and the whole SVU Department in terms of possible upper level involvement in any number of clerical abuse crimes in New York.

However, it was now time to devour some food and prepare to meet this "Wonder Woman" Janet spoke of so highly, Rebecca Bain.

CHAPTER TWENTY-FIVE

Dax was totally unprepared. Janet, being a street hardened cop who banged perverts around like rag dolls, describing another woman as hot, only conjured up thoughts of a brassy, voluptuous type woman, maybe a bit rough around the edges. No, he was not prepared for the woman who stood before him with her hand extended to shake his, as the only word that immediately came to mind was . . . *Stunning*. He told himself that after he got to know her better, he would no doubt experience the persona of the successful CEO she was of an organization that had a worldwide reach. But for now, he could not get his mind past the exquisite beauty he was now meeting.

Rebecca Bain was a perfect example of how striking a woman of mixed race could be. Her hair was wavy, soft and a shiny black that flowed down gently touching the tops of her shoulders. It framed an angular well-proportioned face . . . itself the hue of creamy dark chocolate. Her smooth and unblemished skin only accentuated her larger than normal eyes exhibiting that rare beautiful bronze color so specific to mixed race persons. However, her irises also contained a characteristic that could only be described as golden flecks that caught and reflected light in waves of sparkles. He could recall only seeing that unique combination once before. A perfectly balanced nose, high cheekbones, and fleshy full lips moistened with red lip gloss added to an already staggering first impression. He reached for her right hand in return for hers, and instinctively eyed the ring finger of her left looking for a wedding band. There was none.

"Dax McGowan, Dr. Bain. I very much appreciate your seeing me on such short notice, and I understand from our friend Janet I'm catching you in the process of preparing for a vacation as well." Any residual hint in his voice of this trip being an inconvenience had now disappeared, as Dax was well aware his words were flowing at the peak of his charm.

"Indeed Lieutenant, but no concern I assure you. I have great trust in Janet, and am assured your presence here is well warranted. Please do call me Rebecca, and allow me to escort you back to my office."

Dax appreciated her somewhat old world word chronology, reminiscent of Conan Doyle's time. Her accent held in it a strong New York City influence, more than a touch of an educated New Englander, and a hint of Jamaican islander, his educated ear telling him one of her parents was directly from there.

He attempted unsuccessfully to survey the condition and décor of his surroundings while following her down a long hallway, as he could not keep his eyes off her. She was wearing a very tasteful red dress with elbow length sleeves made of a silky cotton blend, with a wide black belt drawing in on her slim waist. While the fabric was of a modest depth, he could make out that she was wearing a bra and panties close enough to the color of her skin to make them almost invisible. Her arms, swaying rhythmically as she walked, were willowy and smooth, but the toned muscles of her calves, accentuated by her high-heeled shoes indicated the regimen of a long distance runner. He guessed her to be 5'3" shoeless. As his eyes moved slowly up her legs, the sunlight from a far window at the end of the hall passed through her dress silhouetting an extremely enticing heart shaped space at the very top of her thighs, causing his loins to react. Raising his eyes a bit higher, he stopped to admire what most men would consider "a perfect ass," though he cringed at such a low-brow reference being associated with such a refined woman. Each step she took pressed it against her dress, making it easy to gauge its exercised tightness.

In a display of flexibility, she slowly turned her upper body almost ninety degrees as she continued to walk forward, and smiled at him to make sure he was still following her, sensing he had fallen back somewhat. True, it was of his interest in improving his view. It was that position when her profile revealed beautifully rounded and slightly larger than normal breasts for her body size.

"*Who is this woman and why haven't all the rich and famous men in the world knocked down her door to sweep her away?*" He was wishing he had shown Janet more interest in this woman, and asked some of the many questions now flooding his mind about her. He shook his head struggling to reset his mind to focus on his mission as he was having trouble reconciling how he could be experiencing even the slightest of sexually romantic feelings while the loss of his daughter and the drive to kill her abuser were so prominent in his thoughts.

CHAPTER TWENTY-SIX

As he entered Rebecca Bain's office, Dax found the set up incongruent with her status as President of a large global network. The room was small, roughly 7' x 9', with a large cityscape window opposite its entrance door. He smiled. This was the window casting the morning sunlight as they walked down the hallway. Her desk was large for the size of the room, an old rectangular wooden model of a 1950s vintage, much like his own at the NYPD. Behind her in front of the window, were a series of card tables lined up against the wall substituting for a credenza, all covered with stacks of what looked like letters and reports neatly arranged. Copious amounts of paperwork covered her desk, but were well organized.

"Is that sun too bright? Shall I pull the drapes?" she offered.

Grinning more broadly inside than out, "No, please no. We don't want to shut out any sun this time of year. Thank you though."

Rebecca motioned for him to be seated, but he deferred to her and watched, as the matching old wooden executive chair seemed to swallow up her small frame. Settling in, she crossed her legs and clasped her hands.

"Lieutenant McGowan, how is it that I may help you" she said smiling, exposing perfectly white teeth.

"First Rebecca, please call me Dax. I know that our friend Janet has filled you in on some of the details, though I'm not sure how much of my personal situation she's told you about."

"You'll probably soon realize, Dax, that we do a great deal of homework on anyone who enters our sanctuary here, a safety precaution if nothing else. But I would love to hear you tell your own story if you'd like." She stated his name as smoothly as if she had always known him.

He cleared his throat and proceeded cautiously as he knew talking about Grace would affect his control. "As you know, several days ago, my eleven year old daughter, Grace, committed suicide after being raped and abused by a local priest. Rebecca, I loved my daughter with every fabric of my being and am still struggling greatly with her loss. I haven't been sleeping much, and right now the only thing keeping me going is catching up with this . . . man." He was finding it easier than expected to reveal both the facts and his emotions to this perfect stranger, though he struggled to refrain from using the street language he would rather in describing Wendich. "My daughter's death has changed everything. Besides the enormity of the damage I feel personally, my wife and I have already retained an attorney to seek a divorce as we both understood it was really only Grace that held us together."

He knew it must have sounded unusual to be revealing this kind of personal information. However, something primitive in him wanted her to know he was now a free agent. It also occurred to him how much more final the decision to divorce sounded after vocalizing it so specifically to a third person.

He went on. "Though normally not within protocol, I've taken time off from my work as a homicide detective to work on this myself. I discovered that my daughter and one other young boy were the only victims. This little Tommy O'Reilly revealed the abuser to be a Father Peter Wendich, their CCD instructor. This priest managed to escape before we could arrest him, and we have no leads as to his whereabouts. The background we have on him is very thin. Janet and her partner are right now taking a statement from this man's immediate superior, a Monsignor, which may give us more to go on. While he is very motivated to tell us what he knows, he's likely unable to point us to the priest's exact location. That's the reason I'm here seeking your assistance. Janet told me you have a network that may be able to help. I would also like to inquire about a referral for professional help for the O'Reilly boy and his economically disadvantaged family. Janet said you could steer us to the best people on that as well."

He looked up into her eyes having had his head lowered for most of what he said. He was moved to see them tearing, "I'm sorry, I didn't mean to . . ."

"No, no; don't mind me, Dax. These stories always hit me very hard because of my own personal experience. I started this organization when I was still in college because I was the victim of abuse by a priest when I was just a bit older than your daughter. I was fortunate enough to survive more than one decision to take my own life. I was just reminiscing about those painful thoughts of self-loathing and despair that your daughter experienced as you related them to me. I totally identify with the struggle your Grace went through . . . that you're going through. Grace is such a beautiful name, Dax."

He was unprepared for those last words of perfect empathy. His whole body shuddered as tears filled his eyes, and his next words came in almost a whimper, "Well . . . I had no intention . . ."

Rebecca gently raised her hand in a way to softly quiet him. "I never want to lose those feelings. It's what keeps me coming to this office every day to help survivors get through their pain to a place where they might find some solace and maybe eventually some happiness. It's why CABS exists . . . that and to see their pedophiles prosecuted." Her last words were laced with an indulgent revenge. "And, I suppose that in addition to the Monsignor involved, you're getting even less help from the cold blooded Archbishop of New York, Richard James? Let me guess. The diocese has expressed deep regret at your daughter's death and if . . . and I stress the word if, they find the police investigation confirms that a member of their clergy was in any way responsible for this suicide . . . and, I stress the word suicide, normally defined as an act holding only its victim responsible, they will respond further. They will be conducting their own internal investigation, and then, and only then will they release any more of an official statement. Of course, the expected date for the culmination of that investigation has not been determined. Is that pretty close to your assessment of their position? And tell me, Dax, just how successful has your SVU unit been at gaining a warrant to review the diocesan records in an attempt to discover the whereabouts of this Father Wendich?"

He was now witnessing the very driven side of Rebecca Bain, her manner allowing him to shake loose from his emotions. He was impressed with her command of all his circumstances, and the disdain with which she could describe them.

"Well, if it were me who had to describe the status of their position, I would have repeated your words verbatim. As to the warrant, Janet made it clear that the D.A.'s office is a dead end. Even in the past when they had some success early on in these cases, they couldn't do it without huge political backlash coming down on them. Those hierarchical pricks seem to be beyond anyone's reach. Uh . . . sorry about the prick reference."

"No concern. A fucking prick is a fucking prick," she returned with a harshness that surprised him.

"Rebecca, your words tell me that like myself, you're no stranger to the streets," he said fishing.

"You have no idea how much 'the streets' and I are no strangers to each other," she responded.

"Well, I can see we'll have to sit down and trade a few street stories sometime." There was no disguising his blatant attempt at requesting a reason to meet again at some future date.

Unclasping her hands and leaning forward on her desk, she looked squarely at him, "Let's be sure to plan on that," she said warmly.

By now, it was clear a "dance" was in progress that each had no objection to.

Rebecca went on. "Back to how we might help you, our first obligation is of course to all our victims. Because of the nature of the relationships that Catholic clerics have had with their parishioners over the centuries, this pedophilia falls into a category all by itself. It may mirror other forms in many aspects, but it is truly in a class of its own. The trust level could not be any higher. We've all heard the expression, even from non-Catholics, 'If you can't trust a priest, who can you trust?' As we dealt with more and more cases over the years, we came face to face with the consistent stonewalling by the hierarchy, but then eventually discovered, not only a cover up to protect these criminals, but also that they had purposefully transferred known pedophiles to other parishes as a way to protect them from exposure in their previous assignments. These transfers were made with no warnings to anyone at the new locations which only resulted in exposing a whole new set of victims to abuse. We have cases where there were over one hundred children abused by the same cleric at different locations. And Dax, we are now aware of tens of thousands of cases worldwide. We know that's a relatively small number of victims who have had the courage to report them, or who aren't inhabiting alcohol and drug rehabilitation facilities . . . or haven't committed suicide."

"Janet filled me in on much of that. Like most people, I was unaware of the extent of the hierarchy's criminal involvement, and surprised at the lack of the depth the media has pursued in that regard," he said.

"It was the unraveling of that information that led us to devise a way to uncover these 'hidden' priests to protect future victims," Rebecca went on. "To make the long story short, we set up a worldwide network to track as many priests as possible. We had no problem recruiting family members of victims to keep a journal on the movements of all the clergy in their individual parishes. They report when a cleric leaves and when a new priest or Monsignor transfers in. We then match up that information inside a simple database program with everyone else's reports to see who ends up where. If we discover a transferred priest in a new location, who has been under the slightest bit of suspicion at their last, we manage to get parishioner's attentions to that withheld information without revealing ourselves as the source. It's not a foolproof system by any means, but it has been very effective at accomplishing its goal many times. Because everyone is a volunteer and we have the Internet, this process costs us relatively little to maintain, and as you can see from our surroundings, keeping our costs down is something we take very seriously. We are all about service to our victims, not material appearances."

"That's amazing . . . a case where Big Brother helps the little guy for a change. So, what can you tell me about Peter Wendich?"

"We already knew from Janet that he came to the states from abroad, and that you told her his accent was German with a Western European influence, England, or Ireland maybe. By the way, that's an intriguing skill," she said smiling. "We've already begun our search in that part of the world, though, as you can imagine, our network isn't as strong outside the U.S. We may have to cross our fingers on this one. Our initial inquiries haven't yielded anything, but I have some very dedicated people working on it."

"When do you think you might know something?"

"If there is any hint about this man anywhere, we should know in the next twenty-four hours, hopefully by tomorrow. In any event, I'm sure you surmised that Janet didn't send you all the way to Chicago to find someone we might locate and could pass on to you by phone. And, I expect you didn't travel this distance without expecting somewhat of a sales job about how you might assist us. Your case, your talents, and your media image could aid us a great deal in terms of public awareness, Dax."

"Well, I am interested in helping you if I can, but my number one concern is still finding Wendich."

"I know. However, you do now understand how naïve most Catholics and the entire public at large is to the extent of what's really happened, what is still happening, and what will continue to happen if desperate steps aren't taken to change the culture of the Catholic hierarchy. I've arranged a meeting for you this afternoon with someone who will describe to you some very interesting behind the scenes work going on right now, and where you might plug in as a positive force. His name is Seymour Hirsch, and he's part of a group that calls itself the Congregation of American Catholics, C.A.C. being their acronym. Is two o'clock today good for you to meet with Mr. Hirsch?"

"That's fine, and I suppose I'll also then discover how a guy named Seymour Hirsch is so intimately involved in the workings of the Catholic Church." he said grinning.

Rebecca smiled back, "Oh, it's a very good story, Dax . . . that and everything else he has to tell you. Just come back to this building and head to the basement . . . .you won't have any problem finding him."

Feeling he was on solid ground to ask, "I know you're very busy, Rebecca, but I was hoping we could get together . . . maybe for dinner later. We have some street stories to exchange, am I right?"

"Well Lieutenant, I have one story I believe you'll find particularly interesting. However, I'm tied up until fairly late. I could arrange for my housekeeper to prepare a meal at my home . . . say around nine o'clock if that fits into your schedule. I apologize for the late hour, but I do want us to get to know each other better."

"That will be fine," Dax responded. There would be a return flight change to early tomorrow involved, but there was no way he was turning down this invitation.

"Very good. My office assistant can give you my home address and phone number as you leave. Does a filet with vegetables and a salad sound okay to you? I'm sure by that hour we'll both be hungry for something substantial like a steak."

"That sounds excellent," he said as warmly as he could manage.

He reached across her desk to shake on it, and the touch of her hand stimulated a wave of something in him he couldn't quite describe, but very much desired to feel again.

CHAPTER TWENTY-SEVEN

Monsignor Murphy was feeling like the flared end of a well-snapped whip as his taxi pulled into the long driveway back to the rectory. *"That fuck of an attorney didn't even have the decency to offer me a ride home,"* his mind resorting to the street language of his younger years. *"McGowan was right, that prick was only there to protect the Archbishop . . . couldn't care less about me."*

However, the Monsignor's main concern now was for his nephew. As the taxi reached the parking lot, there sat an unmarked police car sitting next to his old Taurus. Annoyed at the time the driver was taking to break a twenty dollar bill, he threw a "Keep the change" at him and grabbed his belongings to squeeze out the door. Almost falling on a slippery portion of the walkway, he managed to stay upright with his feet moving as fast as he could to get to the porch and front door. He ran straight into Ted Laney's chest coming out as he began to enter.

"Whoa there Monsignor. Slow down."

"Are you people finally finished? Can I now call this my home again?!"

"Yeah, yeah, we're all done. I just came over to pick up the last of the police tape and drop off some boxes."

The Monsignor brushed him aside and raced down the hall to his office. "It's gone, it's all gone! My God, did those vultures take everything? Are they going to crucify my Adam now? That bastard Lieutenant promised me goddammit, he promised."

Laney closed the front door and walked back to the Monsignor's office. "Hey, hold on. If you're asking about all that stuff you had on the wall in your office, well, it's in three boxes on the kitchen table. Lieutenant McGowan asked me last night to drop them off to you sometime today. They were at the station house. I guess he had one of our uniforms take all that stuff down, and box it for him right after we took you in yesterday."

Murphy rushed into the kitchen to find all the memorabilia neatly stacked in the boxes as the detective described. "This makes no sense. I just talked to him earlier this morning when he demanded I talk to you and your partner. How could he have known yesterday to remove these things from my office?"

"Hey Monsignor, I haven't even given him my report about our meeting yet, and I have no idea what any of this stuff about your nephew has to do with anything. I'm just the delivery boy."

Laney headed back down the hall and out the front door. The Monsignor slumped into a kitchen chair relieved, but embarrassed that McGowan had foreshadowed his reactions so far in advance. *"No matter. My Adam is safe."* He reached in his pocket for his cell phone and hit a speed dial number.

"Hey, Uncle Mike, how're you doing?" a voice said that brought a huge smile to his face.

"Just great, Adam my boy, just great!"

CHAPTER TWENTY-EIGHT

"Geez Dax, what's all this cloak and dagger shit you've had Ted and me going through? First, he tells me you come up with a way to make the Monsignor talk that involved passing him a note and a phone. Then the guy, who was such a prick yesterday, spills big time. I swear. If we wanted to know his masturbation schedule, he was ready to give it to us. Now, Ted tells me when the Monsignor gets home, he totally wigs out about a bunch of knick-knacks that have to do with his nephew, acting like you played him for a chump. Hey, just tell me what's going on."

Dax had called her from Chicago after his meeting with Rebecca. He related the story of how, upon their arrival at the rectory, he discovered the Monsignor's close relationship with his nephew, and had all the information gathered up as a potential negotiating tool. He apologized for recruiting her partner in the "secret phone and note" process without alerting her first, describing all the culpability factors, and how he wanted to be the only one responsible if the plan went south.

"Hey man, just give me more of a head's up next time," she blurted back. While that made little sense, it satisfied her need to express her role as being in charge, but she was more intent on relating the information she and Laney had extracted from the cleric.

"Damn, Dax. That was the most shit I ever got out of anybody above a priest. Here's what Murphy said went down with Wendich. One day about seven months ago, the Monsignor gets a call from Archbishop James' assistant, a Father Timothy Regan. Regan tells him the Archbishop is about to make a placement in his parish of a new priest, and he needs to prepare living quarters and make any necessary arrangements. The Monsignor starts asking the usual questions, but the assistant begs off, telling him he would soon be getting a call directly from the Archbishop. The Monty is happy as he's been without any help for some time having to cover everything, masses, confessions, sick calls, the works. He also said it was unusual for the Archbishop to call directly about something like this when Regan could have given him the basic information, which was all he would need, or so he thought.

"So, the call comes, and the archy tells him the guy's from Europe, should arrive in another week, and his name is Father Peter Wendich. Based on the name, he asks the archy if the guy's from Germany. The archy confirms that, but says he'd spent the last four years in Ireland . . . which confirms your deduction, Sherlock."

"Okay . . . good so far Janet," Dax said.

"So the Monty tells the archy that if the new priest can just cover the early masses, some confessions and pick up the CCD classes, that would free him up to do all the other more important things in the parish. Then the archy says he's not so sure this guy should be teaching kids, and explains that he's in his late fifties and isn't up so much on what American children's needs are. The M reminds the archy that he's in his sixties himself teaching those classes, and age shouldn't make a difference teaching church doctrine.

"So it occurs to him to ask why a guy this late in life is being transferred to the U.S. He should be a Monsignor by now running his own parish. The archy gets a bit edgy, and comes up with a not so logical reason for the transfer. He tells the Monty that it's been really trying for any priest these days in Ireland because of that major report that just came out about Catholic orphanages there bashing priests and nuns for beatings, starving kids and sex abuse going back to the 1950s. The archy then says he's not sure the guy should be around kids right now because he feels . . . get this, Dax, too alienated from children as a result of the fallout from that report. If the Monty does use the priest in any capacity with children, he needs to keep an eye on him for the possibility of his being over stressed."

"Goddammit, Janet."

"Yeah, and of course, the Monty now suspects that this could be code shit for the guy's a pedophile. When he presses the archy on what "over stressed" means, he tells him that Wendich had been through some intensive counseling for six months, which was very successful, but didn't want the guy to have too much responsibility too soon. The archy also reminds him how hard it is with so few priests coming out of the seminary these days that he should be thankful he's getting any help at all. Finally, the Archbishop tells the Monsignor to go ahead and use him any way he needs to. Just oversee him more closely at first to be sure he's okay.

"Then Dax, as a total surprise to Ted and I, this is where the Monsignor breaks down and starts crying. He tells us that he watched Wendich like a hawk for two weeks, especially when he worked with the kids. He said the guy was a natural. He was kind and the kids loved him. He was sure there was no danger to them. I mean he was broken up pretty bad."

"Two weeks? That's just long enough to build the trust the bastard was so good at. It's, of course, all part of the manipulation process," Dax said fuming.

Janet agreed. "You know, I still don't like this Monsignor, but I think he was also taken in by this perv. He may be somewhat of an arrogant prick, but my take is he would have stepped in if he thought those kids were in any danger. Oh, and he confirmed he was out shopping when the priest escaped, so he claims not to know what transportation he used or if he exited with someone's help."

"Janet, we already know a call was made by Wendich to the O'Reilly's yesterday morning, which is when he found out I'd be talking directly with Tommy. I'm betting there was a call made immediately after that to the diocese . . . I mean within the next few minutes. Since the Monsignor was out grocery shopping, that left only Wendich to make that call."

"We're ahead of you on that. We've got the phone records, and it's clear he made that call and disappeared shortly after. Listen, my next step now would be to take the information on that call and the results of the Monsignor's interview, and press for a search warrant of the diocesan office. We should be able to get that warrant if for no other reason than we have a pedophile priest on the loose and all the records of his transfer are located there. Though, that would likely be an exercise in futility, as it always ends up being."

"You know Janet, I'd hold off on that warrant just yet anyway. It's a great start that we have the Monsignor recorded seriously implicating the Archbishop in placing this pedophile there. But, we need more, and we don't want to spook the archy, as you call him, until we get it. You probably agree, that if we can catch Wendich, we can make a much better case against the Archbishop. Besides, it's likely those records have conveniently disappeared by now; the Archbishop won't tell us anything, and with the usual legal wrangling, it could be a number of days before we could get to question him directly." Dax knew this was inherently true, but was now hoping Rebecca Bain's group could locate Wendich's whereabouts faster. Getting the D.A.'s people involved would only complicate his path to reach him first.

Janet responded. "Okay, I have to agree. However, we still don't have anything on this ghost's location, and if Rebecca comes up dry, what do we do next?"

"We have no choice but to take things one step at a time," he said. Not wanting to break off just yet, Dax changed gears. "You know, we should have had something from surveillance video or a passport hit by now. Anything at all out there?"

"No, nothing . . . bone dry. We're also doing a routine check of tapes from bus and train stations, even ocean liners though no one wanting to get out of Dodge fast chooses those slow mo ways anymore. We also haven't been able to find a cab or limo company that made a pickup at the rectory that day. The guy really is a ghost."

"Hey, can I call you right back? There's something I need to do. I'll call you back in just a few minutes," Dax said, knowing what he must do next. Janet assented.

Her comment about ocean liners was setting off some bells. He needed to lay it out, his hotel room being a perfect place.

"So Watson, let's see what the facts tell us so far as to the whereabouts of this Peter Wendich fellow, shall we? Being a loner, we know that he had few if any liaisons in the city, limiting those to whom he could seek assistance in his escape. It also appears that he did not employ any commercial livery in that effort. That only leaves his method of departure to be a private vehicle. Who then would provide transportation on such short notice for this purpose to this hermit of a man? We can only assume it to be someone who had a thriving interest in supporting his need to avoid capture. From the Monsignor's recounting of events, that would be the Archbishop. But alas, after picking him up, where would the most logical place be to take him?

Clearly, the diocesan office or any of its properties would be out of the question.

His discovery there would be an outright incrimination of the Archbishop, nearly impossible to defend now that the press has all but indicted and found Herr Wendich guilty. No, taking Wendich out of town, more likely out of the country to a place safe from extradition would be the only logical solution. That would also be a reason not to choose any diocesan vehicles for transportation past the initial pickup from the rectory as the outstanding BOLO might lead to it being unexpectedly stopped. It then begs the question: how he could leave the city in the most unobtrusive fashion, avoiding detection by the many security procedures that are available to the police? The answer, my dear Watson, lies in the results of some additional investigative work we must rely on Detective Meehan to perform."

Dax was speed dialing Janet as Holmes' last words trailed off.

"Janet, if we eliminate all the usual ways out of the city that we inquire on, there is one other, though normally an unlikely venue we might pursue. Let's check if the Archbishop or the diocese owns a yacht, and if so, let's see if it's made any voyages of late. Most of those vessels are dry-docked for the winter, though some are left in the water with a bubbler system to avoid ice buildup so they're ready to go if needed by the owner. This works as long as the waterways are not ice bound, and we haven't had low enough temperatures along the coast so far this year to cause that. If we can discover they have such a craft that's made any departures in the last few days, maybe we can find out where it was headed. Then we can check the commercial airlines and travel venues from that location."

"That's worth a try. I'll get right on it," her voice coming across as if she was taking notes. "Hey, how did your meeting go with Rebecca this morning? I was so psyched about what we got out of the Monsignor, I almost forgot to ask."

Dax knew he couldn't possibly discuss the significant attraction he and Rebecca had shared, so stuck only to facts. "You were right; this woman really knows her stuff. She has her best people working on the information and hopefully will have something to report when we have dinner tonight." He then realized Janet was going to take that to mean more than he meant it to.

"Dinner tonight? Hey, I told you this woman was beautiful; was I right?"

"Uh, yes . . . you are correct about that." he said matter of factly.

"Well, tell me more . . . c'mon Dax, what's up with you guys?

Dax felt a bit trapped. He couldn't tell Janet that he re-scheduled his flight and the purpose of the dinner was to swap street stories. He might as well tell her they were on an official date. He quickly came up with a truthful answer to get him off the hook. "If you remember Janet, I have that other meeting this afternoon at two, and because of Rebecca's tight schedule, meeting this evening before I leave tomorrow to discuss that meeting's results was the only time available. Don't read any more into it than that? Please do call me . . . even late tonight if necessary if you come up with anything on the yacht idea," he added as a misdirect, and Janet's "You got it." was how he hoped she would respond.

CHAPTER TWENTY-NINE

The time read 1:58 on the large four-faced commercial timepiece hanging in the center of the Spencer Building's lobby. Once on the elevator, rather than hit seven for Rebecca's floor, Dax punched the B button in search of Seymour Hirsch. During the long wait for its arrival and the ride down, he mentally revisited his meeting with her that morning, feeling a bit like a smitten teenager. That, and the realization every encounter with the growing number of good people helping on his daughter's case was creating a highly stressful tension for him, as each positive engagement with them was in direct conflict with his need for revenge. However, he was pulled back from those thoughts as the opening of the elevator revealed an unusually short and narrow hallway to a single metal door only some ten feet away. It displayed a hand written sign in Magic Marker ink. **"No entrance allowed without a pre-set appointment**." Dax exhaled a one-breath laugh. *"I guess unless you already know who occupies this space, and or the right person to call, you're out of luck."*

He knocked but once and heard footsteps approaching from a distance. The swift opening door revealed the effervescent smile of a middle-aged man greeting him with an outstretched hand. "Dax McGowan! Welcome. Please come in. Seymour Hirsch, at your service." Dax returned his hand which was shaken with enthusiasm.

After his walking the streets of downtown Chicago among nattily dressed executive types, Mr. Hirsch was quite the contrast. His graying blond hair was wavy, but in need of combing, and the large age-faded freckles on his face, were intermittently covered by what looked to be three days of beard growth. He wore tan colored, baggy corduroy pants that broke over a pair of black and white sneakers whose vintage seemed ageless. The well-worn brown leather belt attempting to hold his pants up was mostly hidden under a well-fed paunch. His shirt, a brown and blue checked flannel, would have been more at home in some Upper Michigan hunting camp. Dax thought how much this man reminded him of a somewhat taller version of the deceased actor, Philip Seymour Hoffman. The one matching name only adding to his impression.

"Please follow me. I'm going to call you, Dax, and you're going to call me, Seymour. I've given the staff a special mid-week Christmas shopping break to allow us this private time together."

"Okay . . . ," Dax responded somewhat amused. There was something about this man's commanding and yet friendly demeanor that he took an immediate liking to. He sensed he would be conversing with a highly intelligent fellow as opposed to just some fellow who was going to fill him in on a bunch of salesy information. Besides, he mused, Rebecca spoke highly of this man, and that already carried a value for him.

Their travel down a long hallway took a sharp turn to the right into a large open area that took Dax by surprise. Across from where they stood, about twenty feet away, was a wall of five large flat screen monitors. Under them, across the entire length of the room, forty feet he estimated, was a continuous console of high tech instrument panels with a matching seat station below each screen. Approximately ten feet back and toward them, in the center of the room, was a raised master control panel roughly six feet across, accommodating one large high backed chair. *"Captain Kirk would feel right at home sitting there."*

"Quite the War Room you have here Seymour, or should I say, the Bridge on the Starship Enterprise?"

"It's a beauty, isn't it?" Hirsch effused like a proud parent.

"So, I understand you're part of a relatively new group called the Congregation of American Catholics. How does that tie in with Dr. Bain and CABS, and with me for that matter?" Dax asked, wasting no time getting to the point of his visit.

"Well, I've been authorized by our people to give you the whole skinny on what we have planned. However, before I go on, I have to ask you to keep everything I tell you in total confidence." Hirsch's face was still smiling, but this was said more seriously.

As a rule, Dax never capriciously agreed to anyone's request to keep secrets until he could weigh what conditions might make that promise difficult to keep at some future time. "Then you'll have to give me a minute on that," he said in a friendly fashion.

"Take your time," was the response from Hirsch, spoken in the same manner.

While there was no apparent reason for concern, Dax thought it best to see if he could divine what was going on in this cave-like endeavor. Hirsch was now seated at the master console, swiveled around facing back at him still standing where they first entered the room. Dax turned away from him and began to pace. Holmes was at the edge of his thoughts.

"Whatever these people are planning is certainly something large scale. You don't occupy expensive real estate like this, and invest in what may be a million dollars of IT equipment to plan church potluck dinners."

He surmised that multiple large screens indicated a communication system that likely covered a large geographic area . . . maybe the whole country. Five screens would mean five other groups, a total of six counting this location, all linked together for some major teleconferencing. He ruled out any kind of illegal activity for all the obvious reasons, his own presence included, but the operation had a strong conspiratorial feel to it, the request for confidentiality only adding to the notion. Given the inclusion of the term "American" in the name of Mr. Hirsch's group, what he had now learned about the extent of the criminal activity of the church hierarchy, and a reference to them as "fucking pricks" by a very classy, well-educated woman, left only one logical conclusion, and in his head Holmes pronounced, *"The game is afoot!"*

"So tell me Seymour, when will the announcement be made? I assume you've already chosen a date that likely has some historical significance in the church," he said, feeling not the slightest qualm he may be mistaken.

"Is that an acceptance of your promise of confidentiality, my friend?" Hirsch requested.

"Yes, it is." Dax replied.

"Well, oh most intuitive one, that would be Pentecost Sunday, in June of next year."

Dax knew Pentecost Sunday was the celebration of the ancient time appearance of the Holy Spirit to the disciples of Jesus empowering them to begin the work of building their new church. The Spirit's visitation continues to be commemorated in the Church's sacrament of Confirmation, which bestows on properly instructed Catholic youth, the title of "Soldier of Christ," frequently referred to as the Catholic Bar Mitzvah. "That date seems totally appropriate, and I expect, Seymour, the acronym, CAC, could easily become, ACC, standing for the American Catholic Church," he said hoping he wasn't coming off too smug after uncovering the plot so quickly.

"Your reputation as a quick study is well deserved, Lieutenant." Hirsch said. "Are you now ready for your indoctrination? Actually . . . we're trying to get away from words like that, don't you know," pointing harshly at Dax in a joking manner.

"I'm sure you are," he said smiling. "But, before I get the big sales pitch, pray tell how a guy named, Seymour Hirsch, is involved in leading a breakaway from Rome for American Catholics? I'm from New York City, and most people there would find your name and the Catholic Church in the same sentence a bit of an oxymoron."

Hirsch broke into a full belly laugh. "Jesus, Dax, you're the first person that's ever mentioned that . . . duh!"

Dax laughed just as hard in return.

"I'm one of those converts, my man. Hey, I was a good little Jewish boy. I delved deeply into learning Hebrew and Jewish history, celebrated my bar mitzvah, the whole nine yards. But, I was always intrigued hearing the Torah referred to as the Old Testament by my many Gentile friends and thought I should at least read their New Testament. I decided I really liked this Jesus Christ fellow better than anyone else in the Bible and chose to consider myself one of his aspirants. This all happened in my late teens, much to the chagrin of my parents, and my interest only grew as I became a student of history on into college. That was Harvard by the way, where I first met Rebecca.

"It was there I discovered that Thomas Jefferson and John Adams and I were kindred spirits, hallowing the teachings of Christ, but never believing him to be more than a genius ahead of his time. Did you know that Jefferson took Matthew's gospel and re-wrote it taking out all the miracles and references to the divinity of Jesus? It left just the unbridled essence of his teachings . . . how it was we should love one another and behave like civilized human beings. I was thrilled that I had finally discovered someone who saw Jesus the way I did, and have it be a person of such great intellect."

"Seymour, I'm not one to buy into any of the Gods claimed by their religions, but I could sure see lining up with a thinker like Jefferson as a good place to be. But, joining an organized Catholic religion? How'd you get reeled into that?"

"Well, being of a mind to socialize and enjoy the company of others, and at the same time being considered an outcast in the religion of my own family, I decided to check out a Catholic Church one Sunday and sequestered a good Catholic friend to accompany me. We sat in the back so he could interpret the proceedings, and I was immediately hooked by the music and the liturgy. Being as much a left brained person as a right, I can appreciate an organized religion's practice of people re-stating what they stand for and believe in on a weekly basis. I concluded that I could pal up with these folks even if I didn't buy the divinity of Jesus or the transubstantiation of bread and wine into his body and blood and all the cannibalistic implications of devouring it. Being a historian, I appreciated the connection the current Pope could rightfully claim as a direct successor of Peter who was originally ordained by Christ himself. We Jews get off on those long term tie-ins to the ancients, that, and being able to spend Sundays with a host of wonderful people who just want to make the world a better place for everybody. Frankly Dax, I'm helping lead this charge to break away from Rome because its current leadership appears to be irreparably enmeshed in doing just the opposite."

"No argument from me on that." Dax said.

Hirsch went on, "My hope is that we could eventually force a turnover in the Roman Curia, the men who sit behind the Pope, and who are really in control of the church. I believe operating a successful American Catholic Church here could be just the force to make that happen. We would start by electing our own Pope from a select group of American Cardinals, men who seek as much change as we do."

"While that sounds very ambitious, what of this new Pope Francis, who seems to have caught the liking of Catholics everywhere?" Dax asked.

"Actually, if you follow the news closely, you'll see that every time Francis says anything that would indicate the church might change its direction in an area, like homosexuality, a following quote from a member of the Curia, says something to the effect, the Pope didn't really mean what he said. Then, we wait for the Pope to come back and tell us he did mean it, but we hear nothing more about it. The Curia has no patience for putting up with his liberal views, and will never allow any substantive changes to be made to how they believe the church should be run . . . continue to be run, much as it was in the Middle Ages.

"In any event, that's how I got where I'm sitting at this moment, and I'm a whiz with communications software. It's a hobby, and was one of a couple of other majors of mine at Harvard. I hope I'm not rattling on here. I attempted to tell you all the pertinent facts in the fewest words I could contrive extemporaneously."

"I'll have to admit, Seymour, I haven't paid close enough attention to have connected all those dots before, but what are you guys going to offer that the old regime doesn't? It seems you'll only attract followers if you have something dramatically different for folks to identify with."

"Well, here's the short list. Married priests, no more celibacy, women priests, annual budgets voted on by parishioners instead of some blind tax paid by them with no say in how it's spent. There will be open doors for gay folks, birth control left to people's consciences, abortion dealt with in terms of reality, not blame, and a closer tie between parishioners and the people their money helps.

"Sounds utopian . . . but doable. What about the basic belief system? For guys like me, I--"

"Think there may be a God, just not any of the ones picked so far?" Hirsch trumped in with a know-it-all tone.

"Yeah," Dax started, laughing at the extent of the homework his hosts had done on him, "guys like me."

"Hey, the basic teachings remain the same. There just aren't any tests given or requirements to declare where you are on the belief spectrum. The whole emphasis will be on what everyone can accomplish together to improve the human condition."

"Well, your proposal is both intriguing and makes sense," Dax began. "I would enjoy a more in depth discussion about it at a future date. But the most obvious question for me is how do I fit into this scenery? I'm here to catch a killer, not reform the Catholic Church."

"An excellent question, my man. You're becoming better educated now about the criminal element within Rome's hierarchy in regards to covering up for the pedophiles amongst them, and I'm sure you read about the Vatican Bank being used as a vehicle to launder dirty money. As an officer of the law, even beyond your personal involvement, I expect you have a strong interest in seeing any law breaking institutions, from the Catholic Church to the Mafia, be deflated or ousted if necessary. Am I right?"

Dax nodded.

"So, you use your influence to help us and CABS secure the prosecution of these miscreants that consists primarily of Bishops and their ties to the Cardinals in the Curia who support their hindering of our investigations. A man like you could make a huge difference. Unfortunately, too many Catholics find it easy to be in denial about what our organization and all the victims are saying, but they'd have to listen to a man like you, well known in the most important city in the world. Are you up for that?"

"Whoa there, Mr. Hirsch." Dax was feeling cornered. This was no request to assist the development of a new group, pay some financial dues and glad hand others into joining. This was a crusade that could take him well outside the realm of solving murders. Yet, there was no denying that if he had the opportunity to put away church leaders like the Archbishop, who capriciously put Grace's life in jeopardy by placing a pedophile in her path, there was a primeval justice to be achieved in doing that kind of work. Helping a new church ideology get started mattered little. However, now was the time to remain neutral and diplomatically exit the pressure of Hirsch's request.

"Given all that's in front of me, at this point, all I can say is, that I'll have to watch how you folks come out of the starting gate and see what you actually end up proposing. If you're engaged in something I feel I can support, I'll look for ways I can help."

"That's all I'm asking, my man," Hirsch replied.

As Hirsch went on with some finer points of his proposal, Dax's normally multi-tasking attention was again driven to the overhanging deep-seated stress he had come to call his "dilemma." He wondered if this was what schizophrenia was like. At any given moment, he felt a strong attachment and camaraderie with all these new people he highly respected, Janet, Rebecca, and now Seymour, but also his most powerful desire to kill Wendich. Cold revenge was constantly calling his name. The dichotomy was torturing him, at times almost making him nauseous. Engaging his oft used tic, he shook his head, only this time rather violently.

"Hey Dax. Are you alright there buddy?" Hirsch spoke loudly, sensing it necessary.

Hirsch's strong voice a good remedy, "Yeah, I'm fine. Just shaking loose of some issues in my head."

He was scrambling now, and in an effort to gain control, asked a cop question. "Janet Meehan, an SVU detective and I have been talking a good deal about the previous Pope, Pope Benedict. He appears to have played the largest role as a leader at the Vatican than anyone in terms of the cover up of the rampant sex abuse. What's your take on him?"

"Your SVU friend is absolutely correct about that. Here's the skinny on Benedict. Back in 1981, then Pope John Paul II appointed Benedict, then, Cardinal Joseph Ratzinger, to head the Office of the Congregation for the Doctrine of the Faith, one of the highest and most influential offices next to the Pope himself. This office engages in the kinds of activities its name implies. It keeps track of who's following the rules and who isn't, often dealing directly with any transgressors, and often beyond the knowledge of the Pope. As John Paul became more physically and mentally infirm before his death, Ratzinger's power grew . . . grew enough to be easily named the next Pope. You know Dax, if you consider any sitting Pope, that is in complete alignment with the policies of the Curia, as the Fuhrer, then the head of the CDF would be the leader of his Gestapo. The CDF head is the Vatican's top cop. By the way, before it was called the CDF, it was called the Office of the Inquisitor."

His intellectual interest now overriding his "dilemma," Dax asked, "I have what appears to be an obvious question. You're telling me, this very powerful office exists and oversees the entire church worldwide. Wouldn't it then be logical to assume that both the sitting Pope, John Paul and his top cop, Ratzinger, would have had to be intimately aware of these sex abuse crimes over all those many years because they were happening everywhere across the globe at the same time, and therefore complicit in the cover ups?"

"Lieutenant McGowan, you state it perfectly. Both the question and its answer are that obvious. In anticipation of maybe your next question, I will tell you that in 2005, when papers for a Texas lawsuit filed on behalf of three boys who were molested by a seminarian, named Pope Benedict as a co-conspirator in the cover up, the Vatican claimed head of state immunity. Attorneys for the Bush administration supported that position, voiding any possible claims against Benedict. However, Jeff Anderson, an attorney who has been fighting the church on behalf of victims for over 35 years, has been granted permission by the courts to sue the Vatican in another case based on the supposition that offending bishops and priests are in fact employees of Rome. It's like going after a multi-national corporation, and its CEO for the criminal acts of its employed officers. That case looks like it may have some strong legs."

Before he could respond, Dax felt his phone vibrate against his hip. He politely waved Hirsch off as his Blackberry displayed a missed call from Janet, the signal likely unable to get through to his current basement location. "Seymour, I have a call to make on my case. It looks like Sergeant Meehan tried to reach me about a half hour ago, and I'll probably have to go upstairs to get a signal. Would you excuse me?"

"Of course. Here's a card with the phone number down here if you need to get back in. It also has my cell. Please call me anytime. I only sleep about four hours a night."

"Seymour, it's been a pleasure meeting you. I'm impressed with where you are headed and wish you good fortune. I look forward to getting together with you at some point if for no other reason than to advance our friendship."

De was pleased to read Seymour's hearty handshake and smile as his feeling the same, though the incongruity of his statement with his intentions to murder Wendich, once again, pricked at the front of his mind.

CHAPTER THIRTY

Dax headed for a safety exit stairwell pointed to him by Hirsch. He charged through the door and took two steps at a time that led up to a back corner of the lobby at street level watching the reception bars on his phone fill up in the process. He quickly hit Janet's number and waited.

"This must be my buddy, Dax?" His speedy and smiling, "Yes it is," launched her into her report. "You were right about a yacht as the means of escape. We're still tracking down the person, or persons behind the corporate name on the club boat slip membership, but we got super lucky with a marina service employee who had spotted Wendich. With no direct yacht registrations in the diocese's name, I sent Ted and a couple of guys to check out the more high end boat clubs, passing around our artist's drawing to check if anybody had seen him. We hit pay dirt at the New York Yacht Club where this marina worker, who luckily was working a double shift today, had no trouble picking him out as the priest who boarded a big ass, fifty-six footer, yesterday. He said he'd been called in on a late afternoon, ahead of his normal night shift, to work to get the yacht ship shape for a last minute trip. Besides the likeness in the drawing being so good, what especially stuck in the guy's mind was that he was accompanied by two strange men that he described as either very young priests or over-sized altar boys. What made them stand out--

"Was that their heads were shaved?" Dax injected.

"Yeah, how often do you see a priest with his head shaved, much less two of them? Jesus, Dax, how the hell did you know that?"

"Let's just say I've encountered these ninjas once before, and I've been expecting some link-up between them and Wendich ever since. What about a destination? Did he say anything about where they were headed?"

"No. Most often they do inform someone where they're going or file a travel itinerary with the marina operator, but they're not required to and didn't this time. But, don't hold out on me. Who are those men with Wendich? What do you mean ninjas?"

It was inescapable now. Dax purposefully threw in the comment about their shaved heads as a lever on himself to come clean, or count himself a liar for acting like he was ignorant of their involvement. "Janet, first let me apologize for not telling you this sooner. In fact, I hope I'm not making a mistake by telling you now. But yesterday, as I arrived at home to prepare for this trip, three of those guys were waiting there to take me out. I---

"Jesus H. Christ! Three guys tried to kill you and you decided not to tell me? What the fuck is this all about? I thought we were working together on this . . . total buddies . . . total honesty."

Dax knew he had major damage control to do now. "Janet, first let me tell what went down. These three, who were dressed like priests, ex any white collars . . . yes, were in wait to try and kill me. I couldn't take any mental pictures of their faces because they wore masks. I did manage to outmaneuver them and they ended up leaving frustrated. I have no idea who they are, or who they work for. I had no direct proof they were even connected to my daughter's death until now, though it did seem likely. I thought if we just concentrated on tracking Wendich, we would confirm that in the process. I just couldn't take the chance you'd fall back on protocol and drop me off the case because I was in some kind of danger. I can take care of myself. Can you cut me some slack on that?"

"Look man, I've put my ass on the line for you from the very beginning, treating you like an equal partner. You're even in Chicago now because I revealed to you a closely held, secret information source. There's a great deal at stake here, and I'll admit, if you get killed while we're working this case together, my career would be over. And, I'll also admit that if you told me about the attempt on your life, I would have had to consider the option of blocking you out."

She paused a few seconds, as if considering that now in light of the new information. Then went on. "But, I'm not going to do that. All my chips are in on this one, and goddammit, you'd better promise me two things. First, you never hold back anything else from me, no matter what. Agreed?"

"Agreed," he replied. "What's the second?"

"That you continue using that super brain of yours to keep from getting killed. I don't want to lose my job. Are you feelin' me on this, Dax? Besides . . . I kinda like having you around."

This offer of her sincere friendship ran a knife through his conscience for putting his selfish motives ahead of that. "Yes, I'm feelin' you. Really, Janet, I apologize . . . won't happen again."

Dax grabbed a couple of deep breaths to recover. "Okay, now that I'm repentant for my sins, can we talk about Wendich? It looks like two of these men left with him, likely leaving one still there in New York. Also, wherever that yacht is headed, a boat that size is going to need some major room to dock. That will narrow down the possibilities. We're just going to have to keep making calls to all the possible ports up and down the coast to find it. No doubt, they'll be in a blackout mode for radio contact. By the way, what's the name of the yacht?"

"It's an odd one . . . it's called *2000 Years.*"

"Well, I could think of two hundred potential tie-ins for that name on my own. I'm sure we'll discover its meaning at some point. Who's on tonight in your division at the precinct?"

"Hey, I can get just about everyone to make the calls on this for us, though it's getting late in the day, and I'd better jump on some people before they take off . . . you prick. It's still going to take me some time to get over your holding out on me. However, filling me in on the details of your date with Rebecca tonight could go a long way toward my total forgiveness."

"Is that so?" Dax said, realizing Janet hadn't bought the cleansed description he had given her of the couple's late dinner plans.

"Yes, that's so!"

Still feeling the sting of her disappointment, he decided to entertain her direction in the conversation. "Alright, but any report will have to be of the gentlemanly kind. No sordid details." Then in hopes of escaping any further questions, "By the way, my flight will be getting in mid-morning tomorrow so we can reconnoiter on where we are unless those harbor calls or Rebecca's network pays off sooner." It didn't work.

"So you're expecting there might be some sordid details Daxey boy?"

"Okay, I think I've said enough. Catch you later." As he thumbed his phone off, he began to wonder about that himself.

CHAPTER THIRTY-ONE

After fighting stinging Chicago downtown winds to return from the Spencer Building, Dax found the warmth of his hotel room inviting and was looking forward to relaxing before showering again to re-set for dinner at nine. After stripping down to his briefs, he laid sprawled across the bed.

This had been some day, he thought. He had successfully maneuvered a reticent Monsignor to spill his guts, and with the aid of his alter ego, deduced the manner of his prey's escape by water. Then he met with a very captivating woman who had a rather perceivable interest in him, to say nothing of her commitment to help him track down Grace's killer. He then met a man who made him privy to a major plan for American Catholics to break away from Rome, which would be of no small historical significance. In a somewhat comically ironic fashion, he found himself wondering if this new church succeeded, if it might have some appeal for him, though he was sure being arrested for murder, even of a pedophile priest, might discourage the acceptance of his membership application.

Dax was also at sea in trying to balance the now complex array of his many emotional states. The loss of Grace and the desire for revenge still had his every heartbeat pounding a loud thud in his ears. Despite what seemed to be a completely logical divorce from Darlene, he was aware that the destruction of any marriage, including his lifeless one, would not result in a future without scars. Was the lack of sex and intimacy in their relationship what was driving his interest in Rebecca Bain, to find a home for those long unsatisfied needs? How could all these primitive desires, and feelings of loss and anger, occupy his consciousness at the same time?

There was also the constant the battle of conscience. He had managed to quell its voice until now, but it was beginning to break through. He knew he needed to focus again on the search for Wendich to drive away any thoughts of being swayed from his goal to see him dead. Laying there alone, and in fear of the loss of control over his mind, he instinctively reached for clarity in the only way he knew he might save himself. He next found himself standing quickly to engage in a necessary fit of pacing.

"So Watson, you have been able to observe all of our efforts to date to capture Herr Wendich, as well as our frustrations. Any words of wisdom to share, dear fellow?"

"Well Holmes, frankly I have my concerns. This itinerant priest seems to have disappeared to some faraway place on of all things a yacht that could now be located anywhere on the eastern seaboard. There is no way to know if he's already ashore and taken another form of transportation, undetected to who knows where. Then there are the encounters with these head shaven killers who wear those grotesque masks. Bad business there I fear, Holmes . . . extremely dangerous those ones. How are you going to predict when they will again make an attempt on your life?"

"Well Watson, it would be easy to suppose that they are sufficiently engaged right now with the escape of Father Wendich, and I assume they are feeling rather successful in that pursuit. We could also posit that having left my jurisdiction in New York City, they no longer see me as a threat or seek my demise. However, one of them is still there, and if they have done their homework on me, they have rightly decided that Wendich will never be safe until I'm eliminated. No Watson, killers such as these will not abandon their mission once it is assigned."

"What shall you do then, Holmes?"

"I must discover more about these murderers and their motives, Watson, and I believe I know where I might best find those answers."

"I hope so old boy. That trio gives me the willies," Watson responded, his shoulders shaking in horror.

"Seymour Hirsch here."

"Hello again Seymour, it's Dax. Hey, have you got some time we could get together for a drink? I'm just down the street at the Water Tower. If that doesn't work, I could meet at some other place of your choice. I need help on my daughter's case, and I'm guessing you're just the man for the job."

"Sure . . . glad to. Actually, this is good timing. By this part of the day, I begin to get a little cabin fever down here in the dungeon. I'll be over in a few minutes and meet you in the bar there. Sound good?"

"Sounds good."

CHAPTER THIRTY-TWO

Dax waited in a middle booth in a line of several set across from an expansive mahogany bar that was backed by a wall of large gilded mirrors framed in more of the same hand carved wood. As the required accessories to front those mirrors for any popular drinking hole, the usual brown, silver, and clear bottles of alcohol stood in wait to be chosen by patrons wishing to soothe their day's distresses.

When Hirsch arrived, he had to navigate around pods of business types who had recently arrived for Happy Hour. Dax grinned at his well-worn black wool overcoat had no chance of being buttoned around his torso.

"Pretty cold walk, eh Seymour?"

"They don't call it the windy city for nothin'," he said casting a full chilled body response.

Before he sat down, he caught the eye of one of the busy female bartenders. He raised his hand in a form of sign language. He turned it down and wiggled all his fingers, then made the "thumbs up" sign, the peace sign next, and then just an open hand. Leaving his arm extended, "You all set with that drink you've got there?"

"Yeah, I'm good," Dax said, and Hirsch then nodded to the bartender.

"These folks obviously know you. One of your favorite haunts?"

"I mentioned I get cabin fever this time of day? I'm here a lot."

Despite the mass of people demanding service, the bartender arrived almost immediately with his drink, which Dax noted was an easy translation of his hand signals. A dirty martini, up with two olives. After they completed a "cheers" salute with both libations, Dax launched into the reason for their meeting.

"Seymour, I'd like to pick your brain on something."

"Ah, Mr. McGowan, you are already a man of sufficient mental capacities without stealing any of mine." he jousted.

"Then, let us share thoughts and deductions on a particular subject, leaving neither of us any less diminished." Two strong smiles of instant friends followed Dax's humorous retort.

He began again. "Yesterday, before I left New York, I encountered a trio of what would appear to be either young priests, or as someone else has described them, over-sized altar boys who, shall we say tried to remove me from the planet. All three of these men had shaved heads and wore masks depicting the visage of a wolf . . . the kind you've seen as gargoyles on the rooftops of old European Cathedrals. You're the Church history guy. Any idea who they might be and who gives them their orders?"

"Gulp, Dax! You're telling me these guys tried to take you out, and you're still amongst the living?"

"Uh . . . yes Seymour . . . alive and kicking!"

"All jesting aside, man, I can tell you that over the years there have been people who were considered a danger to the hierarchy of the church, who have ended up unexpectedly dead. No clues to their killers were ever found and the cases just ended up closed. The only piece of information that has come up from time to time that ties these deaths together, is the occasional sighting of what people say are pairs or trios of unfamiliar bald headed priests in the vicinity of the victim's demise.

"Most of these deaths are labeled suicides, a suicide that people who knew the victims said was totally out of character. Rarely, the police have determined the deaths to be murders. Whatever police were involved have never seen these goyles, so there has never been any official connection made between them and the deaths. Since no one has ever reported an attempt made on their life by these assassins, I can only assume you're the first person to ever survive one. What happened?"

"It's a long story but, basically they took a stab at whacking me. I actually overheard them saying they were going to make it look like a suicide . . . obviously their specialty. I see you've nicknamed them the 'goyles'."

JACK HARNEY

"Yeah. A scant few of the reports speak to seeing these dudes wearing those same masks you just described. During the Dark Ages the wolf was considered a mystical protector of the church poised to tear the guts out of anyone who would dare question her authority or besmirch her in any way."

"Well, it appears these wolves are on that same mission," Dax said. "The masks fit in nicely with historical religious symbolism, but it also implies these killers have bought into some kind of religious cult based ideology. These "goyles" were also very young. I would say early twenties. And, another thing, I listened and watched these perps stalk through my house looking for me. Military precision is the only way to describe it."

"Hey, it took me a fair amount of research to discover these same things about them," Hirsch said. "Though I didn't have the advantage you did of actually being hawked by the motherfuckers. Basically, everything you've said holds up to what I've learned myself. Based on their killing expertise and the shaved heads, I started checking them out from the standpoint of a military background. I contacted a retired Marine Colonel friend of mine with Special OPS experience to see what light he might shed on these men. He didn't blink an eye when I asked him who they might be and launched right into an explanation."

"You mean your military friend knows who these killers might be?" Dax asked.

"No . . . not exactly. He described to me soldiers who come home from war after doing Special OPS work that involves seeking out and killing human targets, snipers mostly. The vast majority, with counseling, manage to re-adjust to civilian life again. But, there is a tiny minority of these guys who don't know how to turn off the training to kill. He said there are two types of them. One type really gets off on it, and becomes some kind of mercenary in a third world country getting paid to do what he likes best. Then there are those who still want to kill . . . are addicted to it really, but suffer pangs of conscience and seek redemption, fearing their sins will lead them straight to hell. That's who my Marine buddy thinks these men are."

"And protecting the Catholic Church fits that redemption need perfectly." Dax offered.

"Exactly," Hirsh agreed. "Someone, maybe a wayward chaplain, recruits them into the fold. The Colonel is pretty sure these guys

126

grew up Catholic, though he doubts they are actually priests. He suspects the priest garb feeds their need to be in uniform and provides a psychological perk that keeps them feeling in character. All these killers are wacko of course, but that doesn't make them any less dangerous."

"That all adds up, but the question still remains, who do they work for?" Dax queried.

"And for that I have no answer," Hirsch replied. "We considered a number of possible sources. Since the first reports we got on them were from within the U.S., we considered stateside groups like the Catholic Covenant Group. You probably know the dude who's its President, Wallace Doherty. His office is in downtown New York."

"Yes, I was introduced once, but had little reason to give him much notice, except to classify him as a man with a very large ego."

"You've got that right. The Catholic Covenant Group has basically one function, and that's to protect the Catholic Church from criticism of any kind, real or imagined. Doherty is always out there making the right wing circuit on radio and TV challenging what he considers unfounded disparagements against the church. He constantly paints the sex abuse scandal as overblown. But, we wrote him and his organization off as the boss of these goyles primarily because the guy is so goofy, not able in my opinion to be in charge of such a complicated operation. He's a joke sometimes. He's openly homophobic. He makes ridiculous remarks about how good he is at spotting queers. can tell them a mile away. He also loves to remind everybody how the Catholic Church has been around for 2,000 years, and how that length of time somehow validates everything they do. Of course, he ignores all the other religions and social cultures substantially older than that."

Dax laughed. "I can tell you he had no idea how often he was unwittingly rubbing shoulders with any number of gay people in the upper brass of the NYPD at some of the same city functions we all attended. And your reference to 2,000 years may be very helpful in tracking down something else. Hold a minute would you?"

Dax pulled out his phone and texted fast enough to need less than the time requested. "Okay my friend, please go on."

Hirsch nodded. "Then, we heard of cases where these goyles had been spotted from Europe to South America. So, we started considering the usual suspects like the Legionnaires of Christ who have organizational ties globe wide. That group was founded in 1941 in Mexico by a very power hungry priest named Father Marcial Maciel who was given highly favored status by John Paul II because he was bringing in huge sums of money from high-powered donors, despite numerous allegations of sexual abuse on his part going back to the 50s. However, we couldn't nail down anything solid with them in terms of these goyles.

"Shit Seymour," Dax reacted, "more stories of hierarchy abuse . . . do they ever end?"

"Oh, I'm just getting started. There is also the highly secretive, and powerful group, Opus Dei, highlighted in Dan Brown's book, *The DaVinci Code*. We've thought them to be the most likely candidate. It was founded by a priest, Josemaria Escriva, in Spain in 1928 as a group that strives for perfection in the eyes of God. Opus Dei is believed to have over 80,000 members worldwide, but each is not allowed to disclose their membership without permission. Escriva, an extreme conservative, is known to have said, 'Hitler couldn't have been such a bad person. He couldn't have killed six million Jews. It couldn't have been more than four million.' How's that for moral relativism?

"In 1950, Pope Pius XII, already in trouble with the Jewish community for his silence during the Holocaust, put his seal of approval on the group. Later in 2002, John Paul canonized Escriva a saint, despite outcries from many quarters about his disqualifications, and in 2005 Benedict dedicated a statue to him just outside St. Peter's Basilica.

"As part of their striving for perfection, the Opus Dei people are known for various forms of self-mutilation as a penance for their sins. One of Escriva's better known quotes for what he termed 'mortification of the flesh' is 'Loved be pain. Sanctified be pain. Glorified be pain.' What gives us a stronger possible association with the goyles to these people is that particular predilection. Some members are known to wear what is called a cilice."

"I've read about that little pain inducer," Dax said. "It's a metal chain that's worn around the upper thigh with spikes facing inward to cause pain and discomfort to the wearer . . . literally, a walking penance."

"And just the type of screwed up thinking that falls in line with the skewed view of the mission my Marine buddy sees these goyles believe they're on. In fact, he said it wouldn't surprise him if they wore the cilice themselves." Hirsch added.

"Anyone else, besides them you suspect?" Dax was rolling his eyes in jesting disbelief at what appeared to be a constant run of history about clergy gone bad.

"Well, for a while, we thought it was the top cop at the Vatican, Cardinal William Levada, who succeeded Ratzinger as the Prefect of the Congregation for the Doctrine of the Faith . . . the CDF we talked about earlier. He's an American, and was the Archbishop of San Francisco until 2005 when he was named to that office by Benedict. He wasn't even a Cardinal until elevated to that rank in 2006 after his appointment. He was in total lock step with Benedict's position of maintaining secrecy on the abuse issue. Together they claimed deep sorrow over it, but still fought every attempt made to seek records about priests and the hierarchy who protected their pedophilia.

"Levada's past is going to sound like a broken record to you. Just before his appointment, numerous sex abuse charges and lawsuits had been filed against a slew of Salesian priests, an order based in Levada's San Francisco diocese . . . better called Sleazians in my book. Levada not only proclaimed these priests as innocent, but was caught moving them around and even promoting them to higher stations while they were being investigated, some indicted, and later found guilty. Few archbishops had more experience fighting victims and lawsuits then he did. He was ruthless. So in order for the Vatican to fight the onslaught of lawsuits coming out of the U.S., it was no surprise that Levada got appointed by Benedict as head of the CDF before the white smoke above the Sistine Chapel had dissipated on his election as the new Pope. Aside from the disgust of such a person attaining that position, even amongst some of the Pope's stronger supporters, there was dismay that such an unqualified man was elevated to that rank and office. At the time, the analogies to Cardinal Bernard Law, who was given asylum at the Vatican in 2002 to avoid arrest in Boston, were rampant."

"Damn Seymour . . . no shit on the broken record thing. No wonder you folks want to start a whole new order of things. It seems the old one is corrupt beyond repair."

Hirsch then raised his hand as a judge would in order to call a sidebar to discuss an issue related to a case before his court. "You know Dax, there's a famous quote by Jesus in the Gospel of Mark that he spoke when warmly surrounded by a large group of little children. No doubt, you've heard it. It goes, 'Whoever causes one of these little ones who believe in me to sin, it would be better for him if a great millstone were hung round his neck and he were thrown into the sea.' I'm not one to buy into religious prophecy of course, but I do respect intelligent people's judgments about how punishments should be equivalent to the crime. It seems the downfall we're all witnessing now of the Catholic Church was foreshadowed by the very man they claim as their God. Jesus said very clearly that if you mess with little kids, it's going to cost you big time. What's so inane about this whole affair? These so-called leaders don't even see the connection between what Jesus said and the current demise of their church. To all my Catholic friends, I refer to it as the 'Millstone Prophecy' . . . but I digress.

"As far as our goyle buddies are concerned, linking them to any one source is speculation at best. There's even a chance they act totally independently. We just don't know."

Dax was leaning forward on his elbows watching the timid lighting in the bar dance on the ice in his glass. He knew that if he could spend sufficient time to focus only on those assassins, he was certain he would discover and expose the forces behind them. He decided at that moment, he would eventually make that happen. In the same instant, he pictured himself in a prison cell after being found guilty of murder and unable to meet that pledge. His struggle of conscience was heading toward a crisis now.

But the revelation of the broad areas of the world where these killers had been seen, and the large number of deaths they may have been involved in struck a nerve. "Damn Seymour, in how much danger is someone like Rebecca Bain?"

"That's a reasonable question. However, as far as we know, these goyles have not attacked any very high profile people like her. My guess is they want to avoid what would surely be a relentless, full-blown investigation if they chose a target that was too well known or connected like she is. It's a good question now because you don't sync with who they'd normally finger for destruction either. You're way too high profile. Either they've decided to change their modus operendi, or you represent some kind of special danger they've decided is worth the risk. That seems more like the situation to me."

"But Seymour, I can take care of myself. Who's watching Rebecca's back?"

"Hey, again man, I'm pretty sure that your being a detective with exceptional skills has got somebody very worried. I really don't see that this means any more danger than existed before for Rebecca, and I apologize for even implying that. But, let me tell you, and I'm very serious about this. As much as anyone can be protected, and still have the freedom to do her job, we have Rebecca covered."

Dax mused for a moment about his special interest in Rebecca's safety having just met her, and what his motives were behind that concern. "Hey partner, think you can get that bartender's attention again? I'm feeling the need for another Manhattan coming on."

"Would that be a Southern Comfort Manhattan? Uh . . . my superior senses have deduced the contents from over here."

Dax nodded, thoroughly enjoying being in the company of another person who so appreciated the powers of observation.

CHAPTER THIRTY-THREE

"Good evening. You must be Mrs. Rhigetti who I spoke with earlier." Dax said.

"Yes, good evening, Mr. McGowan. Please come in. Dr. Bain just called, and said she would be arriving near nine o'clock as she hoped. Please follow me," she offered, taking his overcoat and gloves.

Dax noted as part of her welcome she bowed in a decidedly old world manner. Her mostly whitened black hair was pulled up in a bun, and she wore a billowed heavy cotton white blouse and a calf length, navy blue jumper over it. Only her thin neck and face told she was a woman of extremely slight build, and a living relic of the very dignified Italian peasant stock he had always held in high regard and observed so many times in New York.

As he followed her down a short well-lit hallway into Rebecca Bain's condo, he took mental pictures of a large number of family photos on both walls. However, based on less faded areas of paint, it appeared some pictures had been recently removed. At its end, he turned left to see the condo open into a large great room. About thirty feet from where he stood was a floor to ceiling wall of one-way glass exhibiting a spectacular view of downtown Chicago. From the unit's location on the 45th floor, he could see well up Michigan Ave., spying his hotel's spotlight spires reaching to the sky some twenty blocks away. The vantage point allowed him a close up of the thousands of red, green, and white Christmas lights adorning the city he had observed from his incoming plane the night before.

"Mr. McGowan, would you like me to fix you one of those

Southern Comfort Manhattans you like so much?"

Dax was now wondering if Hirsh had been kidding him about being able to divine the contents of his drink at the bar earlier. "Thank you, but I believe I'll wait for Dr. Bain, and just look around a bit if that's okay."

"Of course, sir; make yourself at home. I'll continue my preparations."

He watched her walk to the end of the great room to his extreme right and into a large kitchen containing cherry wood cabinetry and stainless steel appliances.

Peering back to the living area, he observed the floor covered with a plush white carpet maintained in spotless condition. Several all glass end tables were strategically appointed around a black leather sectional sofa and oppositely placed love seat. This arrangement was proximate to the left wall of the room that was entirely covered with a cut-stone fireplace, a rare option available only in the most upscale developments like this one.

To the right of the sitting area and just left off the kitchen was a dining ensemble containing four all glass chairs and dinner table. The edges of those pieces were etched with a beveling that caught the firelight and casted muted rainbow colors in every direction of the darkened room. Beyond the eating area, in the farthest right hand corner, was a very tall, extensively decorated Christmas tree replete with strings of beads and hand painted ornaments of Jamaican origin.

To his extreme left, past the fireplace wall, was a hallway containing three doors. He surmised a spare bedroom and bath on the right and the master bedroom suite on the left, which he calculated would have a direct view of Lake Michigan.

He re-entered the hallway to spend more time with its photos. He was disappointed all the pictures were of recent vintage, hoping to gain some knowledge of Rebecca's past. Consigned to what was there, he concentrated on the pictures of her parents. Her father was a robust, rosy-cheeked man, clearly of Western European descent. Her mother was short and waifish, but a strong looking woman of unmistakable Jamaican heritage. He readily saw where Rebecca inherited her beauty, and the same gold-flecked irises she possessed. Standing close to the front door, it suddenly flew open catching his left elbow.

"Oh my God, I'm so sorry, Dax. I didn't realize you were standing there." Rebecca, wearing a full-length white overcoat, was tearing her brown gloves off as quickly as possible to be able to place her hands on his arm in sympathy for his injury.

"It's okay Rebecca . . . really, no harm done."

"Are you sure? It seemed like the door hit you rather hard."

"I'm fine . . . really . . . no problem. Welcome home. I was just looking over your family pictures. Your parents look like wonderful people, and it's easy to see how you turned out to be so---." Her surprise entrance caught him off guard, and now found him stating something all too familiar, but forced to finish, "you know . . . so pretty."

"What a terribly nice thing for you to say." She grabbed his left shoulder pulling him down for a friendly peck on his cheek. "It has been a long day, and I can't wait to get my clothes changed and relax. Would you excuse me as I get settled?"

"Sure, of course," he said.

"Good evening Dr. Bain, would you like a glass of Riesling before dinner?" Mrs. Rhigetti asked.

"Thank you, Mrs. Rhigetti, and good evening to you. Since we'll be having steak tonight, I think it's time we opened that Merlot that Michelle Obama gave me when they still lived here. Maybe Mr. McGowan would like a glass as well?"

"That sounds good." Dax said.

As Rebecca disappeared to her bedroom, he stood in the space between the seating area and the dining table wondering which they would occupy first. He was pleased when Mrs. Rhigetti brought over the two glasses of wine for him to hold so he could serve Rebecca when she returned. Usually calm in the presence of dignitaries, even Presidents, he found his heart beating faster and both wondered and knew at the same time why. He took small sips from his glass until she re-appeared wearing a shiny blue silk blouse and snug fitting jeans. Crooked in her arm was a medium sized cardboard box containing several framed photos. She walked past Dax, and around the dining table back to the Christmas tree and placed it under there, smiling at him in the process as if knowing some secret yet to be divulged.

"I hope you don't mind my dressing so informally," she began, "but after a twelve hour day . . . and please take off your coat and tie. No reason for you to feel anything but relaxed here in my home. Oh, and I'll gladly relieve you of that second glass of wine."

"Thanks, Rebecca. The word 'relax' has been totally missing from my vocabulary of late," he said as he set his glass down to shed those two items which he laid at one end of the couch.

They spent the next hour enjoying their meal served unobtrusively by her aide as they shared the elements of each other's day. Rebecca had amusing stories to relate about her history with Seymour Hirsch, and his dedication to the cause of an independent American Catholic Church, as Dax related how educational his two visits with him turned out, intentionally avoiding any reference to the specter of dangerous goyles. She apologized that her network had not yet discovered any possible pre-U.S.A. location for Wendich, and he attempted to allay her concern by reporting the potentially positive lead Janet was following up regarding his ocean bound escape.

Seated across from him, and with the expansive window and view of the city behind her, the limited lighting and glow from the fire created for Dax a fascinating illusion. He noticed that if he squinted just enough, the see through glass table and chairs between them virtually disappeared, leaving Rebecca to appear levitated and floating amongst the tops of all the city's buildings, bathing her in sparkling Christmas lights. *"Okay, so maybe angels do exist."*

Rebecca's constantly engaging smile was suddenly distracted by something behind him. He turned to see Mrs. Rhigetti almost completely covered by a simple dark black, woman's overcoat. Her head was topped with one of those non-descript furry hats with large earflaps that were turned up, the strings dangling round the sides of her face. With her hands clutching a small black vinyl purse, "Will that be all, Dr. Bain?"

"Once again Mrs. Rhigetti, you've prepared an excellent meal, and I so much appreciate your staying here later tonight to help with my guest." Rebecca said.

Having stood in deference to her expected exit, Dax added, "Mrs. Rhigetti, I also want to thank you for the wonderful home cooked meal this weary traveler very much needed.

"It was my pleasure to serve you both," she said beaming.

Rebecca retrieved a small white envelope from the edge of a kitchen counter and pressed it into her hands. She gave her a gentle hug, and bade her good night with best wishes to her husband. Then stood at the end of the entrance hallway to watch her traverse it and leave through the front door.

CHAPTER THIRTY-FOUR

"The doorman will see that she gets safely into a cab, and she has more than adequate money for the fare. One of a kind that woman," Rebecca said.

Dax nodded. "It's hard to see anyone that age still having to work, and yet she seems to enjoy it."

"She does, though she does have financial concerns. Her husband is confined to a wheelchair. Actually, her trips to assist me here do give her a break from his constant needs. She is so proper, Dax. I can't ever get her to call me Rebecca, and it's funny because I can't bring myself to use her first name either. How about a refill on your wine?"

"Sure." As she passed him headed for the kitchen, he took in a deep breath of her perfume. There was no denying his strong attraction to her, and understood the wine he had consumed and the circumstances of the evening were pushing some primal buttons. He wanted to be careful. There was something very special about this woman, and he was committed to do nothing but respond to her cues as to how the rest of the evening might proceed.

Upon her return, she crossed the entire room, and set Dax's glass on a table at the end of the couch near the fire. "Let's sit near the warmth," she said. He took a seat near his wine and Rebecca sat at the end of the love seat directly across from him. They both stared at each other for a time silently sipping from their glasses.

"So Rebecca, we have some street stories to swap, do we not? But first, you have to tell me more about yourself. It's only fair as it seems everyone around here, including Mrs. Rhigetti already knows a good deal about me down to my favorite drink."

"That sounds fair, Mr. McGowan. Now let me see . . . I'm not sure just where I should begin," she said as a humorous fib. "I'll begin with that story I mentioned earlier today that I said you might find most interesting.

"As you know from those wall photos, my father is white, Irish like you, and my mother, Jamaican. When they were young and less well off, back in the 70s, their marriage meant limited places for them to live. Being white, my dad's apprentice job on the Long Island Railroad was a decent start for them, but white neighborhoods wanted nothing of mixed couples in those days whether they could afford the rent or not. However, my father was determined that his daughter have every opportunity any white child had. He made sure, that while we were forced by the silent discrimination of landlords, to live in the more segregated part of town, I would attend the all-white public school that was accessible to anyone living in our neighborhood. That was, if they had the courage to attempt to enroll there. My father's registration of me without my presence raised no red flags.

"What was the name of the town on the island, Rebecca?" Dax was sure he'd know it well.

"I'll get to that," she said.

An interesting response, he thought, but leaned in closer enjoying the intrigue.

"As it turned out, when one very mousy little black girl showed up with the right paperwork, and a white father who could stare down the best of them, not much fuss was made. But, despite the lack of any cross burnings on the school lawn, being the only black child in an all-white school was still a nightmare for me. I had to either listen to forced praise from kids prodded by their parents to prove they weren't racists, or when no one was looking, being pushed and beaten up by kids whose parents were racists, and saw my presence as some kind of threat to their cultural existence."

The fire simmered lower and Rebecca ran a hand up and down her arm in a gesture of being chilled. Dax stood and threw two more logs on and stoked the mixture with a poker. As he turned back, he saw that Rebecca had slipped down onto a small throw rug directly in front of the fire. He simply squatted down to join her there. Once settled, he expected to hear more of her story. But she was instead staring at him. He was struck by how the more direct firelight was dancing off the gold flecks in her eyes. Each blink produced bursts of soft yellow flashes that drew him in. He moved his face within inches of hers, but held back remembering his promise to himself. No matter. She breached the remaining distance placing her full lips on his. After a few seconds, he felt her begin to tremble and pull away.

"I'm sorry, I thought about doing that all day, but I guess I'm still not ready." she said.

"Not ready . . . not ready? Of course!"

"Rebecca, I can only tell you that I thought about doing that all day myself, and I'm very pleased you did."

She smiled tentatively looking lost as to how to respond.

Dax knew he was unfamiliar with the challenges faced by sexually abused children, and how they carried that devastation into their adulthood. "Rebecca. That was as nice a kiss as I've ever been given. But you must continue with your story. I feel like there's some mystery afoot, and I think you already know how I am about such things."

A relieved smile replaced her concern as he had opened a door for her to escape her apparent disappointment.

"Of course . . . my story. Where was I? Well I . . . I rarely complained to my parents about my daily travails, as they would hear nothing of it. When I did, the result was intense instruction on the struggles of all African Americans. As I got older, I came to appreciate that of course, but it didn't make it any easier for me at the time in school. It seemed that every day some situation would arise where being the only black child was thrown up in my face, and I would spend many a night crying myself to sleep."

"And I thought my parents always being gone, and me having to baby sit my sister so much was all I could stand," Dax said, shaking his head in self-deprecation.

"I've learned we can all often handle a great deal more than we think if we are forced to, Dax. However, there was one critical event that to this day made a big difference for me. It happened when I was in the sixth grade. One day, our music teacher announced that sometime soon she'd be teaching us ballroom dancing. I was sure that no one was going to want to dance with me . . . not me, that ugly little black girl. I imagined over and over every possible miserable thing that could happen, every possible hurtful thing that could be said. Not knowing the exact day it was to begin, I was unable to pretend to be sick to avoid going to school. Then the worst possible situation unfolded for me.

"As usual, we met for music in the school gym, and as we walked in, I could see that the piano and choral risers, normally stationed in the middle of the room, were pushed back against the wall. My heart was pounding. Our old witch of a teacher announced that it was ballroom dancing day and everyone, boys and girls were to pair up. She always treated me with great disdain, and had to know the position she put me in. The boys that age might normally be shy to pair up with any girl, but not that day. They rushed to find a partner very quickly rather than be the last boy left that would either have to choose me or refuse to. As it turned out, every boy matched up with every white girl, and I was the only odd person out. I was somewhat relieved, as that was so much better than being openly rejected. But that was short lived.

Totally ignoring me, standing alone in the middle of the room, I was mortified as the teacher began to play a waltz and everyone danced around me. Then, suddenly through the gym door walked a boy who had just joined our class mid-year a week earlier, and was late for some reason."

An unexpected turn of his mind was now generating a mass of replays in Dax's head. Times, places, situations were flashing at rapid speed across his memory.

Rebecca continued. "The teacher immediately stopped playing the piano, and instructed the boy to hurry and pair up with me, expecting his refusal. I also expected the worst. But, to everyone's complete surprise, he smiled and without hesitation walked over to me, took my hand, and put his arm around my waist to assume the dance position."

"Becca? Oh my God, Becca, that was you!" Dax's memory tapes were still playing at full speed, her school nickname coming easily to his lips. His parents were remodeling the bar and going through a rough patch in their marriage. He and his sister Eileen had been shipped off to Westbury to stay with their grandparents for a while to give them some space. He now recalled, it was during those days, as the only other time he had observed those gold laden irises.

"Yes, that was me, and I was the proverbial gumpy, ugly duckling in those days. But Dax, in all my six years at that school, virtually every experience I encountered meant pain for me, until that day. You didn't just walk up and dance with me. We talked and laughed at stepping on each other's feet, and had a better time dancing than anyone in the room. No one could ever know what it was like for me to actually feel like a normal . . . no . . . an important person to one of my classmates. You were my hero. I didn't sleep that night either, but for the best of reasons. I was madly in love with you, Dax McGowan, and have admired you from a distance ever since."

"But Becca . . . I mean Rebecca, I was only there a short time. I don't remember you and I spending any real time together after that, and I was gone for good three days after that class."

"It wasn't just the thrill of the dancing and your being the ultimate gentleman that stuck with me, but also the place that experience played out in my life. That one day with you was sandwiched between my six years of misery in that elementary school and what came next. Shortly after you left Dryden Street Elementary School, my older brother, Reggie, who was in junior high, began to show a sexual interest in me. We discovered later that he was only acting out from being sexually abused by a priest. Just like your daughter, Dax, because my father was Catholic, we had to attend CCD classes twice a week after school at a local church. My brother was abused by the priest teaching those classes, and that same priest began to abuse me the next year when I entered that grade level. He continued to abuse me all through high school. Two young black children were perfect targets. There was little chance we would report it, and would not be afforded any credence if we had."

"My God Rebecca, it was just like Grace for you . . . only worse. I hadn't thought that possible. How did you ever survive?"

"In all those twelve miserable years of my education before college, my life was a nightmare except for that one day with you. I held on to that day like a life preserver in a raging ocean. It was my only straw of hope that there was any good in humanity. Your face, your smile, your friendship that day have been with me ever since."

Dax was trying to recall every detail of that class hour, but the power of Rebecca's story was engulfing him. He slid closer so he could put both arms around her neck as she reached around to hug his chest. She lifted her head to see his face, her eyes flashing again from the fire light and opened her mouth in an unmistakable invitation. This time the passion between them lasted as they kissed until they parted. Rebecca's trembling only beginning after, and to a lesser degree.

"I think I did better that time," she said.

He looked hard into her eyes, the gold flashes almost blinding him now. "Oh yes, you did . . . yes, WE did."

"Dax? I . . . there's not much more . . ."

"That's all I can handle myself right now," he said. "Somehow . . . with you, with Grace . . ." He was struggling. His next words abandoned him.

"I know dear, Dax. When I read about your daughter's case, I spent several days in utter distress because her circumstances were so close to mine. I was feeling her pain and yours at the same time."

He was unprepared for the waves of anguish overtaking him. Diving deeply into his daughter's case, the determined anger to destroy Wendich, and his life in jeopardy had insulated him from facing the reality of the full measure of the torture and pain his sweet Grace had suffered. It was now crashing through his defenses. Being in the presence of this caring woman who had endured the identical suffering, and desiring to feel her pain opened the floodgates to Grace's. His whole body was shuddering as he burst into tears. He buried his face in his hands and she embraced him once again.

"That's good, Dax. Go ahead and cry. Don't stop . . . just cry."

For what his formidable memory could recall, it was the first time in his life he had ever completely surrendered himself, all walls down to another person.

It took a measureable degree of time before he felt some relief begin to overtake him, but chose to remain in her arms. "I didn't know I needed this. Thank you for being here for me," he said.

"I've held many hearts in my hands over the years. That I was here for you seems only just for what you've always meant to me," she said, gently rocking him back and forth.

"Dax?"

"Yes?"

"Would you like to stay here tonight? I mean not in the sense of . . . you know . . . but to be together. Am I making any sense?"

"Yes, very much," he said. "There's a place, a beginning we may both want to start. I know I want to, and being here together seems right. I have an early up tomorrow to get to my hotel and pack, but . .

. I hope I'm the one making sense."

Within minutes, they were sliding under the covers of her bed, pressing their bodies against each other. Though cast in near total darkness, they knew each was staring at the other. Dax leaned in to place a full but shortened kiss on her mouth wishing not to test her limits. He then gently pulled away to prevent his growing sexual arousal from pressing against her leg and causing her any distress. She pulled him back. Though recoiling at first to the unexpected erection, she quickly held his face with both hands to kiss him ever so warmly, a kiss he felt held a promise of more at some later time.

As they slowly, very slowly relaxed away from each other and drifted off to sleep, Dax told himself that killing Peter Wendich was now totally out of the question.

CHAPTER THIRTY-FIVE

Friday: December 18th

Dax's cell phone alarm poked its unwanted sound in his head. He had set it early enough to allow the time to discuss with Rebecca an idea that had evolved overnight. He noted her absence from the bed, but the answer to her whereabouts came from the strong aroma of fresh coffee. His entrance into the great room was met with a warm greeting.

"Good morning, Lieutenant McGowan. How did my favorite New York City detective sleep?"

"I had no idea what a full day this mind and body had yesterday until I just awakened and realized how soundly I'd slept. How about you?"

"Well, at first it was difficult to not keep thinking of the first steps we took last night, but I soon fell into a very satisfied state of sleep." She was glowing. "The only thing that woke me early, I wanted to be sure you had a good breakfast, and we had some time together before you had to leave. The eggs, bacon, and toast are ready to go when you are. How do you take your coffee?"

"You mean you don't know?" They both laughed. "I've have a couple questions for you," he went on. "First, would you rather I call you Rebecca or by your nickname?"

She thought a second. "Actually Dax, the only person left that calls me Becca is my father. I think I'd like it very much if you were the only other person who did."

"Becca it is then." As they both sipped coffee after slipping into the same glass dining chairs they occupied the night before, "Do you mind my asking where you're headed for the two week vacation you're leaving for tomorrow?"

"No, not at all. I'm going in today to finish some file work. A high priority of course is making sure our Internet contacts are doing everything they can to track down this deviant priest for you. Tomorrow, I was going to start some research. I'm working with a psychology professor up at Carthage College just north of here in Kenosha on a book that looks at abuse from the abuser's side. It's meant to help identify early symptoms and hopefully intervene in the lives of young people who may be potential pedophiles, and work toward preventing them from turning to the dark side before it's too late, if that's possible. I was going to do some heavy reading the first week and writing the next. What do you have in mind?"

"If you're up for it, how about you join me in New York for a few days? You're already helping me on my daughter's case, and I'm officially off duty myself right now. I certainly don't want to interrupt what you already have planned, and if you can't, you can't. But I think a few days together right now would be good for us. Maybe you could bring along your reading materials and still get that accomplished."

Rebecca response was immediate. "I'm sure that would work. That would be wonderful. I'd much rather be anywhere you are right now."

They quickly stood and met mid-table in the hug of a couple who had just passed a critical first stage of their relationship. Holding her cheek to his, Dax peered out the large window behind her as the faintest hint of morning light was making itself known. He was pleased at her desire to be with him, and felt better she'd be under his protection in New York. Seymour may have her covered, but he would have her covered now as well.

CHAPTER THIRTY-SIX

Upon his return, a perimeter check of his house, gun drawn, revealed no signs of freakish assassins, affirming what his instincts had already told him. He wasted no motions dispensing with his garb and gear and pulled his Blackberry to call Janet.

"Hey Dax . . . wow, I don't know where to begin. Should I catch you up on where we are on Wendich or should I ask you to explain to me why Rebecca Bain called me to see if she could room with me for a few days while she comes here to get to know you better? Holy shit, man. I wanted you to maybe take some interest in her, but now she sounds like you and her are a thing. What the hell went down in Chicago? What did you do to that woman, or maybe I should ask, what did that woman do to you?"

Dax knew this was coming. Upon Rebecca's decision to follow him to New York, she pointed out that it would be both awkward and disrespectful to his soon ex-wife, Darlene if she stayed with him at his house. She suggested staying with Janet so she could ride in with her to the precinct each day rather than make a futile attempt to book a hotel in a convenient location this close to Christmas. He agreed wholeheartedly on the same grounds and for her safety as well. He had decided that Janet's protection was nearly as good as his.

"I know you have a ton of questions about how this all came down, Janet, and the only thing I can tell you is that you're going to have to pry any information about it from Rebecca. There's a long story and personal issues involved, and I'd rather leave it up to her to decide just what she'd like to share. But, I will tell you, that from my end, I was blown away when I met her. Everything you said about her was true."

"Well, I can't wait to get the whole story on this. Jesus, Dax, this is better than the movies!"

Dax laughed in a manner to both acknowledge his friend's sincere interest and allow himself a segue. "So Janet, what's the latest on Wendich?"

"Good news really. Guess what? Before we could discover the location of the yacht, it returned late last night. That same marina employee called us shortly after it arrived. Besides wanting to help us, he doesn't like the people who ride on that monstrosity. He says they treat all the employees there like shit. Also, your text message was right on. The name, *2000 Years* tracks with what the marina guy later confirmed. It's Wallace Doherty, of the Catholic Covenant Group, that frequently uses the yacht, amongst other church notables.

Anyway, the full time captain of the yacht told Kelchuk . . . that's the marina employee, that they took a trip down to DC and turned right around and came back. Here's the problem. We're waiting for airline security tapes from the different airports there because all the regular checks for commercial and general aviation and passport usage have turned up a big zero again. I suppose it's possible that he didn't try to fly out of there and he's hiding in DC somewhere."

"I think that's highly unlikely," Dax retorted. "There are many more places for the hierarchy to hide Wendich in New York than in a smaller town like DC. No, I'm convinced that trip was a ploy to get him out of the country. Besides, the opportunity to hide him in some old haunt in Western Europe would not only provide a better cover away from us, and frankly away from me, but Wendich's background there has to be a factor in his decision of where he'd like to be. There's something we're missing, Janet, some small elemental thing that we're just not seeing."

"Damn, Dax. I've never seen so much drama shit with hunting one of these perps before as I have with this one."

"Well, give me some time to work this out, and I'll get back to you."

"You got it, man!"

CHAPTER THIRTY-SEVEN

Dax was frustrated. This priest seemed to be slipping further and further away. While what was once his determined goal to end his life had now changed, his anger and desire for revenge still lingered. He shook his head violently to gain clarity which pointed him in the one direction he knew gave him his best chance for ideas on how to proceed.

"*Watson! Wake up Watson! There is an inconsistency in logic that must be sorted out in order for us to move ahead with this case. Are you with me, my good man?*"

"*Humph . . . sorry old boy, just dozing off a bit. Had a late night aiding Mrs. Sanders. Headache spells you know. What can I do to help?*"

"*Just be alert my dear friend. We must locate a missing piece to a puzzle. We know who our perpetrator is. We have identified his mode of escape and its destination. Yet, we are totally unaware of his whereabouts after his arrival in Washington, D.C. Unless there is a most unlikely special location to hide in that city, it is only logical, the reason for making the effort to take him there by yacht, would be to allow him the usual escape by aircraft not available to him here due to our intensified net of surveillance. However, there is no evidence, as yet, he boarded any such conveyance. What do you make of that?*"

"*Well Holmes, are you sure that was him getting on that boat? Oh yes, of course, that marina fellow recognized him from the drawing. We also believe it to be him because he was accompanied by those scary goyle fellows. You know the man; you assume his motives for such a trip correctly, I'm sure. Yet his expected means of escape has now become a mystery. I can't fathom a guess why old boy. I'm stumped.*"

"Watson! I believe you've hit on it! Of course, it's so simple. I knew if I could just engage you in logical discourse, the answer would reveal itself."

"Uh, really Holmes, glad to be of service. However, you're going to have to make it clear to me just how I did that."

"Well, you asked the prime question. 'Are you sure that was him getting on that boat?' You see, this is a perfect application of Occam's Razor."

Scratching his head, Watson replied, "Now I'm totally confused. What does what I said have to do with what sounds like some East Asian shaving utensil?"

"Ah Watson, Occam was a 14th century philosopher and mathematician. He was best known for the use in his work of a well-established hypothesis going back to Aristotle that assumes when one is faced with solving a mystery of any kind, it is usually the simplest solution that is most often the correct one. And you dear fellow, went right to the core of it. Your question begs the simple solution that it is not Wendich who merits our pursuit. Oh, it is the same fellow to be sure. But he is either travelling by an alias or his name is not Wendich. However, I suppose the latter, as there was a limited amount of time to produce the necessary false documents on such short notice for him to assume a new identity. No Watson, this man's real name is something other than Wendich, and he would already be in possession of the proofs of his true self.

"You see, this gets at yet another dimension of the undue influence of the church's clergy. The man, a priest, says his name is Wendich. That is further verified by not only a Monsignor, but also the very highly placed Archbishop who referred to him as such. Who would doubt its veracity for even a second? But, not only do we now have a clue which may aid in his capture, but this raises some other ominous issues in terms of the Archbishop's involvement . . . issues that may lead to open salivation on the part of our good friend Detective Meehan. And I believe I have just devised how we may use this information to our benefit in more ways than one."

Dax hit the latest new speed dial number entry in his phone.

"This is Rebecca Bain."

"And what a beautiful name it is."

"Oh Dax, I'm so glad to hear from you. I'm not getting much work done thinking about last night and my trip to see you tomorrow. Has Janet told you that my staying with her will work out just fine?"

"Yes, all goes well on the planning for your arrival, but I have some business we have to talk about. I have a new slant on our Father Wendich, though I'm sure that's not his real name. I'm guessing that Janet caught you up on our frustrations as to his whereabouts after we traced his yacht trip out of New York to DC. "

"She did. Are you saying that his name is an alias?"

"Yes, and I should have picked up on that sooner. It is the only thing that makes sense. Becca, since your tracking system checks on everyone who leaves a parish as well as anyone arrives at a new one, I'm guessing your people concentrate more on the new arrivals, looking to see if there is any danger for the kids there based on the previous assignment of that priest. However, I'll bet there are plenty of times when you register a priest as leaving a location, but there may be a long lag time before he shows up somewhere else for a host of reasons, like family issues, or even his death. Am I right?"

"Well, yes. We keep those names in an open status until we get a verifiable report of an arrival somewhere, or a death."

"Good. In any of the reports your people checked when they were looking for a priest named Wendich leaving an Irish parish six month ago, about the time he arrived here, was there anyone else in Ireland who left a parish around that time who hasn't shown up somewhere else as yet?"

"I have a copy of that report right here on my desk, Dax. Hold on."

Dax told himself it was just a matter of minutes.

"Oh my God, Dax. I didn't find anyone of interest leaving an Irish parish six months ago. However, there was a priest who was released from his parish after the exposure of his involvement in several sex abuse incidents, roughly six and a half months prior earlier. That would have given him the time to be in counseling for six months and then assigned to St. Marks in New York as the Archbishop told the Monsignor, though he may have just been hidden somewhere during that time. And Dax, this criminal falls into the category of one of the worst possible offenders. Once they fully investigated his involvements, over eighty separate cases of abuse were uncovered in three different parishes where he was assigned. And, his name is . . . Paul Werner. How's that for being close, name and initials both?"

"That's got to be our man. Do you have anything else on him?"

"Well, you know about the three year study in Ireland that covered the last sixty years of child abuse there by the clergy? It was that ongoing investigation that caused this priest to be exposed. He was initially to be turned over to the authorities. However, the last notes in our file simply state that shortly after his public outing, his whereabouts became unknown."

"Hmph. It's becoming very clear this, Paul Werner, has received some exceptional assistance in avoiding the authorities at every turn on at least two continents. We can only surmise that the help stems from a source even well beyond Archbishop James here in New York. "

Dax paused a moment, fixing something in his mind before continuing. "Becca, expecting this line of pursuit was going to tell us who this perp really was, I had already hatched some ideas how we might set a trap for our Archbishop friend. If that succeeds, it may take us much closer to capturing this alias toting Werner, once we determine his eventual escape destination. I've got to get on the phone right away with Janet to have a chance of pulling that off. Becca . . . I can't wait to see you again, and I received the email with your travel itinerary. I'll be there to pick you up tomorrow at Kennedy.

"Okay, dear Dax. I'll let you go, but please do call me tonight . . . just to talk."

"Of course."

CHAPTER THIRTY-EIGHT

"Janet? It's me again; I've got better news this time."

"Well lay it on me. Get me out of this dead end feeling I'm having about not catching this prick."

"Peter Wendich is not the name of the man we're looking for. The priest's name is Paul Werner. Wendich is just an alias." Dax then related the gist of his conversation with Rebecca and the history of child destruction left in the wake of this very dangerous priest.

"Wow, that's crazy," Janet added, "a priest with an alias? That's a new one. So hold on while I pull up the passport info out of DC. I'll try Dulles first."

Dax could hear the keystrokes as he waited on her. "Yup, here he is, one Reverend Father, Paul Werner, and he purchased a one way ticket, but not to Ireland. Shit . . . he went to Rome. That can't be good."

"That could mean any number of things," Dax started. "He would certainly be too hot a commodity in Ireland right now, good reasons to avoid going back there. The question is where in Rome? Does he have family or other connections there that would hide him? Was the Vatican his destination? That could be very bad news.

"Janet, please check something else. I'm assuming he bought his ticket at an airline counter as close to takeoff time as possible to avoid sitting in the airport too long and the drawing of his face being recognized from New York newspapers. So let's see if there were any other tickets purchased at the same time at the same counter by two other male passengers either as a one way or a round trip fare."

"Hold on . . . yes on that too. There were two tickets bought just behind his and both were also one way. They are registered to a Thomas Hicks and a Stanley Motherwell. They're not shown as reverend anything, just their names."

"That jibes with my friend's Marine Colonel's supposition about these guys not being priests. Those names also indicate a couple of American men with Midwestern roots, which confirms their speech patterns. Okay, at least we know where our perp went . . . the question is where in Rome we might locate him? As I see it, there are only two people on this end of the planet that might have any idea about that. One would be the Archbishop, and the other would be the goyle who remained behind, assuming he's still here in New York."

"Dax? Are you thinking what I'm thinking? The archy knew all along this guy's name wasn't Wendich?"

"I'm counting on it. And if that's true, the archy, as you call him, is in a whole lot deeper than he would like to be. In fact, based on what you and Seymour and Rebecca have taught me, these higher ups are experts at distancing themselves just enough from these pedophiles to stay out of the grasp of the law. If the Archbishop knowingly placed an abusive priest, and was aware of his alias, he was either being very stupid, or was under heavy pressure from someone to have taken that risk.

"I have an idea to share with you how we may actually employ both the Archbishop and this remaining goyle to help us locate Herr Werner. Let's see . . . it's almost noon already. We're going to have to move very fast on this. We'll also need the aid of the marina employee, Kelchuk. Do you think he would help us if we asked?"

"It seems so based on what Ted said about him. What's your plan there Lieutenant?"

"I'll be there in twenty minutes, Sergeant."

CHAPTER THIRTY-NINE

"Okay Daxman, let's hear it." Janet said.

Despite all the emotions swimming in his head in this most personal of all cases, Dax was about to engage in one of the most satisfying elements of his position as the respected sleuth he was. The laying out of an intricately clever plan, often causing the respectful shaking of heads by his peers.

"Here's what we know. Wendich is really Werner. The goyles know this because they accompanied him to Rome. We strongly suspect that the Archbishop is aware of the alias. It only makes sense, that if he's being manipulated by someone even higher up the ladder . . . say in Rome, he would have all the necessary information on Werner if he's been instructed to protect him at all costs. But, we have to prove that, and still figure out a way to capture Werner by knowing where to look for him.

"Okay, I'm with you so far. But how do we prove the archy has placed a known pedophile with an alias at St. Marks, when as we've discussed, they've probably destroyed any record of that in their offices. While we have a good case against him with the Monsignor's story, it doesn't have him openly admitting to any of that. It also seems discovering the location of this priest on another continent is a separate problem all by itself."

"Actually Janet, I have a plan that I'm fairly certain will work to not only discern the full extent of the Archbishop's involvement, but hopefully pinpoint Werner's location. How to actually capture him, especially if he's in Vatican City, is going to require some strategy I haven't even begun to contrive. But we have to move right away on these first steps before attacking that challenge."

"Okay, give man, give."

"There are three critical elements. First, while we know Werner is the man we're looking for, the Archbishop doesn't know we know that. The second element is the full cooperation of the marina worker, Kelchuk. The third is we have to recruit an undercover cop who has enough of a Russian background to pull off a successful deception. We have to start making this all happen . . . like in the next couple of hours. Ready? "

"Ready, set, go Daxman!" Janet said pounding a fist on her desk.

CHAPTER FORTY

The door to Father Regan's office opened after a soft knock as his secretary, Emily Grayson, slid her head around it looking both fearful and puzzled.

"Father, there's a man on the phone . . . a foreigner. He doesn't sound like a very nice man who insists on speaking to the Archbishop. He sounds a bit crazy actually, but he said I was to tell the Archbishop that he knew everything about a Paul Werner and that the Archbishop would know what he meant. So, rather than just hang up on him, it seemed I should check with you first."

Regan's throat tightened. "Mrs. Grayson, are you sure he said the name Paul Werner, not the name Peter Wendich?"

"Oh yes, Father. Of course I'd know that Wendich name if I heard it!"

"Okay, I'll handle it. Tell the man someone will be right with him."

Regan could feel his blood pressure spike, a mild condition that worsened considerably since taking the position of personal secretary to Archbishop Richard James. Up until Mrs. Grayson announced this caller, he was certain no one but he and the Archbishop knew that name. The only person who might have had any opportunity to discover it was the Monsignor at St. Marks, but Werner had verified before he left town that his identity was secure, even from him. He had to find out what this man knew.

"This is Father Regan, the Archbishop's assistant; can I help you?"

A well-worn raspy voice, clearly of Russian descent responded. "Ya, you can help. I want to speak to da bishop."

"Sir, no one speaks to the Archbishop without an appointment, and as his assistant, I would have to make those arrangements."

"Well you better get me appointment right away . . . today. I want to talk with him about this Paul Werner man, and I not going to wait past this afternoon since I have to work tonight. I must meet with him before five o'clock."

"Sir, that is really too short a notice. What's your name sir?"

"I tell you who I am when I get there. But you tell his highness, if he don't meet with me today, I just take my information and give it to da cops."

"Sir, I can assure you I know nothing about this; so it's hard for me to judge how credible these statements are, and I just can't inconvenience the Archbishop based on an anonymous call. I'm sure you can appreciate that I am also responsible for the Archbishop's safety. You'll have to tell me more."

"Here's da deal. I seen drawing pictures of this Wendich guy everybody looking for and I know his real name. I comin' over at four, and if I don't get to talk to the big man his self, I stop at da police station on my way to work. You got that?"

The phone went dead.

CHAPTER FORTY-ONE

"How'd I do, Janet?" Major Crimes Detective, Yuri Brogovich was convinced he had set the hook in his fish.

"Outstanding, Yuri. What do you think Dax?"

"It's always great working with a pro," Dax added. "If our assumption is right about what they know, you couldn't have played him any more perfectly. If you're ready, Ted Laney will get you set up with your wire now."

Brogovich jumped from his chair where they had huddled around Janet's desk to listen to his unregistered cell phone call to the Archbishop's office. "Yes, let's do this. I don't get to help put away baby and child molesters in my Russian mob work very often, and I want all of this I can get."

Janet pointed to her partner Ted who was standing just outside her office. "I'll be right there in a minute Yuri . . . want to check some details with the Lieutenant here first." She and Dax watched him exit.

"Great guy isn't he Dax?"

"Yes, and being fiftyish with that weather worn complexion, he will easily pass for an old sea salt like Kelchuk. Great pick on him, Janet. I take it Kelchuk is going to let us use his car for this appointment and he's set for tonight as well?"

"Yeah, he's psyched."

"Okay. Let's hope our timing is good, the fish are biting, and no one gets hurt in the process."

CHAPTER FORTY-TWO

"Yes sir, can I help you?" The elderly Mrs. Grayson made the request; one she'd made a thousand times before. She was facing a large man whose head was covered by a dark blue sailor's skullcap. His weathered face and neck were the only exposed skin as he wore a fully buttoned black pea coat, dark blue worker's trousers, and black boots. He removed leather gloves from his large hands exposing the unique calluses and scars of any man who spent his life working at sea. She would never have guessed this Boris Kelchuk was really Yuri Brogovich, a twenty-year veteran of the NYPD who had spent fifteen years on his grandfather's fishing boat in Russia before emigrating to the U.S. to become a New York City cop, his lifelong dream.

"Ya, I got me an appointment with his highness."

Mrs. Grayson was both dismayed and confused as to why she was told to expect this man, and how he could have been granted an appointment in the first place.

"Okay sir, please follow me," she said, as she motioned indignantly for him to come around her desk and they entered a door behind it leading to a hallway lined with three small offices and what appeared to be a much larger office at the very end. Its large hand carved wooden door bore a large brass plate naming its occupant as Archbishop Richard James.

As they entered the last small office on the right, sitting behind the desk was a thin blonde haired man in priest garb. The cleric waved Mrs. Grayson off to leave and introduced himself.

"Good afternoon, sir. Please have a seat. I'm Father Regan who spoke to you earlier." Regan never stood and motioned for Brogovich to sit in one of the two cushioned chairs on the other side of his desk. "The Archbishop has an extremely busy schedule, and asked me to settle any business we might have together on his behalf. How can I help you?"

Brogovich immediately sat anticipating the need to be seated before the conversation began. "Well da first thing you can do is go and get his highness in here. I not makin' no deals with anyone else but the head guy I know for sure can okay it."

"But sir, as I said, the Archbishop –

"Said schmed. I don't care about any of dat. I want to make a deal with da head man. See, I know that these higher up guys are not allowed to lie. It's a church law or somethin', and if he tells me we gotta deal, I know I'm goin' to get my money. You hear me? Either I see his face in here right now or I head to da coppers." Brogovich began to slowly stand as his assurance.

"Please sir, and I still don't know your name. Please sit down. I'll see what I can do." was Regan's disrupted reply.

He quickly exited through a door to the detective's left into what was clearly the Archbishop's adjoining office. A conversation filled with groans of displeasure came from behind the closed door. Finally, after a moment of silence, Brogovich then faintly heard what sounded like a quiet question asked by the other party and a positive response by Regan. The door reopened and in walked a large, chubby man in his sixties, the veins in the cheeks of his face all appearing in a burst condition. He was wearing a black satin priest's cassock with a wide red silk cumber bun. Around his neck was a large gold crucifix hanging from a long gilded chain. On his sparsely covered white haired head was a reddish purple Bishop's cap. His rounded, jowly face confirmed him to be the Archbishop, whose picture the detective was shown earlier by Janet Meehan.

Upon the prelate's entrance, Brogovich stood immediately as if in high reverence and began bowing. "Your highness, it's an honor to meet you, sir. I sorry about all this, but I have a family to feed and my hours are cut back so much, we not havin' much luck with our bills, and it seems only fair dat you folks here who have so much . . ." he was rambling on purposely to better appear to be the oaf he was portraying. He eventually went on long enough to incur the

Archbishop's wrath.

"Sir!" James yelled, his mouth filled with angry words desperately trying to get out, but were held in bitter reserve.

Brogovich reacted appropriately stunned. "Vell, yes, sir. Sorry, sir. I get right to it then. See, I don't want to be a bad man, but I figure my information is worth $10,000." He was counting on his abrupt mention of a specific amount of money to be read as him being a nervous blackmailer, naïve to the possibilities of negotiating a potentially larger sum.

The Archbishop's face was now burning with anger, and it was clear to the detective he was again holding back from reacting. Regan jumped in. "Well, sir, in order for us to even consider your request, you're going to have to tell us who you are, just what information you have and how you came to have it."

By now, the Archbishop was seated at the desk in Regan's chair and Regan was sitting in the guest chair next to the detective. Brogovich had surmised that the agreement he heard from the other room involved the Archbishop remaining silent while the priest did all the talking. The plan was of course to protect the Archbishop from any culpability, leaving only the sacrificed priest to face any potential negative ramifications that might result from the meeting. The detective knew he would have to reverse that arrangement, if he could. As if answering the required question of a teacher, he began his response.

"My name is Boris Kelchuk. I spend most of my life in Russia living with my grandparents after getting shipped dare when my parents, who lived in da Bronx, died in a car accident when I was three years old. I work on my grandfather's boat most of my life till he died. Then I come back to America and get a job at da Yacht Club. I help your priest buddy get on that yacht with those two bald priests the other night. I carry their bags on board and that was when I saw it in his open case . . . his passport. It said his name was Paul Werner, not this Wendich guy. But, it was dat guy in da newspapers alright; dare was no mistakin' it. I don't know what you got goin' on this thing and I don't care. It just seem dare's big trouble if anybody finds out, and I don't think I asking too much. What do you say?"

The Archbishop looked over to Regan for a response. The priest was shaking some now and parsed his next words carefully.

"Mr. Kelchuk, I'm not sure how relevant all this information

JACK HARNEY

might actually be. You see, we have no way of knowing if you're making this up. In one sense, it's just your word that this is true, and there are those who might refute what you've just said."

"Yah, well I whip out my cell phone and snap a picture of dis passport. Come out real good too. Ya know these phones they take pictures better den my old camera."

"Yes, yes I'm sure Mr. Kelchuk." Regan was now trembling. "Do you have that phone with you so you can show us that picture?"

"Oh c'mon now, Father. You don't think I be stupid and bring dat ,with me here do ya? Hey, you give me da cash and at da same time I show you da picture, and hand over da whole phone if you want it."

The Archbishop's reddened cheeks had now turned somewhat white. His face was clear evidence the visitor's story was being taken as all too probable given the circumstances of Werner's escape. He looked at Regan and nodded.

"Okay Mr. Kelchuk, I believe we will make a deal with you for your phone. I have to have assurances however, that you have not discussed this information with anyone else, including your family, and that you have not emailed any copies of that picture to another person."

"Hey, dis information ain't worth nothin' if I tell anybody, right? I wouldn't take da chance of screwing myself by doin' that, and I have no idea how you send pictures with my phone. I don't think my plan let me do that. I got da cheap of cheap plans ya know," he said nodding in a doltish manner.

"Okay Mr. Kelchuk, we will make your deal with you."

"So I get da $10,000?" He responded with glee. "Yes, you will Mr. Kelchuk." was Regan's reply.

Wanting to seal their agreement, but still be left with the opportunity to plan other potential scenarios the priest immediately continued. "Mr. Kelchuk, you said you work nights at the Yacht Club. How about we send someone over with the money, and meet you there for the exchange sometime this evening?"

"Dat sound good to me. I there by myself this time of year with it being winter and all da cutbacks. Better come after ten. Da party people are usually gone off their boats by then. I be in da repair shed at da end of da dock. We have privacy way out there. Uh, one thing though, just to be sure." He stood and leaned over Regan's desk, his

162

face but inches away from the Archbishop's causing the seated prelate to recoil. "You gotta tell me yourself your highness that this is goin' to happen. My family needs this money bad, and I know if you say it gonna happen, I can trust it."

He remained still, with the look of a child waiting for a present he had been promised, and never let his eyes move from the cleric's gaze. The Archbishop looked over at Regan who shrugged back indicating there was no choice but to respond.

"Yes, this will happen," was the Archbishop's reluctant reply.

Brogovich stood at attention with the smile of a man whose troubles were all about to end. He reached out to shake their hands, then quickly backed off as if suddenly realizing hand shaking was not something his hosts might want to engage in under the circumstances.

"Er, sorry about dat, I guess. Oh, well, see you tonight." He purposely addressed the Archbishop as if he foolishly believed the prelate would personally complete the transaction. Bowing reverently, he turned and walked out the office door. Aware that their eyes were on his retreat, he managed to walk the slowed gait of a tired old seaman as he navigated the hallway to the front entrance. He left them unaware of the thrill he was experiencing . . . the thrill of knowing he had just finished acting out one of the best undercover performances of his career.

CHAPTER FORTY-THREE

"Hey Ted, how's Mr. Kelchuk doing?"

Laney laughed hard in response. "Janet, it's a good thing I'm driving. This guy is packing away the beers like he'll never get to drink another one as long as he lives, that, and the most expensive steak dinner on the menu."

Sitting across from him at Ivy's Steakhouse in Manhattan, Boris Kelchuk was taking in Laney's end of the conversation, as he was enjoying the free dinner and beers at the expense of the NYPD. "Tell that Meehan lady I'd like to spend a night out with her instead of you sometime," he said, his large toothy grin causing the gravy soaked mashed potatoes on the edges of his mouth to slide faster into his lap.

"Hey Janet, this guy wants a date with you when this is all over. You interested?"

"Yeah, funny Ted. You just keep him happy with his unexpected evening off, and thank him again for helping us out with his car and all." Meehan thumbed her phone off as Dax entered, closing the utility van's door behind him.

"Well, Mr. Kelchuk is happy and I just checked in with the guys at the end of the dock a few minutes ago. Yuri is all set up in the repair shed with the two guys from SWAT and it's almost 9:45."

Dax and Janet were seated in what appeared to be a Florist Delivery Van, purchased by the department for surveillance purposes. The late evening, and the shaded glass everywhere concealing their presence. They were located a hundred yards down the road from the street entrance to the New York Yacht Club.

Dax rechecked the time on his Blackberry. He knew he had stretched his assumptions that the Archbishop would be able to somehow make the connections to employ the remaining goyle in New York to take Kelchuk's life, in the hopes of recovering the cell phone containing the incriminating pictures of Werner's passport. He was replaying in his head Holmes engaging in a conversation with Inspector Lestrade where he confirmed to him that such a leap of logic was well within the limits of probability given all the facts in the case. However, he was sitting in the darkened van right now as the more nervous Dax McGowan, not the more confident Sherlock Holmes.

"You know Janet; I've sure pushed the envelope of expectations that this goyle is going to be a main player in this plot tonight. I hope I'm right."

Janet added some necessary encouragement, "Hey, it all makes sense to me based on you describing how these goyles like to operate. They sneak in, make a kill, and leave unnoticed with nobody the wiser. The bastard just doesn't realize we're on to him."

"Thanks, but let's hope we accomplish our most important task tonight, catching this monster alive. How fortunate we were from our end that Father Regan suggested the meeting take place at the Club docks before Yuri had to suggest it. Even he saw the location as a good place to commit a murder with the best chance of leaving no evidence. The Club management bought our story of closing off the dock area from the building for a late night terrorist test exercise in the bay?"

"Sure did. They were cool about it, especially with us starting so late after the members have gone home."

"Good. We just have to wait now. Is the sound system working okay, and you've confirmed the sonar set up to detect the goyle's arrival by water under the dock is working properly?"

"Yup we're all set," Janet replied. "We're not hearing anything from inside now because those guys are in total silence mode."

"How about the people on the boat out in the bay? They're ready to rush in once we've detected his arrival? Getting this guy alive is critical."

"All set. Hey Lieutenant, I get you're not liking having to hang back on these arrangements so your Captain doesn't get his nose out of joint, but I've got this covered old buddy. Really, we're as set as we can be."

"I know . . . I know . . . just the control freak in me talking."

The radio receiver in the van began its crackle in anticipation of someone's report.

"Detective Meehan, this is Shorty out here. It's only 9:55, but we have faint sounds coming from the roof, and nothing from sonar on anything below us. Should we check it out or hold our positions?"

"What do you think Dax?" she asked.

Dax quickly went to his mind's eye to re-picture the setup. Yuri was standing in the dimly lit workshop at the door facing the clubhouse as if naively awaiting his visitor coming from that direction, and Shorty Williams and Ben Billard, both decorated SWAT cops, were hidden left and right of him under work benches facing the water side of the building. The roof sounds were disturbing. He concentrated more deeply to re-see the exterior of the building on its backside facing the water.

He grabbed the mic from Janet. "Shorty, just across from the south corner of your building on the outer edge of the dock is a tall nesting pole with wiring extended from its top to attract mating Osprey Eagles. It's possible that our perp has anchored his boat away from the dock and managed to loop an access line to the top of that pole and shimmy high enough to swing from there over to the roof without coming in low enough or close enough to set off the son—

Before Dax could finish, the sounds of two silencer muffled shots, each accompanied by the ping of bullets piercing glass suddenly filled the van's speaker.

"Shorty!" Dax yelled, "He's on the dock behind the building now!"

The speaker was now returning the sounds of dozens of automatic rounds firing in rapid succession . . . then silence.

"Shorty, tell me everyone's okay. Is Yuri okay?" Dax was now in fear for the lives of his fellow officers. He knew that much fire could mean any number of outcomes, most of them not good.

After what seemed like too long, "Sergeant Meehan. Shorty here. Yuri's been hit. Goddammit, his left ear is torn off. We need that bus here right now."

Before she could respond, one of the two EMTs added as crew to the intercept boat in the bay responded. "No worry Sergeant, we're pulling up to the dock right now. We heard the shots and hit it hard to get here."

"What about the perp Shorty?" Dax jumped in.

"Ben's already signaled to me from the back door that we got him, but he ain't alive. Sorry Lieutenant. We had no choice. He fired first and we couldn't hold back. Sorry sir."

"No worry, Shorty . . . this is my fault. You did the right thing."

Dax leaned to exit the side door of the van and Meehan grabbed his arm. "Oh no. You stay here. We're not going to mess this up any more by you getting involved. Shit, those shots have probably been heard by some of the neighbors on this street, and no doubt, all kinds of cell calls and tweets have gone out. Please, let me handle this?"

Nodding repentantly, "Okay, but promise me as soon as you get out there, you'll call to let me know what's going on," he said. She nodded back and ran up the road to the Club's entrance.

Her voice finally came over the speaker moments later.

"Okay, here's what's up. You were right. The perp was on the waterside dock behind the building, and was attached to some kind of line that was hanging from that wiring you described at the top of that pole. Man, we are definitely going to have to identify this guy from his fingerprints or DNA. There's so little of his head left after Shorty and Ben blitzed him, I doubt there's enough left of his mouth to do a dental check. The good news is Yuri took one slug in the back that just barely pierced his vest . . . may have a broken rib. The other did take off his left ear. It's plenty bloody, but both EMTs say he'll be fine . . . should be able to re-attach it."

"That's good news at least. I'm sure the eisenglass played a role in saving his life."

"What do you mean eisenglass?"

"The waterside window panes on that building are made of eisenglass. It's actually a form of thin-sheeted mica, not regular glass. It was standard issue for buildings by the water back in the day when this old yacht club was built because it held up better in the elements. You'll see it's rather opaque, which would have hampered the goyle's ability to see his target clearly, and get the kind of perfect shot a trained killer like him would otherwise have. Regular glass and . . ."

"Jesus, Dax. Is there anything that brain of yours doesn't have stored up?"

"Hey my friend, I'm not feeling very good about the fact that it never occurred to me that the flagpole could be used in the way it was until it was happening. That mistake could have cost Yuri his life. By the way, is the perp bald and was he wearing a wolf's mask?"

"Oh yeah on both counts. Only it's hard to tell where the mask ends and his sinus cavities begin. What do we do now that we didn't take this guy alive?"

"I'm not sure. I was counting on getting the goyle to give us something that would determine our next moves." Dax paused to consider something that was becoming clearer to him by the hour. "You know, Janet, when we take everything into account, the Archbishop's heavy involvement, the attack on me, and now a marina employee, it only makes sense that a trip to Rome equates to his hiding in Vatican City to be housed by a powerful source of highly placed assistance. The only problem with arriving at that certainty is it may leave us at a dead end. We have the man who killed my daughter thousands of miles away, in a place that may not be penetrable by any legal means, and the leverage of a captured goyle's information is no longer an option. It's bad. It's very bad, and I had better head out before anyone sees me here."

"Hey, Dax. I know how good you are, but nobody is a hundred percent on this job. We pretty much have the Archbishop by the balls. It'll be the biggest arrest I've ever made thanks to you. That's something, and I know if that motherfucker ever sticks his head out of Vatican City, you'll be there to snatch him before he takes two breaths. Of course, I'll always be there to help. You know that. I don't mean to sound like I'm giving up. I just don't want you to be beating up on yourself when you've managed to take an abuse case farther than anything I've ever done."

"You're being super, Janet. I appreciate that, but there's still a part of me that's saying this isn't over. I just need to get into that place in my head and see what we should do next. I'll be in touch."

CHAPTER FORTY-FOUR

After returning home and mulling over the missed opportunity to capture the goyle, Dax decided he needed to let it go for a bit and keep his promise to call Rebecca. It was eleven Chicago time, and midnight in New York. "Hey beautiful, how did the work go today? Are you ready to come and visit this guy who's been missing you ever since he left you yesterday?"

"It's so great to hear your voice, Dax. Actually though, I was expecting you to call me sooner than this. What were you able to do with the information I gave you about Werner?"

Dax proceeded to fill her in on how well the undercover meeting went with the Archbishop followed by the assault and wounding of Detective Brogovich. He realized he could no longer keep the subject of the gargoyles from her. He was about to broach the subject when she asked about the issue herself.

"Dax, who tried to kill that detective? Was it one of those bald headed priests . . . those goyles that Seymour has me looking out for?"

Dax shook his head. Of course, it made sense she would know. While Seymour and company would be aggressively protecting her in as silent a manner as possible, there was no reason to keep her in the dark about potential dangers she might face. He was still unsure if he should tell her about the attempt they made on his life.

"Yes, it was, but unfortunately the goyle involved was killed in the process of the attack, eliminating any opportunity to question him.

"You must have set a very good trap. Seymour tells me, no one has ever confronted one of those creatures, much less captured them. I hope you're using your head and watching out for yourself."

"Ouch, now I have to tell her."

"Becca, I now know these goyles are here amongst us because of my daughter's case, but I didn't at first until they paid me a rather unsocial visit. However—

"Oh my God, Dax, these assassins tried to harm you? Why didn't you tell me this before?"

"Actually, you and I had so much else going on in one short day, and I hadn't made up my mind yet if I should worry you with the information. Besides, they never laid a hand on me. I'm not your everyday easy mark as these men found out," he said, strong ego flaring in his voice.

"Dax, it just hit me how I'd feel if something happened to you. I don't like those thoughts, not at all."

"I know. I've had the same thoughts about you. Maybe Seymour mentioned my concerns for your safety. You know, it's kind of funny, the two of us getting hooked up so suddenly and living so dangerously at the same time."

"Actually, I've never worried that much about myself, and it sounds as if a brave detective like you just takes it in stride. Please Dax, let's both stay safe for each other's sake. I can't wait to see you tomorrow. I'll feel safer for both of us when we're together."

"My thoughts as well, but I should tell you that with the death of this goyle, we may have lost any leverage on whoever is hiding Werner and the chance to get him back here to the states. Assuming he's somewhere in Vatican City, as we suspect, he may be untouchable. Of course, I'm not giving up, but I also don't want your choice to spend part of your vacation with me to be a disappointment in any way."

"First, my dear, Dax, no one understands the concept of capturing these clerics better than I do. Getting the opportunity to help you, someone who has meant so much to me for so long is only going to make this vacation a wonderful one. I know our time together will be worth it regardless of the outcome on this sociopath."

"Thanks Becca. I can at least put that thought to rest as I work on something new."

CHAPTER FORTY-FIVE

Saturday: December 19th

Dax threw off his covers and managed to reach a sitting position. His nightstand clock read 5:30. He had given up more than an hour ago trying to get back to sleep. What little sleep he had managed before that was filled with constant interruptions. His mind had been swimming, mixing images of a warm embrace from Rebecca to a daughter's hug from Grace, to wounded cops and dead wolves, mental chaos totally unfamiliar to him.

He grabbed his bathrobe and made the trek downstairs to the kitchen. The blinking answering machine reminded him of Darlene's message from the night before upon his return home from the yacht club. She would be spending Christmas this Friday with her mother and father. He perceived she chose the machine to leave the message in order to avoid a direct conversation with him on his cell. He hit the erase button desiring not to re-listen to the words, "I see no reason to drag out our separation, Dax. Seeing each other around Christmas without Grace will only make it all the harder." He couldn't agree more, though a slight sadness overcame him as he speedily revisited some much earlier better times with her for a brief moment through the power of his memory.

He poured coffee from its maker, though the brew was now two days old. He shoved a full mug of it into the microwave, setting the time long enough to produce a substantial amount of steam, rationalizing he had killed off any unfriendly bacteria that laid in wait for him. A lot of milk would likely offset the old coffee's acidic taste. He was wrong. He drank heartily anyway, knowing how much his body needed the jolt.

As he began to dwell on the holiday's arrival, he caught himself trying to push aside the thought of a first Christmas without Grace. He felt a touch of fear that he would somehow not be able to survive that day without her, maybe the single day of the year when he gauged her joy to be at its peak. He knew it was better to concentrate on tracking down the man responsible for her death. He pointedly allowed the surges of anger and disgust he could conjure up at will now to displace that fear. He knew his anger had taken him this far, though it carried less power, as the decision to kill Werner was now reversed.

He sat with his hands holding the sides of his head staring at the now empty mug in front him. The inability to capture a live goyle the night before had created an apparent dead end in the search of Grace's killer. He knew what he must do next to lead him away from any thought of failure.

"*Watson! Care to work through a problem solving construct with me?*"

"*Why of course Holmes. Let's hear the known elements.*"

Watson managed a strong "humph", his oft used method of expressing grave interest in anything his good friend was about to say, as he crossed his legs and nestled into the leather chair that was his custom to occupy in Holmes' apartment.

Holmes began to pace with his right index finger placed upon his pursed lips, in the ready to strike out to emphasize the more salient points of his thought processes.

"*Well, my good man, we do have the identity of the paedophile well established, and I would say I have neatly tied up the loose ends on who we may prosecute locally for injecting this sociopath into our lives in the first place. With the help of the CABS organization in tracing this perpetrator's past history and alias, the incriminating recorded interview of Monsignor Murphy, and the aid of the recorded and exceptional theatrical performance by detective Brogovich, I believe that as the expression goes, the Archbishop is toast.*

However, our paedophile, who has currently fled to Rome, is most likely hidden behind what has been, heretofore, the impregnable walls of Vatican City. Our conundrum, my friend, lies in that virtually every attempt to enter those grounds, and or extricate one of its inhabitants, has been met with absolute failure. The Magisterium of the Catholic Church has managed to claim any and all forms of religious and diplomatic immunity as well as intimidate legal officials; even to the point of implying they can influence the direction their souls may travel after death should they cross them. Ah Watson, a wall of fear, which these prelates are masters at creating, can often withstand outside pressures better than the solid stone walls that surround that city . . . any ideas as to how we might gain entry?"

"I see your dilemma, Holmes, and I'm at a loss as to a possible solution. I am the last person to know of any way to circumvent the vagaries of diplomatic affairs. As to the fears the police experience due to their religious affiliations, it seems beyond logic to me. And not being a man of faith, I suppose I'm unable to speak to their negative effect on the mind's reasoning powers. I suppose that if you can't get in, the solution lies in somehow getting your suspect to come out. However, short of trying to burn him out with a good fire," Watson chuckled loudly, with his hand over his mouth, "I'm at a loss as to how you might accomplish that."

"Hmm Watson, you may be on to something there my friend. A good old fire started in the right place may be just the ticket."

"By George, Holmes, you're not considering starting some kind of blaze at the Vatican, are you? I can't imagine you even considering such a plan!"

Holmes began to speak more softly as he was in the process of a developing solution. "Well, my dear Watson, there are all kinds of flames. There are the flames of fire and there are the flames of fear. It makes sense that if we face a wall of fear, then a fire of fear may be just the required remedy. As usual, old chap, you have aided me in reaching a potentially workable strategy. Yes Watson, the construct is piecing together quite nicely."

"As is always the case Holmes, I do much enjoy working on these mental exercises with you, and appreciate your respect for my part in them. However, once again you are going to have to inform me just how it was that my input made the difference."

"My good friend, it seems that you often provide a link to a problem's solving by producing an appropriate metaphor. Alas, the simple mentioning of burning the bastard out immediately led me to the solution. You'll have to tell me my good man how it is you readily conjure up these analogous offerings."

Watson's response began with a full clearing of his throat . . . a trait he would inevitably employ before making a tempered boast about himself. "You know Holmes, I suppose it comes from the many unique and expert observations made by any good country doctor such as I, in dealing with the travails of life for so many of my patients."

"Indeed Watson . . . indeed."

CHAPTER FORTY-SIX

"Shit, Dax. It's only five-thirty. Do you know how late we were out there last night finishing up at the yacht club? Jesus man, I didn't hit this bed till after three."

"I know Janet, I know. But calling you as soon as possible was critical."

"Oh, this better be really good then. What's up?"

"Questions first. Were there any civilians or club people around who saw you remove the goyle's body last night? Also, did any press show up, and how much do they know?"

"God, I'm whipped, Dax. Okay, let me think. What little club personnel were left on duty by the ten o'clock hour . . . maybe half a dozen, they never passed by our police tape out to the docks at all. As to press, shit, the club people never let them in the front door. They thought they were helping us as part of our terrorist practice gig, and enjoyed telling the press to get lost. And only a couple of press people showed at that."

"What about from the water side . . . any action there?"

"You know, with winter and the time of night, we only had one boat with two crazy drunks who pulled up when they saw the emergency lights on our NYPD boat at the dock. By the time those two sots got there, it was already pulling away at top speed to get Yuri to the hospital. They had also loaded mush face to take him to the morgue."

"So, at this point no one knows anything about our dead goyle," Dax offered, "and there were no other outside medical people called in on this, just the two EMT's who took care of Yuri?"

"No, I'm sure there weren't." she yawned in response.

"Okay, that's good. Now, this is very important. Please call everyone on your team last night and tell them that it's your idea, not mine of course, that we not release any information about this dead goyle. All we want to let the public know is that there was a shooting, there is an ongoing investigation, and we have a suspect in custody . . . a dead suspect, but no one needs to know that just yet. Do you think we can get your people to keep that quiet, including whoever was last night's morgue attendant . . . well, for at least a couple of days?"

"Ooh, I don't know. A couple of days is a long time to keep something like that hush-hush, but we might be able to hang with that for most of today, maybe part of tomorrow. As you know, it was really just my best hardcore people involved, so no worries there. Shorty and Ben, who we borrowed from SWAT, would be willing to hold their report a day or two, I'm sure. I'll have to see what I can do with the EMTs, and we'll have to keep any media away from Yuri in the hospital. Damn Dax, the only way this is going to work, of course, is if I get my ass out of bed and contact all these people before the rest of the fucking world wakes up." Hesitating, but only a moment, "But, I told you I'd be there for you and whatever you've got planned, no matter what."

With a new bounce in her voice, she changed the course of the conversation. "Hey, this is going to really scare the shit out of the archy, won't it? He's going to think if we have a live goyle and a live Mr. Kelchuk, we have him stone cold on this attempted murder. And he doesn't even know we have him on CD making the blackmail deal. We'd better arrest him now while we have him dead to rights."

"Actually Janet, we need him to remain free for one or two more days if my plan is going to work."

"Really? Okay, but we'd better put him under full-time surveillance so he doesn't skip on us. We don't need another perp escaping to Rome like Werner has. You gotta agree with me, that if the archy shows his face anywhere outside his residence, and looks like he's going to skip, we're going to have to cuff him."

"Actually, I think it would be an excellent idea, Sergeant, to make it very obvious that you're watching him so he doesn't try to escape. Have black and whites parked in plain view in front of his residence and office. Besides keeping the Archbishop put for now, it will also leave him accessible to be reached with information we want to be sure gets to him so he can unwittingly help us with our plan.

"In addition to the Archbishop's assistance, we are going to have to apply our next set of pressures somewhere much farther away, and hope we can pull off yet another trap that will be much more difficult to set than our unsuccessful attempt last night."

"Hey Daxman, I'm more than a little lost here; tell me how this is all going to work."

"Janet, you're always telling me that any time you even think about getting near the Archbishop with a subpoena, he gets wind of it somehow. I'm assuming that since the people in your office are secure, the leak is likely in the D.A.'s office. Am I right?"

"Oh, that's where it is alright. One of the assistants to Moyers, you know the head D.A., is a guy named Dennis Sullivan. Word is he hangs out with that fat fuck, Wallace Doherty of the Catholic Covenant Group, and keeps him informed on any negative actions we might have planned for the clergy so they can scurry away or destroy records. He drinks a lot, and I've told the street crew that if they ever pull the motherfucker over for drunk driving to call me. I personally want to be at the scene, and see if I can create an excuse to personally drive his fucking face into the sidewalk."

"Whoa, Janet. Why don't you tell me how you really feel about the guy?" Dax knew she was wide awake now. "Sergeant, we are going to make that grapevine work for us this time. But first, I have to get some help from Becca to nail down some other players in this plan. If we time this all correctly we just might get Werner on the run again. When the three of us are all together later after her plane lands, we can go over the whole thing then . . . does that work?"

Janet chuckled. "Sure, that's fine, but hey, Dax, who is this Becca person. Anyone I know?"

Dax laughed, realizing using Rebecca's nickname exposed yet another intimate item about his relationship with her. "Oh yes, Janet; remind me to introduce you to her when she arrives. Nice lady. You'll like her," he said teasing.

"Okay hotshot, I can see things have really heated up between you two. What nickname does she call you? Big D? And what does that actually mean?"

"You're incurable, my friend."

"Hey man, for me who works eighty bazillion hours, this soap opera with you and Rebecca is the best entertainment I've had in a long time.

"Hey, glad to be of service. I'll either call you, or Becca and I will just show up at your office."

"You got it Big D!" They both heard laughter from the other as they hung up.

CHAPTER FORTY-SEVEN

"Good morning, Becca. I hope I'm not calling you too early or catching you heading out the door to the airport?" Dax waited until six o'clock Chicago time in the hope what he had just said was true.

"Good morning to you Lieutenant. It wouldn't matter when you called. I'm finding hearing your voice so often now, as music to my ears. But I hope you slept okay after your crazy night and almost losing one of your good detectives."

"Yes, well, sleep is overrated till you get done what you need to get done," he said in jest, but meant it seriously for himself. "Actually Becca, if you have a couple of minutes, I have some critical things to get in place as soon as possible, if you can help."

"Sure. What do you need?"

"I'm going to need the assistance of that network of yours again. I'm assuming that with all the thousands of victims and their families you've had contact with worldwide, you've managed to accumulate a substantial amount of personal information about them, like how they make a living. I very much need to locate a couple of agents in Europe who work for Interpol. Are there any victims or victims' family members you're aware of who might work in that capacity and would be willing to help on our case? Would you feel comfortable contacting them on that basis?"

"Well, one of the sacrosanct promises we hold for our members is not only anonymity, if they wish it, but also keeping confidential any information we may have about them. However, there have been many occasions where we've sought assistance from them on things ranging from childcare to legal matters using our database as a human resource center. We approach it by sending out a group email to potential individuals asking if anyone will volunteer their services even though we may already know who those persons might be. We just never assume anything. I can tell you though, that when most of these victims and their families see an opportunity to help on someone else's case, they often jump at the chance. I can get my staff to work on the logistics this morning, and I'll work from my laptop at the airport, and on the plane so we can get that communication out soon after I arrive there later today. Given the time difference between here and the continent and people's work schedules there, we may even get responses by this evening. You asked about Europe. Is there any specific area you want us to narrow our search to?"

"Ideally, I'd like to enlist an agent in Switzerland, just north of the Italian border and one in Italy, if possible. It's going to be important that you make your invitation non-descript in the sense that it says nothing about me or my daughter's case. I don't want to raise any red flags about what we have afoot."

"Of course. I don't think we'll get any fewer responses if I simply word the need for assistance as an Interpol legal matter. If we get a volunteer, you can explain your plan, and let them decide whether they want to be involved or not. Consider it done. Dax, just what is your plan?"

"As you know better than anyone Becca, the walls of Vatican City are virtually impenetrable when it comes to extraditing a member of the clergy from there. I've devised a plan that I hope will create reasons for those harboring Werner to believe it is in their best interest to move him to another location. What I'm looking to do is start a credible rumor within the New York legal community, that we are pursuing Interpol's cooperation in the extradition of Werner from Vatican City. If I can get the assistance of a couple of Interpol agents to extend that rumor there in Europe, we may successfully utilize an intercontinental grapevine of sorts to make this work. We must convince whatever Vatican officials are involved, that Interpol is ready to implement a never before attempted plan to once and for all break down the doors of the Vatican to capture a cleric. We have to make this seem so real a threat to them, they will decide to transport Werner out to hide him elsewhere rather than allow such a precedent to be successful, or have him captured and reveal what we suspect he knows. Tracking how and to where they might remove Werner creates another set of challenges, but our hands are definitely tied where he is now."

"I think that's an excellent plan, Dax, and actually you'll be getting some unexpected help. I know you've been totally involved with what's come down in the last few days with your daughter's case so you may have missed some of the breaking news. I know Seymour has filled you in on the wide extent of the abuse cases in the U.S. and Ireland. But, all of Europe is now exploding with hundreds of new ones. They're pouring in from Australia, Switzerland, The Netherlands, even Brazil, but more importantly, Germany. There is a case that surfaced there that implicates the previous Pope Benedict, in the transference of a known pedophile priest to a new parish when he was in charge as Archbishop of a diocese there."

"Benedict himself? Now that's going to rattle some cages."

"Even his brother, Georg Ratzinger, is now also under suspicion. You've probably heard of the famous Regensburg Boys Choir in Germany. There's a boarding school attached to that program and previous students there are coming out now exposing naked beatings, sexual abuse and all forms of excessive corporal punishment. Georg Ratzinger has been the Cathedral Bandmaster there since 1964 and may be implicated. There is certainly no way he could not have been at least aware of those conditions as he claims.

"But, here's maybe the best news of all to help your plan. At one point, the Belgium press had exposed some of the most incriminating evidence of hierarchical pedophile re-assignments, where in the past, the police may have been complicit themselves in a cover up. As a result, to now prove their sincerity to seek real justice, at one point, the police raided the home and previous office of retired Archbishop Godfried Danneels confiscating all his documents and computers. On top of that, they took another unprecedented step. Literally, leaving no stone unturned, they actually opened the graves of two previous Archbishops who were buried at St. Rombouts Cathedral in Melchin looking for more hidden documents. The Vatican was of course totally incensed, but all of our members are ecstatic that someone's police force had finally stepped up and treated these crimes like they should have been from the start.

"So Dax, if the hierarchy was ever going to fear that the legal community will no longer consider the walls of Vatican City as sacred, that time has come. The Vatican is in crisis mode for a host of reasons now, which should only amplify the fear you're planning to inflict on them."

Dax's mind was also tabulating the effect of this new information. In a typical New York City boy's bent toward sports metaphors, he saw this particular European scandal as the designated hitter that could possibly drive home all the base runners. "That's outstanding news," he said. "Though I suppose it's both good news and bad news. On the one hand, that all works to our advantage, but it also means many, many children in those countries had to have been abused for that information to be true. Damn Becca, we have to somehow make sure none of these kids have suffered in vain."

"My dear, Dax, you really have become one of us now. You totally understand what my life's work is all about. I wish I was there so I could kiss you."

"I wish you were here so you could kiss me too," he said. "See you in a few hours.

CHAPTER FORTY-EIGHT

Dax felt the verve in his step as he pocketed his guest ticket after passing through security and walked down the B Gate corridor at JFK. The United flight scheduled for 12:30 at B-14 was listed on airport monitors as on time. His anticipation of Rebecca's arrival had been mounting all morning. He caught himself walking faster than needed and smiled to himself knowing why. A few observations left and right picked up a good many people recognizing him from all the latest media coverage. He was passing B-12 when he noticed that a group was already deplaning at B-14. Rebecca's plane was early. He rushed now, not wanting her to disembark and not see him waiting. He arrived just as she stepped through the gangway door and passed the attendant's desk.

"Becca!"

"Dax!"

She ran a few steps and quickly dropped her briefcase to free her arms to hug him. They squeezed as hard as they could without hurting the other, both wishing it were summer, eliminating overcoats and allowing less clothing between them.

"Has it only been a day and half, Dax?" She whispered in his ear.

"I was thinking the same thing," he was quick to add. "It's crazy, I know . . . to feel this way so soon . . . but I like it."

Still holding tight, they pulled their heads back to stare at each other. A shared split second concern over a public display of affection dissolved into a warm kiss. It took the third round of flashes from cell phone cameras before they realized the attention they had attracted and headed for baggage claim.

"Well Mr. Detective, I see you really are a famous person around here."

He smiled and thought. *"Ouch. This isn't going to play very well at mom's house. But also, no trembling this time . . . none at all."*

Once on the road, with catching up on Rebecca's progress to enlist help from Europe, and Dax's explanation of more of the details of his plan, it wasn't long before the high pitched whine of airplane engines was replaced with the crescendo of sound that was the uniquely sophisticated clamor of New York City.

Soon thereafter, "We're here Becca, at the Four-Five . . . Janet's place." Dax had just turned onto Barkley Ave. for Rebecca to view the organized chaos of uniformed and trench coated men and women revolving around an ancient looking government building on a typically cobblestoned New York City street.

CHAPTER FORTY-NINE

Dax was torn between the enjoyment of watching the two women hugging, their delight at seeing each other again, and his impatience to move ahead with his plan. "Ladies, we're running out of time . . . much to do," he said cringing, expecting blow back for the remark.

Rebecca smiled in understanding; Janet would have nothing of it.

"Hey man, I've been up since five-thirty with less than three hours sleep working on your plan, and I'm entitled to a little time here with my good friend. Besides, she tells me you two are headed for the Essex Hotel tonight . . . la, di, da . . . and our night of catching up is already looking to be postponed."

Despite them living apart for the days ahead, Dax and Rebecca had decided to spend another night together to feel their way forward in their budding relationship and its dealing with nightmares past. Rebecca's enthusiasm for the step forward had him excited about the possibilities and cautious about the process at the same time. They were committed to all the baby steps that may be required.

"Sorry, Janet," he said blushing a bit. "Just my control issues again."

Rebecca jumped in to help. "It is true that the three of us are here because there's work to do. So Janet, as you and I have said so often on the phone together . . . 'Let's get these guys.' Though I do believe we substitute other words for the 'guys' portion of that sentence," she said with a knowing smirk.

They moved to the long table set up in Janet's office displaying a laptop, three yellow pads, and a box of Dunkin Donuts.

"As you can see Lieutenant, I'm well prepared. Rebecca, that's my laptop I brought in for you to use. I can't set yours up on our secure network, as it's not been properly debugged. It's already logged in for you. Hopefully we'll have something intelligent to write on those legal pads and the donuts, they're about all I've been living on lately. There's enough for all of us. As to phones over the next few days, we'll just have to use our cells with the door closed. Your boyfriend here has me jumping through all kinds of hoops pushing the envelope on protocol, so staying private for now is important. On that note, I have to catch you up, Dax, on where our public position is on mush face." She halted a moment at her poor word choice in front of a civilian. "Uh, our public position on the health of our goyle friend."

Dax glanced at Rebecca's grin catching the terminology had rolled off her back. "So what's up on that?" he said.

"Ted, that's my partner Ted Laney, Rebecca, still has to track down the EMTs from last night to be sure they keep the goyle's death under wraps. It seems we have everything else covered, except for me. Dax, I went way overboard last night by not telling my Captain about the terrorist exercise ruse I used to get those elitists at the yacht club to allow us to use their facilities. Though, I've kept you out of it of course, I've only given him just bits and pieces of our crazy new plan. I'm also not supposed to tell the press anything without his approval, and I've already spread the word to them that we've arrested a suspect in an attempted murder last night. He's out of town until Monday, but he isn't going to allow me to use that as an excuse for not calling him and giving him every detail of what we're up to. But I couldn't take the chance of him telling me we couldn't proceed because your plan would seem so outlandish to him and lose the upside for us if it works."

"Hey Janet, I don't want what we're doing to jeopardize you in any way. I did make the assumption you had your Captain's ear on this, though wondered how you were going to pull that off, and keep any knowledge of my involvement out of it."

"I know, and it was up to me to get that right," she said. "I've just been so revved about the spot we have the Archbishop in, I went full speed ahead on everything. Besides that, it appears one of the employees at the club last night bragged about being part of some national security gig to a reporter. I've already had a call from the

"Daily News" wanting to know how the shots heard by neighbors tie in with a terrorist related exercise. I told her that we were involved in an unrelated criminal investigation that didn't have anything to do with that practice exercise. It's just a good thing we stayed as late as we did so we could clean up the entire scene. Except for some broken . . . what's it called . . . eisenglass, you wouldn't be able to tell anything happened there last night."

"Your Captain has a reputation for being a pretty tough guy on the rules. I've got to believe though, that for such a good cop, he'd cut you some slack." Dax said.

"Yeah, the problem is I'm also on his shit list sometimes because of my so-called aggressive arrest tactics. I just hope we can make some headway on this before he gets back in town or I'm dead meat."

"Dax, are you going to be able to help Janet on this? This sounds very serious." Rebecca said.

Once again, Dax was finding himself caught in having been so one minded about the pursuit of his daughter's killer, he had not considered the possible unintended consequences of his strategies on others.

"Look, Janet, I've instigated most of these moves, and should take some of the heat on this. You've placed your trust in me, and if you end up suffering any kind of negative departmental action, it's really going to be my fault. I promise you, I'll do everything I possibly can to prevent that from happening, sacrificing myself if necessary, explaining that it was pressure I've been applying that's the cause."

Janet waved the back of her hand at him demonstrating that wasn't going to fly.

"That's great pal, but I knew I was screwing with the system all last night and this morning. I'm a big girl, and my Captain isn't going to buy for a moment that I was pressured into anything. He knows I can't be. No, I'm not asking you to do anything to take any bullets for me. Just use that brain of yours and see if you can save me from myself in the next forty-eight hours. You feel me?"

"Yeah, I feel you." Dax realized he had led Janet over a cliff, and now knew what he had to do to catch her. That would mean a very uncomfortable meeting with his own Captain. For now, there was much work to be done before what he hoped would be a singular night with Rebecca at the Essex Hotel . . . certainly not the disaster that awaited them there.

CHAPTER FIFTY

Sunday: December 20st

Except for the light of his bedside clock reading 5:04 am, Dax once again rose to a winter's morning of darkness. Only this time being without any sleep for the three short hours he attempted it. In addition to reliving the events of the previous evening over and over in his head, the gunshot wound to his left side, burning all night, had him wishing he had not turned down the pain medication he was offered while it was being street dressed by an EMT in front of the Essex Hotel. His hotel date with Rebecca was nearly a date with death.

After a long day, he and Rebecca not only needed a break, but were looking forward to the more private time together. For Dax it meant romancing this new woman in his life, sensing a soulful intimacy that had always been missing with Darlene. For Rebecca, it was an opportunity to further pursue a relationship she once thought never possible. But all that was not to happen.

Being the Christmas season, the lobby of the Essex was crowded with wealthy out-of-towners wanting to experience New York City for the holidays. Dax and Rebecca managed to navigate past loaded suitcases and their well-dressed owners, to the desk of the Concierge, Dominic Garza. Dax had called in a favor based on helping Garza's son out of a jam in a manslaughter case where Dax was able to successfully advocate the boy's innocence and release before producing the hard evidence that eventually proved that.

He and Rebecca were headed for a small out of the way room usually reserved for visiting hotel corporate execs, the only thing Garza could manage on such short notice in season. After a wink and a handshake filled with fifty dollars, they headed past the front desk down to the end of a long marble-floored hallway lavishly lit by art deco, crystal chandeliers. They passed through an "Employees Only" door then down a short flight of stairs to a basement room at the very back of the building, an elderly bellman leading the way to ensure they found its more remote location.

The bellman, holding their one small piece of luggage in his left hand, slid the room key through the reader and opened the door with an extended right arm for them to pass. As Dax entered first, an outside exit door at the end of the room flew open. He reacted immediately. The wolfen mask worn by the intruder was unmistakable. The assassin's weapon was being raised from his hip to fire in Dax's direction.

"Get down!" Dax yelled in his loudest voice.

His training took over as he moved hard to his right inside the room and began to draw his firearm. Before the sound of the blast from his attacker's gun could reach his ears, he felt the edges of skin and rib bone on his left side tear and splinter. The instant pain didn't slow his reaction as his gun came up and he fired two shots into the chest of his assailant, throwing him back through the door he had entered and against an outside stairwell wall. After a moment's pause, to be certain the attacker was well down, he wrenched his head sideways to look for Rebecca. He had no thought for the bellman, stepping over him to get back into the hallway to find her in a state of overpowering fear.

He swept her into his arms whispering, "It's okay," over and over until he could feel her breathing finally begin to slow. It then struck him the bellman was not moving. It was clear that Rebecca had not quite made a full turn into the room from the narrow hallway, and the bellman must have turned from his position against the door toward the room in front of her upon seeing the back door open. With the bellman lying on his left side, Dax could see an exit wound in the middle of his back, a bullet likely piercing his heart. He realized, had he not moved to his right when he did, that would have been his fate. Quickly checking his pulse and eyes, he confirmed the man was dead. He gazed up at Rebecca with a look communicating that. She began to cry quietly in empathy for the man. He returned to her side, and put his left arm around her as he reached with his right hand for his phone to call it in.

What was most puzzling to him was how the goyle knew just when he and Rebecca would be walking into that room. After a short interrogation of his concierge friend, Dominic, he was convinced he was not the source. He had only given Rebecca the details of their tryst on the way to the hotel. No one else aside from Dominic knew about them. The only other person privy to those details was the cab driver they flagged down to go there, and his potential involvement was too much a stretch of logic.

Besides this second attempt on his life, making it clear someone wanted him dead very badly, it dramatically exposed some unexpected security concerns. Any assumption that the goyle now lying in the morgue was the only one left in the city was incorrect. The impact of the two forty-five slugs he put into the Kevlar vest of his attacker's chest would have rendered him nearly helpless to escape the scene as quickly as he did without substantial assistance. Dax had decided to trade his .38 service revolver for the more high-powered weapon after his first encounter with them. Clearly, there were more of these monsters roaming the planet. Likely, a small army of them, he surmised. What stressed him most, however, was the realization that keeping Rebecca close by his side may only be endangering her, the opposite of his intention when inviting her to vacation with him in New York. Besides the call to be all the more vigilant now, he would have to make sure he kept Rebecca at a safe distance. As he considered what he saw as his most probable next move to capture Werner, he was both disappointed and relieved that it would likely separate them by thousands of miles.

In addition to reliving the events of the previous evening during his short and unsuccessful attempts at sleep, his thoughts also converged on an early meeting he had set up with his Captain about Janet, spending mental time rehearsing what he would say.

He also remembered drinking all the old coffee in its maker the day before. He would have to brew a new pot. He was sure he would need to consume all of it.

CHAPTER FIFTY-ONE

It was ten-thirty, and Dax felt the effects of all the coffee he had downed already on the wane. His impromptu meeting earlier at eight o'clock with Captain Pressioso had left him unsure of what might result in terms of Janet's dealings with her Captain. Even his most intense attention to his Captain's reactions discerned little, as during the entire meeting, Pressioso appeared in a state of uncertainty as to what action he might take. All Dax could do was await the outcome. Earlier at seven, he had received a call from Rebecca with a "my first thought as I awoke" interest in the condition of his wound. After a convincing report of, "no problem at all," she said she would stay at Janet's condo for the morning so she could check for responses to her emails sent to Switzerland and Italy looking for Interpol volunteers. She wanted to work on her own laptop without the restrictions of Janet's in her office. She told Dax there were also many follow up calls to make to Europe in regards to the explosion of new clergy sex abuse claims there. Membership in CABS was spiking and her staff was swamped. He was amazed at how by morning she had already compartmentalized the previous night's attack and death of the bellman. No doubt a well-honed coping technique for clergy abused victims, he thought. However, she was also effusive in thanking him for his warm embraces at Janet's condo as she drifted off to sleep before he left for home. He was especially pleased that she expressed the desire to make sure the missed night together be re-scheduled as soon as possible.

While exiting his car in front of Janet's precinct, his phone rang. It was Rebecca again, and clearly in a positive mood. "Dax, I've got good news for you. I received a communication from an Interpol Agent in Switzerland who said he'd be more than glad to help. I told him you'd have to explain the details of your plan, but he was very positive, that based on what I told him, they could likely pull this off. I hope you don't mind, but I remember this man and his case very well, and felt I could introduce him to the basics of your idea to gain his interest. And, as I mentioned before, once he knew he would be helping another father track down a pedophile priest, he was thrilled to help. His son is still in therapy some fifteen years now trying to deal with his abuse. This man has heard of you, Dax. It seems your reputation spans the globe."

"That's super news, Becca. Only right now, depending on what happens between Janet and her Captain, we may or may not be able to employ this strategy. Her partner, Ted called me a few minutes ago to say that she's in his office right now taking a special weekend call from him. I'm concerned my overzealousness to get this killer has put her in terrible jeopardy. Some brainy detective I've turned out to be."

"Dear Dax, your strategies have been brilliant! And, I can tell you after hundreds of cases of frustration I've been through, I have never seen a member of the hierarchy so cleverly trapped. It's also clear you have other people in high places feeling in grave danger of exposure, as last night's encounter readily proves. All that has to count for something."

"Becca, how you manage to always say just the right thing at the right time is some gift you've got. Thank you . . . you're a sweetheart. However, let's just hope Janet doesn't have to pay for any mishaps I've pushed on her."

Still high on her results, Rebecca went on.

"I have more good news for you, Lieutenant. While I didn't get an Interpol agent's response from anyone in Italy, the Switzerland agent said he would be able to recruit one for you. By the way, you'll enjoy this. The Swiss agent's name is Poirot, Stephan Poirot, a Belgian. I thought you might enjoy hearing the name of another famous detective being involved. In any event, he has a close friend who's also an Interpol agent in Italy who will help. These two, probably in their early fifties, go back with each other to their academy days. The Italian agent is stationed in Rome and is godfather to the clergy

192

abused son of the first agent. His name is Roberto Bellini. Poirot was going to call him as soon as we hung up, and said he would await instructions from you. How about that? Does my network produce or what?"

"I'll say. Your network rocks!"

At least for the moment, the news was an adrenaline fix helping to evaporate some of his exhaustion and immediate concerns about Janet. He had entered her office while on the phone awaiting her arrival. He turned to see her at the other end of the bullpen heading his way.

"Becca, I see Janet coming. Except for her legs moving, her whole body seems rigid. The only way I can describe the look on her face is . . . is disbelief. Can I call you back later?"

"Of course, but please let me know as soon as possible. It's going to prey on my mind until I hear from you . . . and Dax . . ."

"Yes?"

"I . . . just want you to know that . . . I have every confidence in you." She ended the call.

Dax peered at his phone wondering. *Was she going to say something else about how she felt about me?* Janet then entered her office requiring an immediate change of focus.

She walked by him and sat at her desk. Smiling now and looking squarely at him, "Hey Lieutenant, all I can say is that if this plan of yours is going to work, we'd better get our asses in gear and make it happen."

She jumped up and hugged Dax around the neck, then quickly let go, realizing her soft side was showing to all the other detectives on the floor peering through her glass walls. Her potential reprimand had been the fodder of precinct gossip all morning.

"Okay, Janet, I'm guessing that phone call from your Captain went a little better than expected?"

"Better than expected? Hey, my Captain thinks I'm a genius. Oh, he gave me hell for not briefing him with more information sooner, but . . . ya know, Dax, I think he thinks I'm another you! Somebody had already filled him in on what went down both Friday night at the yacht club and with the goyle last night at the Essex. He knew it all and acted like it was all my planning. Who told him that? Did you?"

"No, I haven't said a word to your Captain . . . promise."

"Well, somebody did. But, I don't know how he got the

impression that I was behind all the thinking on this. That's been mostly you. I'll tell you, and I hope you don't mind, I didn't cut him off and tell him he was wrong. I just let him go on and on about what a great detective I was. There was no chance I was going to screw with how he saw it. I was just so fucking relieved."

Dax was laughing now, her happiness and his relief feeding it. It was time to move on. The mystery of what he knew have come from his Captain, and said to her Captain, would have to wait.

"So, tell me Sergeant, how fast do you think this fabricated information we want to circulate will take to reach this Sullivan guy in the D.A.'s office? Then, how long before he contacts Doherty, and he then contacts the Archbishop?"

"Shit, Dax. No one has ever attempted something as radical as storming the Vatican before. My guess is news like that would travel at the speed of light."

"I hope so. We both know keeping the goyle's death a secret has an unknown expiration date. We have to hope a lot of dominos fall in succession very quickly before that happens. Once the Archbishop gets the news, we have to hope he immediately contacts the Vatican and scares the hell of out of the right people there. Certainly though, we expect they will check it out with a contact they must have at Interpol in Rome to verify the threat. And Janet, I just talked with Becca and she's recruited just who we need over there to back us up. Unfortunately, with a lot of different players involved, thousands of miles apart, anything can go wrong, especially when all this is nothing but a big con job. I'd better get on the phone right now with our new European friends and set things up. What's the first step on this end?"

"Well, I call my good buddy, Manny Berkowitz, at the D.A.'s office and get him rolling. I've already briefed him with all the reasons you explained to me yesterday, like the Belgian police raids, why our case for extradition would appear so strong, and he'll figure out how to make the rumor sound credible within his office. He's a helluva good guy, and he gets just as frustrated as I do on these cases. He's gonna love putting one over on that dick, Sullivan.

"I have to say, I was a bit skeptical at first. Think about it. We have a hard enough time getting a goddam warrant for an Archbishop's office much less convincing anyone we have enough juice to storm the gates of Vatican City. But now that I see how it might all play out, I'm psyched. Of course having my Captain behind me on it now sure helps. It'll be worth it just to know that we monkeyed with the grapevine these pricks use. They sure as hell won't be so fast to trust it again."

"That's the key, my lady friend. We want each person along the way to think they've delivered the most critical grapevine news they've ever latched onto, expecting to ingratiate themselves all the more within their conspiratorial club. Say, isn't it pride that goeth before the fall?"

CHAPTER FIFTY-TWO

Sunday afternoon traffic was atypically snarled due to the hordes of Christmas shoppers in town. Dax was double-parked in front of Janet's condo to pick up Rebecca. He enjoyed watching her walk the lengthy distance to the car from the deeply recessed front entrance set back in a portico, as a waft of winter air made her hair float upward around her head exposing her long and beautiful neck.

"Ooh Dax, its cold out there." She said sliding into the car. "The way the wind swirls between these tall buildings and chills a person, I'm not sure Chicago has anything on New York in that regard."

She recovered quickly enough and leaned over to plant a small kiss on his lips as he leaned her way in expectation. He gently pulled her back for a second much longer one, netting deep breaths from them both. Leaving the car to idle, he turned more fully toward her.

"Still signing up new members for CABS at a rapid pace?"

"Actually Dax, my staff is stressed out right now. I'm wishing we had a translation program on our website accommodating the different languages of our new members so they could navigate it easier. Our Chicago office has brought in friends to act as translators to help. We're also starting to get a greater number of new American members who feel more empowered as a result of the outbreaks in Europe. As reluctant as I was, it got to a point where I had to offer to go back home if they needed me, but, my National Director, Daniel Corbin insisted that I needed my vacation and didn't want to see me in the office until it was over. His abuse story is as sad as any you've heard, but his recovery has also been remarkable."

"Well, selfish me is very glad he was so insistent on your staying. I like the guy already."

"So how did your call go with our Interpol friends, and your meeting with Janet? Is she going to be okay with her Captain?"

"Janet couldn't be better. It was nothing but praise from him for her work. She's much relieved, as am I."

"Oh that's wonderful . . . and with Poirot in Switzerland?"

"You were right about him. He couldn't have sounded more interested in helping. It didn't take long for him to catch on to the basics of what we wanted to accomplish, and he was excellent at filling in the details for his end of it. He said his friend Bellini, in Rome, would spread the word that the New York D.A.'s office had contacted his good friend Poirot in Zurich about planning an unprecedented arrest of a priest within the walls of Vatican City. Zurich was to prepare and complete all the necessary paperwork ahead of time, only looking to get Rome to sign off at the last minute, so there would be no time for anyone in the Rome office to alert the Vatican it was coming. Poirot said Bellini did confirm there was actually more than one person in the Interpol Rome office that warns the Vatican about any legal issues that might impact them negatively. So, I called Bellini myself to be sure we were all on the same page. To strengthen the gravity of the matter, he's going to tell those leakers of information, this all concerns the death of the daughter of one of NYPD's most highly decorated detectives." Dax gestured to mean no bragging intended.

"You don't have to create any justifications in my mind, Dax McGowan. I have a scrapbook at home full of the news stories about those awards."

Avoiding a desire to crow on that comment, Dax continued. "Janet already has our end here at the New York DA's office in the works. Since you indicated that my name may have already made its way to Europe, Bellini is also going to act dumb and say he thinks the detective's name is McGowan.

"You know Becca, I've created some interesting traps for killers over the years, and most of them have been successful. This is the first time, I'll have to admit, that with such a large number of players involved, there are a lot of chances for something to go very wrong."

Dax watched Rebecca produce a smile that said he had her total confidence.

Accumulating street traffic and the illegal blare of a taxi's horn from behind them broke in. Dax put the car in gear and headed back to Janet's precinct.

CHAPTER FIFTY-THREE

Dax's phone was rang.
"Hey Janet, we're downstairs on the way up. Be right there."
"Hurry Dax, hurry!"
Before he could end the call, another was coming in. It was Bellini from Rome.
"Roberto, what's up?'
"Signore McGowan, it is happening."
"What's happening?"
"The priest, this Werner fellow, he has just left the Vatican. I am behind them now."
Dax looked at his watch it was just after 3:00 pm in New York which meant it was 9:00 pm there.
"Are you sure, Roberto? This seems too soon for them to react."
"Sir, I assure you I am correct. As soon as we talked earlier, I stationed some of my men at possible exits from the city in case this "faccia di merda" should attempt an escape. He was seen leaving as a passenger in a small gray Mercedes about one half hour ago. In addition to the driver, there was a third person in the back seat behind him. I had my men follow them north along Via Flaminla until I could pick up the trail myself just north of Rome on E35. I had to waive my men off as we are still yet unofficial on this."
"Excuse me Roberto, but it is dark there now and . . ."
"Signore McGowan, you must trust me. Yes, it is evening here, but the main entrance to Vatican City, from where they exited at Via della Conciliacone, is well lighted. It is like the daytime . . . so bright, and the artista pittura you faxed to us made the identification

unmistakable."

"Excuse me Roberto. I trust you totally. It is just my grave concerns getting ahead of my good thinking."

"No problema, Lieutenant. I do the same." Then, checking a roadway sign, "We are well north and into the country now, and I have no idea of their destination." Bellini laughed a bit. "This may be a good direction for me. I can visit my good friend Poirot in Zurich should we travel far enough. This is the same strada I always drive to see him."

It made perfect sense to Dax they would travel by car. Having planted the Interpol deception in their heads, any form of public transportation would be considered too dangerous with their expectation the law may be watching those venues. He began to replay in his head the geography of northern Italy he had memorized from Google Earth's program for that entire section of Europe, anticipating the need to do so as soon as he formulated his plan. He recalled there were no other major cities left in Italy in the current path of Werner's escape. This increased the chances, he deduced, he and his chaperones may be headed out of the country, but to where was the question. Another check of his mentally encoded map steered him to turn to Rebecca.

"Becca, Werner is already on the run."

"What? This soon?" Oh my God Dax, your plan . . ."

"Yes, it appears they were concerned enough about Werner being caught, they must have skipped any double check with Interpol. Undoubtedly, our correctly predicted call to Rome from the Archbishop was all that was needed. I'm amazed myself at how fast this came down, but, Becca, I need your help again. We know Werner is originally from Germany, which is just northeast of Switzerland, which is just north of Italy. Would you have the information on exactly where in Germany he is from . . . where his family resides?"

"I'm sure we do. Once we discover a priest to be bad, we build an historical account of his life. We can often tell one of these jackals things about their past they don't know or remember themselves."

Rebecca pulled her phone out of her purse as they continued up the stairs.

"Hello, Jeff? On my desk, you'll find a file on a pedophile priest, a Paul Werner. It's right on top of everything in the middle. Would you please run there and find it. I'll hold."

After a short wait, "That's good. I need to know this man's hometown in Germany . . . where his family lives? Okay. I'll wait." Rebecca spied an empty desk in the open bullpen on the way to Janet's private office and sat there grabbing a handy pen and sticky note. "Great, I've got all that. Please email those two pages to my phone. Thank you, Jeff, and wish everyone there my best."

Rebecca jumped from the chair and headed to Janet's office where Dax was already being filled in by Janet's news.

"So you two, Manny Berkowitz called me maybe an hour ago to tell me what went down over there. I knew you both were on your way here, but I couldn't wait any longer to tell you his story . . . why I called. Anyway, Manny tells me he approached the paralegal he knew was the biggest gossip in their office, and also did a lot of work for Sullivan. He explained to her that he was working with SVU on an important hush, hush case, and wanted her to help him draw up the paperwork to have Werner arrested in Vatican City. She was also to gather the information on the Interpol contacts needed to be approached in Zurich to begin the process, as they didn't want to alert anyone in their Rome office prematurely that this was coming down. And please, he told her, to keep it to herself until he could get Moyers, the head D.A., to sign off on the completed package.

"He then told this assistant he had to hit the head, and would get back to her in a little while with all the evidentiary information he'd pulled together. So he says, he makes it to the head, takes a long leak, washes his hands like a good boy, and as he's coming out of the john, he practically gets run over by Sullivan who's rushing out of the building. Manny said Sullivan was extremely uncomfortable and uncharacteristically speechless during the encounter.

"See what I mean about the speed of light on this? Then you tell me the Rome guy has already called and this prick is on the loose? Shit, Dax, Sullivan must have gotten to Doherty right away who was likely on the phone to the archy just as fast. I'll bet with all our guys out in front of his place, he's was sitting with an open line to the Vatican ever since the word got out we had a live goyle in custody. This plan is goddam brilliant."

"Thanks Janet, you pulled off your end of this perfectly. Now we have to find out where Werner is headed. I assume Manny Berkowitz is working on the real arrest and extradition papers for Werner so our Interpol guys can nab him legally later, right?"

"Yeah, being processed as we speak," she said. "We just need to let him know when and in what country. He did say depending in which country he's nabbed in, and his country of citizenship, we may not be able to extradite him."

"I'm familiar with some of that from my law classes." Dax said. "The country of citizenship can claim the right to try him for the same or similar crime committed here. But right now, hopefully Becca may have the answer to the possible where and when for the arrest. Am I right?" he said leaning toward her.

She smiled in satisfaction and began, "Well our infamous priest hails from a small town in Bavaria called, and I'll spell this, M-A-R-K-L-T, A-M, I-N-N. I'm guessing it's pronounced Mach-Til om Inn. My office tells me it's maybe a hundred kilometers east of Munich."

"That's a very small town." Dax said squinting hard, "I can barely make it out."

Janet was shaking her head. "Geez Dax, are you looking at that town on a map in your head? I'll never get over this shit. You think he's headed for home, or I guess homeland would be a better term?"

"It makes sense that he's like any other perp on the run. They have nowhere to hide in public view so they seek out familiar surroundings and maybe some assistance from relatives. In Werner's case, it's the most logical place now since he's totally persona non grata everywhere else he's been."

Dax was calculating his next move; one he had anticipated as soon as it was confirmed Werner had left the country. He pulled his Blackberry from his coat pocket and began sorting through various applications.

"Dax, did your Interpol buddy say if the goyles were with him?" Janet asked.

"Yes. There are two men with him and I presume them to be his latest travel companions." Dax was hitting his phone's keyboard rapidly and answering at the same time. "I'm sure they want to get him to his hometown, and satisfy themselves that it's remote enough he'll be under the radar for at least a while."

"Okay then," Janet said. "I guess we call that into Manny and wait for the paperwork for the Interpol agents to arrest him. You know, I hope those guys realize how dangerous those killers can be. They're gonna need backup."

Finishing his task on the Blackberry, "I'm going to be their backup," he said to the puzzled faces of both women. "Here's the situation. We have one Interpol agent who has literally gone off the reservation to help us because sexual abuse by clergy has touched the lives of his good friend and his godson. The other Interpol agent who's ready to join him in the chase as they drive by his home in Zurich, is the father of the boy who was abused, but both will be out of their jurisdictions entering Germany. It's going to take Berkowitz a couple of days to get the paperwork and evidence right on this before Interpol will act officially. I know; I've been involved in a couple of these extraditions before. I can see only one way to proceed. I have to fly there myself to support these men until all the legal maneuvers can be sorted out."

"Dax, that seems physically impossible; can't you just wait for the legal system to take its course?" Rebecca asked. "As long as Werner stays put for a while, Interpol can arrest him soon enough, right?"

"Well, I actually can pull this off quite easily. You see, travelling by car from where they are right now, just north of Rome, Werner and the goyles are going to take eight and a half hours to reach Marktl am Inn. It's an eight-hour flight to Munich from New York and there's one on Austrian Air leaving JFK in about an hour and a half that I just booked on my phone. That's a total of nine and a half hours for me to get me there. I'll ask agent Poirot, who's in Zurich, to make the drive to the Munich airport to pick me up. We then have to add another hour and a half to drive from there to this little town. That puts Poirot and I in Werner's home town eleven hours from now. He and I will arrive only two and a half hours after Werner does himself, and Bellini will already be there keeping an eye on him and his friends in the meantime. Even if we are wrong about Werner's final destination, which I don't expect we are, Poirot and I will be in the general vicinity soon enough that Bellini can direct us to the correct destination by phone. We'll have three armed and dangerous officers of the law in place while we wait for the necessary paperwork to clear, and Bellini and Poirot can get the proper Interpol people up to snuff in the meantime so when the D.A. submits the request they won't be starting from scratch."

Despite what he thought to be a totally logical and well-explained scenario, he could tell Rebecca still had concerns. He was also picking up a similar sense from Janet, the two of them sharing something yet to be revealed. He went on hoping it would help.

"Please understand why it's so important for me to be there. First, I've seen this kind of paperwork always take more time than expected. Governments never communicate correctly the first time. It just happens. The three of us will need to spell each other on surveillance over those two or three days. Also, I know these goyles better than anyone now, and my presence there would be a better guarantee for the safety of both Bellini and Poirot. Despite my instructions to them, I'm not sure they know just what they are up against with these killers.

"But of all the collars I've ever been involved in, I have to make sure this one happens. I can't take any chances that this man might escape somehow. With the church's reach all over the world, if he manages to get out of our sight, there's no telling where he could be hidden, never to be found again. If for no other reason, I owe that to Grace." Dax's eyes began to tear at saying her name.

"Dax? You won't do anything rash over there, will you? You will let the law take its course and deal with Werner as it should . . . right?" Rebecca pleaded.

Forestalling an immediate answer to what he now understood, "Hey, I have to get moving so I can catch that plane and security may take longer with me having to register my gun box. Becca, we need to talk outside a minute before I leave," he said gently squeezing her shoulders with both hands.

"Hey, Go Gettum, Lieutenant," Janet said. "But don't do anything dumb over there, hear?" She knew he couldn't be stopped now, and held out hope he would do the right thing. Despite her fears, her instincts as a cop could do nothing but back him all the way.

"I'll be good . . . promise," he responded.

He clasped Rebecca's hand leading her out of Janet's office to a back corner of the large open room for what limited privacy it afforded. He pulled her in close.

"Becca, I'm sorry about this. I hope you know that I'm not abandoning you. I promise I'll be back as soon as we have this man in custody. I have to admit that I thought this might happen, which is why my passport and a couple of days' clothes are in the trunk of my car. I didn't bring it up sooner because I couldn't know all the circumstances until now."

"I know, Dax. I understand you're a detective and what your job entails. As our relationship moves ahead, you'll likely find yourself in the same place I'm in right now with my ever-constant responsibilities. But I'm concerned because . . .

"Because you're afraid I might kill this guy. Please hear me on this. I will admit that I began this manhunt with destroying this priest as my intent. I imagine Janet has expressed her concerns to you on that. At first, it didn't matter to me that it went against everything I stood for as a cop. He tortured and stole my daughter's life. I was blinded by that, and there's a part of me that still wants him dead. But, then I met a most dedicated cop who began to rely on me to make Grace's death mean something more in terms of getting justice for so many other children. Then I meet a man who introduces me to the world-wide extent of all this insanity, but most of all I met with you Becca . . . or I should say met you again. With busy schedules and ducking bullets, we haven't had much time to really talk, but we know there's something we both want from our relationship . . . something that's been missing in both of our pasts. How can I possibly mess all that up through a selfish act of revenge?"

All the time he was assuring her, he could see her peering deeply into his eyes gauging his sincerity.

"Thank you for being honest with me, Dax. I so want to believe you, and I think I know you well enough that you mean every word you're saying," she said . . . a tinge of fear still apparent.

She wrapped her arms around his chest and kissed him hard several times on the lips and face. "Listen, Dax McGowan, you have to promise me you'll get this done and come back to me unharmed."

"You can count on it," he replied.

After donning overcoats, they walked out together so Dax could retrieve his things from the trunk of his car. He would leave it for Rebecca's use and take a taxi to the airport. As luck would have it, one was heading his direction from down the block as he approached the curb, and raised his arm to hail it.

CHAPTER FIFTY-FOUR

"JFK please . . . Austrian Air, and I'm really pushed for time."

"Yes sir," the cabby replied.

With all the security issues after 9-11, it was a good thing that cops could still travel with their guns as long as they were in a locked box in checked baggage. However, that always meant more time consumed verifying identity. For a change, Dax was hoping the security person he would encounter might recognize him from his press coverage and that would somehow translate into speeding up the process.

He began to picture the corridors and gates he would have to navigate as well as calculate what margins of time he had, when he had a sense of something strange, not out of tune exactly, just unusual. What for a lot of people might be interpreted as a déjà vu experience, for Dax it was the realization that he was in the very same taxicab he and Rebecca rode to the Essex the night before, a fairly low odds coincidence, he considered. He "played his tape back" to the few minutes before he entered the cab and noticed that it had pulled away from the curb from a good distance down the block as he was exiting the Four-Five, almost as if it anticipated his need, he now wondered.

Wishing not to openly react to his discovery, he held his phone up in front of him and pretended to be texting. This allowed him the freedom to spot elements in the cab to further confirm his suspicions. He spied an old piece of pink chewing gum stuck to the floor behind the driver's seat, mostly blackened from daily exposure to city traffic soot. Just below and between his feet he saw a cigarette burn in the vinyl flooring he remembered as being shaped exactly like a miniature banana. As he allowed his memory full reign of what his eyes were taking in, countless other matches came into view including the back of the driver's head, who he had noticed the night before was wearing a toupee. Given the hairless domes of his rather persistent assassins, this carried yet another reason for his alarm. It now made sense that it was the taxi driver, *aka* goyle from the previous night who was privy to Dax's detailed description of their Essex accommodations, and whoever else was also listening in that set up the ambush at the hotel. He surmised some additional observations would confirm that.

"There it is." Just below the driver's picture on his license display, a place nearly every passenger observes at least once on every ride . . . was a tiny camera lens, a match to the one he had seen protruding out of Grace's window spying on him at home. No doubt, he thought, there was a microphone equally well placed. However, discovering its position was of no priority now. The certainty of its presence was not in question. Determining what they may have planned for him was; that and eliminating any distraction from getting to the airport on time. There was only one way to be sure he would make his plane, and not fall prey to yet another ambush. He grabbed enough of the sticky, blackened gum from the floor to smear over and cover the camera lens. Then leaning forward on one knee, he positioned himself closely behind the glass partition between himself and the driver and very close to his ear. He spoke in a clear voice.

"Okay George, or whatever your name is, you gargoyles sure are a bunch of stupid fucks. This will make the third time you bastards have tried to kill me. Don't you ever do enough research on your targets? Didn't you know I'd recognize this as the same cab as last night? Didn't you realize I would have noticed how awfully convenient it was that you rushed to pick me up before I even hailed you . . . you worthless piece of shit?"

Dax was hoping the whole cult of goyles was listening in to hear the string of insulting epithets he rarely used in succession, but was hurling at them for the pure satisfaction of it.

"Listen, I have a plane to catch, and I have a 45 magnum aimed right at your heart. I want you to get to the airport as fast as you can, or I'm going to blow your insides all over that dashboard. And listen motherfucker, I know the shortest route there with my eyes closed, so you'd better know it too or you're a goner. Are you getting this?"

"Yes, sir." was the driver's military fashioned response.

Nothing but silence prevailed until their arrival at JFK. Dax grabbed his travel bag and was about to exit the cab. "Good job there you mercenary prick. I'm right on schedule. Sorry there's no tip in it for you though . . . or fare for that matter."

After stepping out of the cab, he leaned in with one last comment.

"Listen, all of you, there is no way you bastards will ever stop me from reaching the man who killed my daughter. Even you less intelligent half-wits must understand that by now. But, I want you to know something else. As soon as he's out of the picture, I'm coming after you next. After Werner is no longer an issue, you motherfuckers better not ever close your eyes . . . even to sleep."

Dax slammed the car door hard and peered around in all directions as the driver pulled away. He knew there had to be a trail vehicle to stay in contact with the camera and voice signals, but he was unable to spot it. He removed his hand from his now holstered gun and turned to enter the terminal.

CHAPTER FIFTY-FIVE

Dax shifted in place several times to no avail. Airline coach seating was rarely comfortable under the best of circumstances, but his wound made it impossible to find a position that didn't leave him in some pain. It had been nearly twenty-four hours since the attack at the Essex, and he had hoped to have less pain by now from what he considered only a bit more than a flesh wound. Despite his discomfort, he expected the eight-hour flight to Munich might be the first time in the last ten days he would be taking a break from the near 24/7 involvement this manhunt had become.

As he sat in an aisle seat, a woman approached eyeing the seats to his right, announcing she would be his row mate. Her greeting was friendly and pleasant. With an extended hand, "Morgan Montgomery here. Ready for this bus trip?"

She was attractive in a masculine sort of way, he thought, in her mid-thirties with a pallid face surrounded by short dark hair. Dax caught that her green eyes, and the facial lines around them projected the toughness he had often observed in women whose careers involved piercing the proverbial 'glass ceiling'. As she slipped by him to her window seat, he noted she was carrying Dan Brown's latest novel. Knowing his books were page-turners, he hoped it meant she would be sufficiently engrossed to allow him whatever rest this trip might afford.

Smiling at her reference to eight hours of airtime being akin to a lengthy bus ride, he returned his hand, "Dax McGowan, nice to meet you, Morgan. I'm sure looking forward to catching up on some much needed shut eye. It's been a rough week." He was hoping she would get the hint, but not take it as unfriendly. Apparently not.

"Dax . . . that's an unusual name . . . must have a history I expect?"

Rather than respond in a way to encourage more conversation, "If I wasn't so tired, I'd tell you more about it. There actually is a good story behind it, but I must get some sleep. There's a good deal ahead for me in Munich. Please forgive me if I break off for now."

"Oh, but of course," she blurted, acting as if she had missed the earlier hint. "You get your rest. Maybe we can visit some later."

Immediately closing his eyes to appear serious about being allowed to rest, Dax began to register some suspicious impressions of this new acquaintance. He thought her an interesting anomaly of fashion. She wore an expensive business pants suit. Having attended countless city department meetings, told him it was Armani. Yet, her rather low heeled shoes, while stylish, fell into the "I take long walks on my lunch break," category. Her makeup was flawless, balancing her features and color perfectly, yet her fingernails were cut nearly to the quick. While her skin appeared femininely soft, her forearms, showing below her elbow length sleeves, revealed exceptional muscle definition. On the surface, she appeared to be a normal female business traveler. However, Dax thought she was just as much built and dressed for speed as anything related to commerce.

Her immediate interest in engaging him in conversation and other observations had raised his antenna. As she settled into her seat, he noted the boarding pass protruding from her small purse placed her elsewhere in coach. From his aisle seat vantage point, he now recalled, she was not only the last passenger to board, but after spying him, headed directly to his row, never pausing as she passed the seat she was assigned.

He found himself wondering if paranoia from being so frequently targeted for death was raising his suspicions unnecessarily. *"Relax,"* he told himself. He assumed it was his exhaustion getting the better of him, and that nothing was likely to happen over the next eight hours at 40,000 feet, though both the Dax and the Sherlock in him each held an ounce of concern.

Surely, after nearly a week of sleep deprivation, he would drop off like a newborn puppy, no matter the throbbing in his side. It was, however, his thoughts that would not shut down as he attempted to sort out the chaos since his daughter's death. So much had happened so fast, even for a man like himself who could normally juggle a host of balls in the air at once. He realized that it is one thing to deduce solutions to mysteries like Sherlock Holmes with the coldness of disciplined logic, and quite another to attempt to control a large array of disparate happenings when every intense human emotion you possess is entwined in the process.

After several minutes, he began to realize closing his eyes had become more than a ruse for the benefit of his row mate. The plane's engines were now slipping into an even flowing hum, and the pain in his side began to fade as a full moon might disappear slowly behind an evening cloud. He found himself drifting off into a sleep his body demanded that would no longer allow his mind to interrupt.

CHAPTER FIFTY-SIX

Monday: December 21st

"Dax . . . Dax McGowan, wake up. We're at the gate." A hand was roughly shaking his right shoulder.

Dax wrenched forward, and winced as the sudden movement created a biting reminder in his rib. Confused at first, it then came to him he had slept the entire flight, and was experiencing that drugged feeling such a deep sleep often produced. Before he could respond to his row mate's rousing, she had gathered herself to cut in front of him to the aisle.

"I'm sorry, Mr. McGowan. I'm in a hurry to meet someone. I hope you enjoyed your rest. Clearly, you needed it."

"Wow, I was out . . . really out." He shook his head in order to jolt his remembrance of meeting Morgan Montgomery when boarding in New York, a time that seemed more like days ago instead of hours. He watched, as she wasted no time heading toward the cabin door. She turned, looked back at him with a quick and vacant glance, and that was the last he saw of her.

It suddenly occurred to him that agent Poirot was waiting for him and he had to get moving. He was also thinking he would feel a lot better once he got to take a leak, being nearly ten hours since his last one. Coming out of the airport restroom, which included a stop at the sink for a cold water face wash, he dialed Poirot to discover he was downstairs just outside the door from baggage claim. As he descended the steps to that level, he was beginning to feel a surge of new energy. Good, he thought. He was going to need it to survive what he knew would be a lengthy surveillance.

CHAPTER FIFTY-SEVEN

Poirot launched immediately into a French-spattered update for Dax before he had time to settle into the passenger seat of a Volvo station wagon. Remembering their previous phone conversations, while friendly, Poirot was an all business, straight to the point type, and now meeting him in person, he saw he looked nothing like the mustached and more rotund, Hercule Poirot character. This Poirot was rather tall, thin, and his pale and hairless face portrayed more of an Ichabod Crane persona. His husky and raspy voice, more suited to a bigger man made his physical appearance seem all the more incongruous.

"Monsieur McGowan, Roberto and I have already spoken. You were correct that their destination was Marktl am Inn, just into Bavaria. It is but a tiny ville, and Roberto is parked about 300 meters from where the Mercedes of this rogue is located. He reports they arrived there one half hour ago, and Herr Werner and two men, in stealth like manner, entered into a very small maison, a house, a short distance down the road from where they parked. He divine that they may have wished not to awaken others who live there. It is of course still early, and there won't be any light for another hour or more at this latitude.

"Roberto has a souci, ah, a concern that they may have . . . as you Americans say . . . made him. They were the only autos on the road for most of those early hours. They drove through the center of the ville, which is but a small circle of just a few rues, and travelled east from there, maybe another one or two kilometers to this remote maison. He drove past them out of the ville so as not to arouse their suspicions. He then waited some time, and returned to his current position with his auto lamps off. He is simply not certain if they are aware of his presence."

Remaining in the officious tone of his host, Dax began, "Thank you agent, Poirot. Good morning to you. I calculate it will take us approximately an hour and half to get there from here, is that correct?"

"Oui, that is correct . . . no more than that, I expect."

Poirot wasted no time after Dax had closed the car door to exit the airport to the highway, and they managed to get well down the road during their conversation. He was famished and expected so was Poirot, but there was no time to stop. He was anxious now to once more eye this animal, this despicable man who expected others to address him as, Father. His mind could not help imagining various scenarios where Werner might attempt to escape and he would be justified in killing him legally. He remembered his promise to Rebecca, but momentarily, allowed the sweet drug of revenge to course through his veins.

As the trip progressed, and it became more feasible to wake the appropriate people, he listened as Poirot was on his phone in contact with his Zurich people to explain his whereabouts. He went into detail about Werner's escape from the Vatican and how his friend, agent Bellini from Rome had been in pursuit and tracking him throughout the night. In his overhearing, Dax was pleased to discover Poirot's expertise in terms of handling the necessary procedures to successfully arrest Werner by properly processing the request from New York through his office in Zurich, giving him the temporary lead on the case, and eventually coordinating with Interpol's Munich office that would have ultimate jurisdiction.

He controlled a strong impulse to call Rebecca primarily due to the 1:00 am hour in New York, and wanting to have more privacy for the things he might want to say to her. He settled on calling her later when he would have more to report.

It was coming to a head now. The very eventful and often dangerous search for this wretched criminal would finally reach a righteous conclusion. His heart began to beat faster at the thought of standing in front of Werner as they put the cuffs on him, enjoying the satisfaction of letting the bastard know, it was Him who ultimately tracked him down. He had managed to quell his desire to kill him, but wondered if he could possibly hold back from spitting in his face.

CHAPTER FIFTY-EIGHT

Dax estimated they were no more than ten minutes from their destination when Poirot's cell rang.

"Oui, Roberto . . . oui. We are almost there. No! It cannot be true! How long ago? What of . . . sortir?! And the gendarmarie? Oui, we will drive there directly. Au revoir."

Heading directly east on the last leg of the trip, the rising sun streaming through the windshield revealed that the conversation with Bellini had depleted Poirot's already pale face of all its color. The one thing that registered immediately with Dax from the phone call was the word sortir . . ."gone."

"Stephan, has Werner escaped?" His voice, laced with anger, held back, but ready to explode.

"Non Monsieur. Werner is dead! He is hanging by a rope in a bedroom in the maison he entered earlier."

"What! Are the two men he travelled with still there? How does Bellini know this?"

"Non, the men left an hour ago, he said. In the dark, he had moved closer to the maison on foot, and watched them rush out without this priest and speed off in their auto. At first he saw no reason to do anything but wait for us, not aware of who else occupe the habitation or Werner's condition. It appears this is the house of his mere and frère, his mother and brother. They woke to find the priest hanging from a rafter and oui, they called the gendarmarie. When they arrived it was then that Roberto entered, identified himself, and discovered what had happened."

"Dead!? Dead!? Of course, he's dead!"
Dax was incensed and now doing Holmes in his head.
"I should have anticipated this, Watson. Werner, if arrested, might have been able to provide all the information needed to implicate many of the players in the chain of command who had abetted his escape from New York. He could have named the guilty hierarchy who arranged his surreptitious transfer from Ireland to the United States in the first place. Of course, he's dead! My well conceived plan to force Herr Werner's ouster from behind the Vatican's walls, based on the false premise of manufactured suppositions, was clearly successful. However, I'm afraid I have outdone myself, for I also caused his protectors to face all the potential liabilities he posed for them if captured. No doubt, my request to be taken to the airport and the Austrian Air terminal with the goyles listening during my cab ride would have only added fuel to the fire of their concerns. Oh yes, old boy. He is dead alright. And while I had made the decision to no longer seek my revenge and fire a pistol into his head, I surely caused that noose to be put around his neck as if I had played the role of hangman myself."
"Monsieur McGowan . . . Monsieur McGowan, what do you suggest we do?" Poirot asked.
Dax was now observing the scene unfolding ahead of them down the narrow, two-lane road they were travelling. On their right, was a dense stand of snow covered pine trees lining the road for a good mile or more, and there appeared to be a house nestled somewhere within those trees. The only visual evidence of that from their current position was a driveway with two cars parked side by side in what appeared to be a front yard. The one closest to their sight line was a police car with a rooftop red light swirling at a very slow pace. The other was harder to make out, but was clearly a much older car not far from its demise at a junk yard. On the road, on either side of the driveway, were a half dozen other cars with people milling around . . . the neighbors and passersby that always stop to see what's happening. Well down from there on the left side of the road, sitting in isolation was what Dax presumed was Bellini's car where he had parked it for surveillance.
"Sorry about being so distracted my friend. I don't know just yet what we shall do. Let's see what we find out about the recent events at this house first." was Dax's eventual response.
"You believe this is not a suicide, but a murder, Monsieur McGowan?"
"Oh absolutely, Stephan. There is no doubt."

CHAPTER FIFTY-NINE

As Poirot pulled into the driveway of the Werner's house, he veered far enough to the right so as not to block in what was an elderly model of a Ford Crown Victoria police car. While it displayed the emblem of the village of Marktl am Inn on its doors, there were remnants of a previous city's logo underneath it. Numerous rust spots pocked the vehicle front to back, also evidence of a small village's tight budget.

Dax observed that the Werner residence was more a small cottage than a house. The siding was of a drab gray asphalt shingle. Across the face of the structure, small pieces of it were either torn or eroded away. The exposed portions were a light brown, a contrast that made the house appear like it suffered from a bad case of acne.

The roof was covered by weather worn black tar paper lying in wait for expected shingles that had never arrived. Two paint-faded, white trimmed windows were placed equidistant on either side of a hollow core plywood front door. Never having been painted, its corners were pulling apart as its glue had succumbed to years of brutally cold Bavarian winters. It was easy to conclude, thought Dax, that poverty was also a resident of this household.

As he exited the car, the front door opened and Bellini emerged, jumping down two front concrete steps in haste to welcome them.

"It is wonderful to finally meet you, Signor McGowan," he said enthusiastically, extending his hand. "Salve, Stephan. Unusual we should be here under these circumstances, eh, my good friend, and not sharing cold ale together?"

"Roberto, what do you have to report?" Poirot's words beat Dax to the question.

"Well, my friend, this Werner fellow is hanging by the neck, the victim of one of his own cinctures, and as you can see the polizia is already here. I should say only one Polizia Capitano. He is not a cooperative sort. As much as I tried to appear in deference to his position, my Interpol credentials seemed only to anger him and place me in his mind as an intrigante. I have not told him you were coming so as not to, what are the words . . . freak him out? Nor have I told him the purpose of our presence. Maybe your personal story to him, Signor McGowan, would be the best form of introduction. His name is Capitano Kohl . . . Frederick Kohl."

"Si, Roberto, I'll take it from here," Dax answered.

He led his new partners through the front door, both he and Poirot with their IDs in hand. It opened left to right against a side wall into a small living room with a kitchen just beyond, both rooms completely open to the other. The only separation was a centrally placed Franklin stove with wood logs piled next to it, the only apparent heat source for the dwelling. The wall, wearing numerous doorknob gouges, stretched a short distance to the back of the house, except for a hallway about halfway going to the right. Based on Bellini's information that the home was inhabited by a mother and her son, Dax assumed that area housed two small bedrooms and a bathroom. Though it occurred to him that if Werner was hanging in one of the bedrooms, and had not been discovered until they awoke, his brother and mother must have been sleeping together in the other. Looking up, it was apparent how easy it would be to be hanging from a rafter as the entire house was without a ceiling. Bare joists were open to a pitched roof with insulation between the studs of it.

In the kitchen, a uniformed policeman in his late forties was standing and rolling his officer's cap around his fingers while speaking to a man of similar age dressed in pajamas who was seated at a dining table for two, Dax concluded to be the son, Werner's brother. As he passed the hallway on his right to the kitchen, he could hear the faint voice of an elderly woman repeating some phrase in German he could not quite make out.

The captain turned toward the three of them with a look of scorn.

"And who is this now?" He looked beyond Dax and Poirot at

Bellini. "Do you bring more of your kind to descend upon me? This is my dorf and my jurisdiction. What is your purpose here? Tell me!"

Brandishing his Lieutenant's gold shield long enough for the captain to have no doubt about its authenticity, he proceeded on Bellini's suggestion. "Hauptmann Kohl, my name is Lieutenant Dax McGowan of the New York City Police Department and this is agent Stephan Poirot of the Zurich office of Interpol. Paul Werner is wanted in the United States for the rape of a minor child, and as a result, the cause of my eleven-year-old daughter's suicide. These agents have been assisting me in tracking this man. It appears we have arrived too late."

The Captain was speechless at first. He had never seen the world famous gold shield of a New York City detective, and Dax detected his urge to reach out and touch it. However, it was the power of Dax's words that left him most unbalanced. Attempting to regain control of himself, he moved closer to Dax, now in a friendlier manner.

"Meneer McGowan, I must offer you my condolences on the loss of your daughter. My own son fell the victim of an auto crash three years ago and I know your feelings well. These abusive priests and what they do to children is disgusting. I don't doubt your accusations in any way, especially in the case of this man."

The Captain's edging closer alerted Dax to the man's heavy smoking habit, and what he guessed was a previous night of substantial drinking. He attempted to observe unnoticed, his food stained uniform and unpolished shoes, these and his demeanor, all signs of a man with a large ego caught in a dead end job.

"Thank you, Hauptmann. I appreciate your understanding, and let me offer my condolences on the loss of your son. We certainly do not wish to infringe upon your official capacity here, sir, but as you are now aware, we have great interest in your proceedings in this incident. May we ask questions and observe your work? We would be in your debt if we could gather enough information to report to our superiors and close our case."

"Oh, but of course. By all means, please feel free," he responded magnanimously. "However, I do not see much to report beyond this man's suicide. His bruder sitting here states that he and his moeder were unaware of his presence in the house and had not seen him for years. He was not expected. The son awoke . . . he often sleeps in the chair by his moeder's bed."

Making sure the man sitting in the kitchen chair was still faced down in grief, the Captain raised his hand and made the sign of a circling finger about the temple to indicate his mother's mental state. He went on. "She has got the Alzheimer. He awoke and went into his bedroom to change clothes, and discovered his bruder hanging by one of those priest ropes, the one they tie around their waist?"

"May we view the body, Herr Hauptmann?" Dax bowed in deference.

"But of course. Herr Werner has offered to make us some coffee and I will keep him company." The Captain winked in a false expression of sympathy, as though he was going to spend time consoling Werner's brother in their absence, though Dax was sure he had more interest in the free coffee.

As Dax led Bellini and Poirot down the short hallway, Bellini leaned forward to whisper from behind. "Well handled, Signore . . . well handled."

The first door on the left was a full bathroom. On the right was the mother's bedroom and Dax could now make out that the woman was constantly repeating the phrase, "Dass ratten . . . dass ratten." He turned back to Poirot shrugging his shoulders with his palms faced upward as a silent request for a possible motive for the words meaning, "the rat." Poirot returned a matching gesture as a response of, "I don't know."

They proceeded but a few more steps to enter the smaller bedroom on the left just past the bathroom. As described by the Captain, Paul Werner was hanging by a brownish hemp colored cincture cord from a ceiling joist. His feet hung just below and a couple of feet away from a smoothly made twin bed jutting from the wall on their right. As was the case with most hanging victims, his face was extremely distorted from the writhing and gasping in vain to catch a breath until his neck could no longer support his body's weight and snapped, putting the rope's inhabitant out of his misery. The congestion of petechial hemorrhaging about his face and eyes with his tongue extended well beyond his lips were not unusual manifestations, especially for a person of such excessive weight. Dax accepted there was no question of this corpse's identity, though his now hideous countenance looked little like the Paul Werner, alias Peter Wendich he had met the previous Monday at the cemetery.

Dax now stood unable to move, as he re-visited the events that led him to be standing thousands of miles from his home, the place where but ten days earlier, each day was a joy to live in the presence of his precious Grace. It was clear the despicable man in front of him had endured a torturous end, experiencing the greatest of all fears, that of inevitable death. Yet, Dax knew it was not enough. There could be no horror to beset this beast that would equal the terrors he had visited on his Grace. He imagined that if he could have captured this devil and tortured him interminably, he would have never reached a point of gratification that justice had been served. No, he was sure that even the crime of murder fell behind the heinous violations of the sexual abuse of a child, and that no punishment existed to claim its equivalence. Had he shot this man dead, he would have only carried the weight of that unrelenting dissatisfaction the rest of his days. It was time to release himself from the demon of revenge and be the man, the cop he was best known to be, the man and cop his daughter loved and was so proud of.

He instinctively moved in and pulled up on the sleeve of Werner's cassock to check out his left wrist. He motioned to Bellini and Poirot to look. There were barely noticeable ligature marks present from some form of binding used to restrain him from grasping at the cincture around his neck and delaying his demise. Both men nodded in agreement. He then moved over to check the other wrist with the same discovery.

"Gentlemen, the freshness of these marks would indicate that Herr Werner was not likely bound until the last minute before his hanging. Clearly, he had been fooled into thinking his fellow travelers were bringing him to a place of hiding, only to discover it was going to be the scene of his death."

Dax moved in closer to the body's chest and face area raising his head like a hound searching the air for some unique odor and locking in on it. As he expected, acetone was used to clean around Werner's mouth to remove any trace of glue from duct tape or other muzzling element to prevent him from arousing his sleeping mother and brother. Dax made a hand motion as if wiping his mouth with a napkin drawing nods of agreement from both Bellini and Poirot.

Dropping to one knee, he then lifted the thin cotton bedspread to look under the nearby bed. Then stood and moved closer to his partners and whispered his observation.

"There is no stool or chair for him to have kicked over leaving the bed as the only place to jump from to commit an act of suicide. Wasn't it thoughtful of this victim, that in the last moments of his life, as he struggled so desperately for air, he managed to somehow smooth out the bedspread with his feet so as not to burden anyone to have to make the bed after his use of it?"

Dax's humorously sarcastic remark, laced with contempt for the Captain's concluded cause of death, was met with hearty, hand muffled laughter by both Europeans.

He was now fingering his chin in an attempt to make a decision about how they should proceed. He offered, "Roberto . . . Stephan, we know who murdered this man. We could inform this Captain and offer our assistance. However, he clearly has no facilities to build any kind of case; no CSI facilities likely for many kilometers. I'm sure the only Medical Examiner at his disposal is the local undertaker. More than that, I presume he lacks all interest. I'm asking myself if it matters that we tell him. Your thoughts?"

Poirot jumped in. "Monsieur McGowan, you are correct. I'm sure my good ami, Roberto, like myself, does not want to get involved with degrade´ of paperwork that will lead to nothing, and just take up our precious time when we know we will not likely be able to prove who killed this man unless . . . Roberto, you are able to make a certain identification of these men?"

Bellini made an instant hand gesture of frustration. "Non. The lighting at the Vatican gates gave us a surety of Werner's face only, as the speed of their auto did not allow us further identifications. It was also extremely dark in this wooded area, and I was not able to see the faces of these assassinos when they either entered or exire the casa . . . ultima deludente."

Poirot continued. "These wolf-like ghosts that you have told us about Monsieur have likely left us few clues and now have a large lead on their escape. You know vous-meme that without a direct connection to the victim, these mercenary killings, promulguer by outsiders, are a gaugeure to ever prosecute successfully. Am I not right, Roberto?"

"Most certainly, Stephan. We would be best to call it done. We are not even on an official case. We are out of our districts. We are here as friends attempting to help our dearest, Dr. Bain. We should just depart."

Dax was torn between the logical strain of their conversation and his own abilities to solve even the toughest of crimes with the most miniscule of starting evidence. The Holmes in him yearned to embark on the challenge, but Dax McGowan reconsidered. *"I have a life to live thousands of miles from here, and I will be tracking these bastards down as promised anyway. I can better start from my home base in New York, where there is already a dead goyle to begin with as evidence."*

He looked at both Poirot and Bellini whose stares of anticipation were immediately replaced by ones of liberation at his words. "I am in agreement, gentlemen."

Before they could turn toward the door, the Captain entered the bedroom carrying a cup of coffee. "See my good men . . . a simple case of suicide. I will tell you that this man has been in trouble his whole life. He is hated in this dorf. There will be no mourners at his funeral."

Matching that up with what the Captain had expressed earlier as no surprise that Werner was an abuser, Dax pursued the remark.

"Hauptmann, what is the nature of this man's history here in Marktl am Inn?" Keeping to the script of his earlier stated mission, he continued. "If we are to put down that this man committed suicide, some insight to report as to why he would commit such an act would be helpful."

"Of course, I see that," the Captain began, missing that Dax was rolling his eyes in contempt. "As you see, we are a small dorf and we all know each other very well. As a boy, this man defiled the name of the priest at our Catholic Church, St. Oswald. He told a freund in his class that he had been touched in the wrong places by a priest and claimed it happened many times. That freund told his mutter and she informed one of the church women who prepares the altar for mass each day. I am telling you only what I've been told; I did not grow up here. However, I was informed that the priest, I don't recall his name, a much older man at the time, was well loved by all. When asked to directly name the priest, the Werner boy refused. His mutter also refused to speak about it to anyone. But there was no other priest in the ville; we had only the one, and no other had any such complaints about him.

The dorf has held a groll . . . a grudge against this woman and her son ever since. All were disgusted when it was told this Werner had himself become a priest. The only motive guessed was that he did it to atone for his sins. The times he did return to visit his familie, no one would even look at him. He has always been an outcast in Marktl am Inn. Good Befreiung . . . 'Good Riddance' will be the words on his marker."

Dax could hear the front door open and close as he responded. "I have heard from a very good source, Hauptmann, that on rare occasion, a sexually abused child may become a sex abuser himself. Is there any chance that might have been the case here?" He knew the conjecture would displease him.

The Captain began to strongly protest his remark, but Dax wasn't listening. Aloft from the cold breeze that entered the front door as it opened, the unmistakable scent of a woman's perfume made its way back to where he was standing. Around the corner into the hallway walked Rebecca Bain. Not even thinking, he brushed by the Captain to reach her.

"Becca . . . how? It's so good to see you!"

They embraced warmly. Rebecca pulled back to face him with a wide smile as she continued to hold onto his arms. "I did some work on my Blackberry too, Dax McGowan, and there was a flight to Munich just forty-five minutes after yours out of La Guardia. So here I am."

"Well, here you are. Wow! What a surprise; I'm thrilled."

"Dax, I need to speak to you alone to explain. Oh my God!"

Dax could see she was looking past him at Werner. He quickly, but gently, turned her around and escorted her back to the living room.

"Of all the horrors, Dax. I've seen enough dead bodies now to last me forever. I'm glad you're the homicide detective and not me. I can't imagine facing that every day."

"Sorry about that, Becca, but as you saw, this Father Werner's case is now closed. The goyles did him in. The local guy here is buying suicide, but we all know better."

Bellini and Poirot had followed them from the hallway into the open room. Dax could see the Captain had returned to the kitchen to sit next to Werner's brother, but only after casting a look of disgust his way.

"Becca, please meet agents Roberto Bellini and Stephan Poirot . . . I assume, for the first time in person."

Before she could respond, both men were bowing in homage and exclaiming all the wonderful work she was doing for them and their families. Dax could only stand back and enjoy their reactions. It also gave him a moment to re-visit his conversation with the Captain. He had learned from Rebecca that it was extremely uncommon for any child to claim being abused unless they had been. His despising of Werner aside, the detective in him was wondering who was responsible for his abuse. It was not a major leap of logic to blame that person as the instigator who set Werner on his own course of rape and destruction. It was probably moot at this point, he thought. If it was the elderly priest in the village, nearly forty years ago, he was long dead, and any trail of evidence would be ice cold by now.

Their greeting and adoration completed, Poirot decided to walk with his friend Bellini down the road to get his car and bring it up to the house, leaving Dax and Rebecca alone in the living room. The Captain walked up to them.

"I assume your part of the investigation is complete, Herr McGowan. If not, that is too bad.

Mine is over and that is all that matters. I have closed the door to the bedroom and I will bring back two of our firemen who will be strong enough to remove the body and take it to the mortuary."

"Yes, we are done, Herr Captain. Thank you for your cooperation. We'll be leaving soon." The policeman exited the front door followed by the accompanying sound of squealing tires and the roar of a hole in his car's muffler.

"Okay, Becca, tell me everything. First, how did you find me?"

"Finding you was easy. This town has one main circle where all the businesses are located. There are only four roads that come off that circle and I decided to look down each one before I called you. I spied the police car's red light and told myself that Dax McGowan couldn't be too far from what appeared to be the only action in this tiny place, and I was right."

His pleased smile matched hers till her face became more serious.

"Now, please don't be angry, Dax. What I'm about to say does not for a moment mean that I think you lied to me, but, I have worked with many abuse survivors, and, as we've already discussed, you are also an abuse survivor. Those survivors have often looked me in the eye, and promised that they would never do anything extreme as they dealt with the residues of their experiences which they were working to reconcile. However, managing those memories takes time, and the reactions I've seen from some of have ranged from writing death threats to physically accosting their abusers, which often caused their own incarceration. You can't blame them of course, but those actions only led to them suffering more harm at the hands of the law and their own guilt. I know that when you told me you would not murder this man, you meant it. However, based on past experience, I could not do anything but fly here and make sure. Can you forgive me? Can you understand why I'm here?"

Dax looked warmly into her golden eyes, and could only stand in appreciation of her good intentions for him. He also wondered if she wasn't right. Werner's murder eliminated any direct test of his will. He recalled the number of times over the past few days when he wanted to destroy him so badly, it blinded his decision making processes and caused him to push the edges of reason, negatively affecting others around him. Despite his commitment to restrain himself, was it possible that if he had been left alone with Werner, and he had said anything negative about his dear Grace, he would have lost it and blown his head off? Maybe Rebecca better understood the potentials for disaster than he did.

It hit him once again, that in such a short time he found himself falling for this woman who had just travelled across an ocean for his benefit. With Werner's demise added, he felt in a state of released joy. He slowly pulled Rebecca deeply into his arms knowing it was now that time.

"I think I love you, Rebecca Bain."

"I think I love you, Dax McGowan," she returned, and pressed her body tightly against his.

Not concerned about anyone who might be listening, Dax began, "You know, it looks like we could be stuck in this tiny town until at least tomorrow. Let's say we pick up where we were about to enter that room at the Essex, only some place around here?"

"Oh, I can't think of anything I want to do more," she replied in full voice.

Before turning toward the door, Dax noticed that Werner's brother was still sitting at the kitchen table. He realized he hadn't spoken a word to him since his arrival. He pointed to him telling Rebecca who he was. Recognizing his grief, the counselor in her wanted to at least provide a word of consolation.

"Herr Werner? My name is Rebecca Bain, and I just wanted to

offer you and your mother my deepest condolences. These next days will be very rough for you and I wish you both the very best."

The man, still in his pajamas, with yet uncombed wavy brown hair, looked up accepting of her kindness. He was clearly younger than his priest brother but appeared pale and physically wanting in terms of normal vigor.

"Frau Bain? Are you the woman who helps children who have been assaulted by priests?"

"Yes, I am."

"I have heard of you. Mine bruder mentioned your name to me on more than one occasion. He said he had wished there had been someone like you for him when he was a little boy many years ago."

"Your brother had been abused by a priest, Herr Werner?"

"Yes, dear woman. He demanded I never speak of it, but he told me it was so, and I believed him."

"Was the priest ever identified?"

"No, he had fears about naming the man. He would not tell me, but I believe my mutter knows. She of course, has been in her current condition for some years now."

"Becca," Dax injected, "the Captain told me there was only one priest in town at the time Werner claimed being abused, and based on the opinion of the townspeople there was no reason to suspect him. Of course, you've heard that disclaimer before."

"What is your mother saying, Herr Werner?" Rebecca asked.

"Oh, she has been saying that since we found our Paul this morning. She saying 'dass ratten', dass ratten. I yelled when I first saw my bruder. It was such a surprise. My mutter came into to see and began saying these words. But she says many things. She can't help it."

"Oh my God, Dax!"

"What's wrong?" Dax asked, uncharacteristically confused.

Recovering quickly, Rebecca reached over to shake Werner's hand wishing him well one last time. She turned and looked at Dax with a sideways glance and face to be interpreted as meaning, let's talk outside.

Dax bowed to Werner and followed Rebecca out the door to her rental car parked across the road. Everyone was gone now except Bellini and Poirot whose cars were now parked in the front yard. They were sitting in one of them and appeared to be swapping stories.

Dax entered in the passenger side of her vehicle.

"So what's up?"

"Dax, right after you left Janet's office to fly here, I got another call from Jeff at our office. He informed me that further down in Werner's profile was a cross reference to another priest who was born in this town of Marktl am Inn."

She waited.

"Okay, I'll bite. Who is it?"

"The Pope Dax. Not Francis, but his predecessor. And you of course know what his name was before taking Benedict?"

"My God, Becca, it was Ratzinger! Is that the rat Werner's mother is referring to?"

"Doesn't it make sense that while he didn't pastor or work here, he would have been in town on many occasions visiting family in those early years?"

Dax nodded pensively. "It sure could explain why some low level priest got special care to get moved from Ireland to the U.S., then once exposed there, received high level assistance to escape to Rome and then here to Germany. Even the Archbishop in New York took what we know to be unnecessary risks to protect this guy."

"And let's not forget those goyles who have made attempts on your life, darling. I'm glad that's over now." Rebecca said with a nervous shutter.

Dax leaned back in his seat. "I'm not sure where this leaves us. Unless we could get Archbishop James in New York to report a direct line to this retired, Pope Benedict, we have no real evidence implicating him. Besides it being highly unlikely he would do that, it's just as possible Benedict played no direct role with him anyway. That would be the normal modus operandi . . . someone down the line would have engineered this.

"The people who may have helped Werner along the way of his escape, like possibly Doherty of the Catholic Covenant Group, would likely also know very little. He'd say he was just meeting a request to transport someone whose name he would claim he didn't know, and likely be telling the truth."

"And dear Dax, there is also the possibility that it could be the past Pope's brother, Father Georg and not Benedict. His name is Ratzinger too, and he has already been accused of being complicit in the heavy handed corporal punishment on those choir boys I told you about yesterday on the phone."

"That's right . . . it could be either one of those rats. It seems the only two people who could possibly tie one of the Ratzinger boys to this, if they are guilty, are a woman suffering from dementia and an overweight priest hanging dead inside that house. Frankly, all we have is pure speculation, but all the facts surrounding Werner's past and present escapes sure give that hypothesis some traction."

"And Dax, it could also explain why Benedict dragged his feet to defrock priests or act directly against any of the hierarchy. Maybe his mandate for secrecy back in 2001, when he was head of the CDF, was an all-out attempt to quell the scandal motivated by a fear of his own potential exposure."

"That motive would be a powerful one," Dax said. "But, for something we have no proof for that happened that many years ago, I suppose we had better not make any unfounded accusations."

"That's true, but that's okay," Rebecca began. "Benedict already has plenty to answer for based on his clear access to information about the child abuse that was going on worldwide all those years he was head of the Congregation for the Doctrine of the Faith. I'm also sure his unprecedented early retirement that apparently, has him cloistering himself within the walls of the Vatican, tells us something."

Nodding his head in strong agreement, Dax reached to open the car door to exit. "Maybe we should say our goodbyes to Bellini and Poirot so they can get back to their families. Then we can check out whatever sleeping arrangements we can find in this village for tonight."

Her face changing from the stern predator of pedophiles to a woman highly aroused by this new man in her life, "You know, Dax, I'm thinking there may not be much sleeping involved."

He could hear both the tentativeness and yet the resolve in her voice. Already halfway out the door, he turned back, "No arguments from me on that plan."

CHAPTER SIXTY

Walking together toward the axis of the center circle of Marktl am Inn, along the street leading from their rental quarters, Dax was lodging a feigned complaint. "Becca, I'm stuffed. I'd gone so long without eating I gorged myself on that huge meal."

"You sure did put it away, detective," she said. "I feel like I over did myself. The food was delicious. I normally never eat corned beef, and I can't remember the last time I had real German sauerkraut. It was wonderful."

Their Bed and Breakfast was located about a block and a half off the town's center, and they decided walking off their large meal, arm in arm, would be a good idea. Despite the frigid evening temperature, the stillness of the proverbial sleeping village had a warm invitation about it.

"Look at that full moon and the stars," Rebecca said. There's not a cloud anywhere. No wonder it's so cold. I'm glad there's no wind tonight, or this walk would have been a bad idea in these rather thin coats we brought with us to Germany."

"But Becca, we have to work off some of this food because we have other things to do tonight since we won't be getting any sleep. Am I right?" Dax was feeling the full effect of the two bottles of Riesling they'd polished off with dinner. "Do you think we upset anyone with all the noise coming from our room this afternoon? The walls are so thin, you can hear everything going on in that old place."

"They did seem a bit put off by us at the dinner table. We may have made the other three couples staying there jealous, or they were reacting to our color mix . . . or both," she said smiling slyly.

"Frankly Scarlett, I don't give a damn." Dax's slurred, Rhett Butler, had them both laughing.

They finally reached the town's main circle, and had a chance to observe it in the bright moonlight, with only portions of it hidden by shadows cast by the commerce center's buildings. They both expressed their enjoyment of the old world feel of the village's almost medieval setting. The florist shop, the shoe repair, the candle store, the apothecary, all appeared as if they had been taken from a photo, if one could have existed in the era of Charles Dickens.

The core of the village's circle was surrounded by a cobblestone street for auto traffic, though one could easily visualize horse drawn produce wagons and private carriages just as appropriate in this timeless setting. A step up from the circling curb was a full sidewalk traversing the circle's entire circumference, which led to a grassy area encircling the village's heart, its central masterpiece. Standing wide and tall was an exquisitely ornate marble fountain featuring the figures of angels, pixies and little children, all engaged at play. It was unexpectedly grandiose as it rivaled the statuary more common to cities like Munich, Paris and Rome.

"Oh Dax, this little town must be so beautiful in the summer, when this fountain is turned on, and families come here to spend the day watching their children playing in its watery spray."

A slight breeze began to pick up and Dax put his arm around Rebecca to warm her while imagining the scene she had just described.

Without warning, a malevolent voice bellowed from directly behind them. "Too bad neither of you will live to ever see that."

Dax reacted with a one hundred eighty degree pivot to confront the threat, while also picturing his gun still placed in its locked travel box back in their room. The never before experienced emotion of true fear began to cramp the middle of his chest. As Rebecca made the same move more slowly, he pulled on her to a position somewhat behind him to more singly face the danger. "So it's you two. I would have thought making a clean escape after murdering Werner would have found you well on your way to whatever cave you killers hide in."

Psychotically reveling in his obvious position of power, the goyle responded. "Now, why would we want to just eliminate Werner when you afforded us the convenient opportunity to trap you here in this faraway place, Lieutenant? Besides, you made a pledge that you would hunt us down after Werner was out of the picture . . . did you not? I will pay you some respect, sir. We have not yet encountered a man of your abilities, and thought it best to eliminate you before you might make good on that promise. And, it's either a pleasant coincidence, or God's will, that your unexpected arrival allows us to remove you as well, Dr. Bain."

Dax remembered the voice as the leader of the three uninvited guests to his home. His mind was racing, trying to come up with any possible exit strategy. Both men had guns with silencers trained on each of them and were standing a good ten feet away. There was no opportunity to rush them at that distance. He would be soon dead, leaving Rebecca at their mercy. His only weapon was continued conversation until he could devise some other method of escaping what appeared to be a no win situation. "It does seem you have us in a bad spot. But tell me, which one of you is, Hicks and which one, Motherwell?"

"Oh, very good, Lieutenant. It's Hicks, though that matters little now."

"Listen, Hicks, tell me something. You've got nothing to lose. Why do you do this? I'm guessing you were a damn good soldier who unfortunately was required to take a few too many lives in the service of your country. But those were the lives of our country's enemies. Why would you want to take the lives of civilians, abused kids who have grown up to be mentally tortured adults, or good people like Dr. Bain here who work every day to help them?"

"You don't get it, McGowan. There is no greater purpose than serving the Mother Church. She is God's shield on this earth, and we are the soldiers who support that shield. Anyone who challenges her authority must be smote by God's hand, and we humbly perform that service in his name."

No surprise at that response. These men really are the cultish wing nuts Seymour's military friend said they were." Dax realized he was running out of time and words, but before he could launch into more stalling, Rebecca jumped in.

"Tell me, young man. If you are so proud of what you do, why is it that you must hide behind such ugly masks? Are you so fearful that your work is so despicable, it causes you to cover your face?"

"Ouch." Dax was now concerned that Rebecca's challenge would put the two men over the edge.

"We are not hiding behind these masks," Hicks retorted defensively. "They are part of who we are. The wolf has always been the symbol of the protector of the Mother Church. Here, we will show you, we have no reason to hide from our work!"

Both men removed their masks, revealing men so young, the term "baby face" came to Dax's mind.

"Look Dax, these are not men." Rebecca was now in full on righteous disgust. "These are boys who have lost their way. I have met hundreds of boys like you, abused boys who no longer know who they are. You two are no less abused. Just like the priests who stole away the childlike innocence of so many, the church has stolen yours. Just as those other boys were used to satisfy the despicable demands for sex from the clergy, you are being used by them to satisfy their need for power, and to protect their money. You may kill us, but I will tell you right now that you will never forget what I have just said to you, and it will haunt and plague you the rest of your days."

Impressed at Rebecca's raw courage, Dax expertly read the growing anger on the assassins' faces. They were at the limit of their patience, and he was slipping ever more in front of Rebecca in what he knew was a foolhardy attempt to allow her but a mere second more of life.

Suddenly, the breeze that had come up earlier was carrying the odor of cigarette smoke. In the same second of his notice of it, Dax heard a sizzling noise, much like that of a 4th of July sparkler, as a brightly burning cigarette was tumbling through the dry air from his right between them and their captors. As if in slow motion, the flaming stick rose in an arc to its apogee just above their heads, paused, and then began wafting in the direction of the ground. He was about to turn to discover its source when two silenced pistol rounds were fired with only their mild "phoot" to be heard. Instantaneously, each shot was followed by the sound of shattered skull bone exploding at impact, and the flush of spattered blood being soaked in by the night's thin air.

Dax and Rebecca watched in amazement as the two goyles collapsed in unison before them.

Rebecca moved quickly in front of Dax and buried her head in his chest. "My God Dax, what just happened?"

"I'd say someone just saved our lives."

His heart still racing, he turned and peered to his right awaiting the entrance of their savior from out of the lunar shadows of a nearby building. A woman's voice broke the silence.

"So, Dax McGowan, are you finally going to tell me just where you got that first name of yours?" A dark haired woman in a jumpsuit holding a smoking nine-millimeter pistol stepped into the moonlight. He immediately recognized the voice of Morgan Montgomery from the plane ride to Munich.

Rebecca raised her head, and with a smile of relief shouted, "Morgan! Oh my God, Morgan. I thought you would never have to save my life, and yet here you are . . . and you saved us both!"

"Hello, Dr. Bain. Just doing my job."

"Whoa!" Dax interrupted. "Are you the person Seymour Hirsch engages to protect Rebecca?"

"That would be me."

"Morgan," Rebecca added, "I'm so glad I called in yesterday, and let Seymour know I was following Dax here to Germany, or I'm afraid we wouldn't have survived this night."

"It sure made for some crazy travel for me," Morgan began, "but, I'm glad you did as well."

"Morgan?" Dax asked. "You didn't follow Rebecca to New York from Chicago?"

"No. I was supposed to, but my flight was cancelled. Seymour wasn't as concerned with the gap in coverage because she was meeting you and thought she'd be safe under your protection. However, after the attack at the Essex, I was put in a rush mode. As soon as I got off the plane from Chicago at JFK, I got the call that Rebecca was heading to Munich from LaGuardia. Since I didn't want to take the chance of leaving JFK and not making her flight from there, with the time so tight, I literally ran to the international terminal and caught the flight ahead of hers you and I were both on, out of JFK. That was pure coincidence. It still fit into my plan, as I could just wait in Munich for Dr. Bain's arrival there. While Rebecca and I have met and know each other, per Seymour's instructions, I just hang back in the shadows to do my job."

"Well, literally back in the shadows I see," Dax said, putting his arm around Rebecca's shoulders. "I have to say, I was at my wits end trying to come up with a way out of the fix we were in. And my dear Becca, I was impressed with how brave you were, and that you were ready to go out fighting, but those psychos had reached the end of their patience with us." He turned to Morgan. "Hey, the flying cigarette was an excellent diversion."

"Yeah, those guys were ready to start shooting. I needed the extra second to position myself so I wouldn't miss. Both my shots had to be dead on. A miss, and one of them would probably have fired at you out of sheer reaction. I guess it's a good idea I haven't given up the filthy habit just yet. Anyway, it was a justified kill. Uh, sorry for the graphic reference, Dr. Bain."

"No complaints from me, Morgan. My heart is still pounding. I'll never give Seymour any more grief about my need for security."

"Damn." Montgomery was now lamenting. "Talking about justification, I'm going to have to wake this little burg up, and go through all the crazy paperwork, my authorizations for protective firearm's use and all that jazz. This is going to be especially messy with two dead guys in tow. I wonder how hard it's going to be working with the local cops around here."

Dax turned to Rebecca, shaking his head and smiling. "Should we tell her, Becca, or let Morgan find out for herself?"

EPILOGUE

After some well deserved partying and rest over the Christmas weekend, Janet was seated at her desk enjoying a degree of satisfaction she had always hoped for on the job. Grace McGowan's case had finally led to bringing at least one member of the Catholic hierarchy accountable for his criminal activity. The Archbishop's self-incrimination during the "blackmail" meeting he had with undercover Detective Yuri Brogovich, and the attempted murder of marina worker, Boris Kelchuk, acted out by Brogovich, resulted in the prelate's arrest. Groups like the Catholic Covenant Group, as well as Bishops countrywide chimed in to claim the action as blatant persecution of the Church, but to no avail.

"Even those chicken shits in the D.A.'s office, have no choice this time. There's more than enough evidence to cover their sorry political asses," was often heard to be said by Sergeant Meehan in the cackle of a wicked witch, as a prelude to the well-deserved justice for "her" children, now clearly in the offing.

In a TV interview, he made special arrangements to schedule, Dax referred to the absolute silence of the Vatican in the matter as "conspicuous by its absence."

The adventures and near death experience in Germany for Dax and Rebecca was the daily fodder of every New York newspaper and all the wire services. The entire NYPD had to scurry so its divisions could get their stories straight about who had what level of jurisdiction in the various crimes involved.

SVU at the Four-Five took the lead position in terms of Grace's sexual abuse. However, Captain Pressioso demanded that the Four-One's homicide division take a share of it arguing that Grace's death be considered a de facto homicide in terms of Werner's despicable role in her death, that and the tie in with the attempted murder of Detective Brogovich at the yacht club. It was an unorthodox position to assume, and everyone knew that his prime motivation was to protect his best detective, and put a stamp of approval on any actions he had taken in the case. Since Werner's death meant no trial would proceed on the sex abuse case, and any weaknesses in protocol would not be an issue, everyone involved, including the D.A.'s office, offered no objections.

It was during this process to determine precinct pecking order that Dax learned the nature of the conversation that took place between his Captain Pressioso and Janet Meehan's, Captain Hughes. He expected his admission to Pressioso of his unauthorized involvement would result in an apology to Hughes, and a plea to him to forgive Janet's stepping over the line at times as a direct result of Dax's insistences to breach protocol. However, Pressioso took a completely unexpected approach. He chose to downplay Dax's involvement by claiming all the plots and plans to be of genius level detective work on Meehan's part. He went to great lengths to compliment Hughes on what a great cop she was and that, "It seems our precinct now has to compete with yours, Jeremy, for who's got the sharpest detective in house." Hughes was apparently flabbergasted to be complimented so enthusiastically by the highly regarded John Pressioso, a man well his senior. The net effect left him with nothing to do but praise his Sergeant for her exceptional work, with only a mild rebuke for not keeping him better informed. In the end, it was clear to Dax that his Captain's prime motive was to protect his "son" at all costs.

Janet's ecstatic mood was also being fed by the surprise solving of her sister Karen's murder by Dax, with the legwork help of her ex-partner and Dax's homicide division associate, Dick Daley, all accomplished during the lengthy manhunt of the last two weeks for Paul Werner.

In that Cold Case, the original lead detectives, as well as Karen's five apartment roommates, were certain that the building's superintendent, Darren Horton, was the guilty party. He had a previous record of assaulting another woman, and lied about his whereabouts during the strangulation murder and post-mortem rape of Janet's sister, Karen. However, the original detectives were unable to produce any hard evidence linking him directly to the crime with no science to back them up.

The murder weapon used was a large hand towel discovered in a Chinese restaurant's dumpster days later. In addition to Karen's epithelial cells all over it, there were also another thirty-four other substances detected on the towel ranging from exotic Chinese food sauces to various forms of dumpster grime. In the end, Dax was able to match up traces of formaldehyde on the towel with the attendance in a Gross Anatomy class that very same day by one of Karen's roommate's boyfriends, an Arthur Goldblum. He was attending Mount Sinai Medical School and had direct contact with the substance while working on a cadaver. Due to the high suspicion regarding the building superintendent by the lead detectives, any serious investigation into Karen's friends and associates had never been done. Daley's delving revealed previous stalking and other threats to women by this new suspect.

Later, Dax, Rebecca, Daley, and a host of her cop friends stood in prideful camaraderie as they witnessed Janet cuffing Karen's killer in his penthouse apartment in an upscale area of Chinatown. Goldblum's attempt to look away during the process, rather than acknowledge Janet's presence, resulted in an attention getting hard fist to his jaw by her, with no protests by anyone present.

Fighting unsuccessfully to avoid the inevitable, after Goldblum was dragged away, Janet fell into an outpouring of tears. Turning to Dax, "You know, there's no way I can say a thank you that would ever be enough."

"Listen, Janet, there's no way this city, or the kids and families that live here can ever pay you back for the kind of cop you are, and probably a good deal of it due to your sister's death. You turned that tragedy into an amazing career of saving people. What I did was only a small bit of payback from everyone who owes you so much . . . me included."

Being the only two people left after everyone had exited the suspect's home, Dax then turned to Rebecca to catch her beaming at him. "You know, Dax McGowan, I have to say, I'm more than a little impressed with what you've done these last two weeks, something very dear to my heart, solving two sex abuse cases."

She moved into his arms as they shared what each thought was a perfect embrace. They turned their heads, and kissed with what each would describe more as love than lust. It was only the primal need to breathe that led them to pull apart, and step toward the elevator for the ride down to the street.

Arm in arm, they treaded slowly across the sidewalk to Dax's car.

"You know, Lieutenant, my office has just been contacted by a friend of a female New York City police officer. She reports that this young cop just recently began to suffer from extreme bouts of disorientation. Some of the mental health professionals think it may be a result of some form of abuse, likely sexual abuse when she was younger. They have no proof it was a priest, but her friend thought with our experience, we could be of help. No one wants to believe that happens . . . repressed childhood memories taking over in a person's adult life, but I've got files full of those cases. Would you like to help us on this one? It's right here in your backyard? "

"Well Becca, at least I can always say you love me as much for my mind as my body."

"I would readily confirm that to be true, my dear, Dax."

Pulling him around into her arms again, and with a shudder of passion, she said. "I love you, Dax McGowan . . . all of you."

While he deeply meant every word of his response, "I love you Rebecca Bain . . . all of you," his mind drifted to the plight of this woman cop, caught in the hell of depression and likely facing a wall of distrust from her fellow officers. It was much later that Dax was to find out that the mystery surrounding this woman's condition was going to come looking for him.

THE END

My Dear Readers,

I hope you've enjoyed Millstone, and discovered some synergy with one or more of its characters. I invite you to seek out my next Dax McGowan mystery on Amazon. (Available late summer/early fall 2015) The title is "Six." Janet Meehan seeks Dax's aid in solving the case of a serial killer raping and murdering nuns in Mott Haven, the poorest area of The Bronx. However, this assassin chooses only those rare women who still wear the old-fashioned, veiled habits. The case appears to be connected to an old, closed case murder that took place eighteen years earlier.

Once again, thank you for your interest in my work, and if you feel it worth your time, please place a review for "The Millstone Prophecy" on its Amazon page. A link is available through my website, www.jackharneyauthor.com, where you can also contact me directly if you like.

JACK HARNEY

ACKNOWLEDGEMENTS

I owe thanks to the famed writer, Mary Jane Clark and successful author, Julie Compton, for both specific suggestions and needed encouragement early on. I'm also in debt to Stephen King for his book, *On Writing* as a cold shower cure for the naïve belief in the perfection of first drafts, second drafts, third drafts . . .

Most assuredly, I want to thank all my beta readers. They took the time to preview my work at different stages, providing kudos when earned, along with well-deserved and stingingly honest criticisms of its weaknesses. My hats off to Heather Awad, Leila Awad, Diane Bernick, Julieanna Blackwell, Todd Blackwell, Gary Croskey, Hope Croskey, my wife, Nancy Harney, Yuliya Harney, Loraine Smith Rhodes, and Laure White.

I owe special gratitude to Therese Albrecht, herself a clergy abuse victim, for sharing her harrowing life experiences with me, and, as a previous member of the NYPD, her assistance in learning a good deal about the culture of the department. Much thanks also to Lena Woltering, the parent of a clergy abuse victim, for dispensing her expert knowledge, and supplying me with critical research material. Finally, I offer a warm thank you to my son and screenplay writer, Axel Harney, who over hours of review, literally parsed portions of my work, at times down to individual sentences to help his dad.

JACK HARNEY

ABOUT THE AUTHOR

Jack Harney grew up in the Mott Haven area of the Bronx, still one of the poorest and more diverse areas of New York City. Irish born, it was no surprise he chose his main character, Dax McGowan, to have a parallel background. It is also no surprise Harney's lifelong interest in everything Sir Arthur Conan Doyle and Sherlock Holmes, Dax would employ a similar skill set in his work as a detective. Spending most of his adult life in the world of business, and despite being known for applying a creative flair in those pursuits, Harney describes those years as his Left Brain Period. Five years ago, he entered what he now calls his Right Brain Period, doing what he has always desired to do most, write.